"I want to believe you, but you've already admitted you lied to me."

When Jud turned to her, Liz realized how close he was and how far back she had to tilt her head to look into his face. Uh-oh. Big mistake. Those blue-gray eyes bored into hers and suddenly she felt as though her blood pressure was careening off the charts. He was too close.

And then he was closer. She didn't remember lacing her fingers behind his neck, but she felt his arms around her waist, his body leaning over her, lifting her as those giant hands moved her against him. She felt open, exposed and, above all, hungry.

He kissed her urgently. Mouth met mouth, tongue met tongue without hesitation or pretense.

She fought to remain rational while waves of unreasoning heat and longing rolled through her.

He killed his wife, he killed his wife, he killed his wife...

The heck he did.

Dear Reader,

Liz Gibson, a trained police negotiator, is nearly killed in a negotiation that goes horribly wrong. Recuperating in the cold case squad, she's assigned to find evidence against Jud Slaughter, a man the police are certain murdered his wife seven years earlier. He escaped arrest only because no body was ever found.

This is one wife killer who won't escape Liz.

The more Liz learns about the case and the better she knows Jud Slaughter, however, the less she believes he killed his wife. He's trying to manage a difficult teenage daughter—who hates Liz on sight—run a business and deal with the cloud of suspicion that hangs over his head.

Against her better judgment and certainly against police policy, she finds herself falling for him, and even enlists his help to discover what really happened to his wife.

Just as Liz and Jud discover that their feelings for one another have grown way beyond attraction, the events of seven years ago come back threatening to destroy them. Liz must use all her skills—not to convict Jud, but to save him.

I hope you enjoy this as much as I enjoyed writing it. I love to hear from readers! Write to me at Harlequin Books, 225 Duncan Mill Road, Don Mills, ON M3B 3K9, Canada, or check out my Web site, www.carolynmcsparren.com.

Carolyn McSparren

HIS ONLY DEFENSE
Carolyn McSparren

HARLEQUIN®

TORONTO • NEW YORK • LONDON
AMSTERDAM • PARIS • SYDNEY • HAMBURG
STOCKHOLM • ATHENS • TOKYO • MILAN • MADRID
PRAGUE • WARSAW • BUDAPEST • AUCKLAND

Recycling programs
for this product may
not exist in your area.

ISBN-13: 978-0-373-78277-2
ISBN-10: 0-373-78277-2

HIS ONLY DEFENSE

Copyright © 2008 by Carolyn McSparren.

www.eHarlequin.com

Printed in U.S.A.

ABOUT THE AUTHOR

Carolyn McSparren lives in the country outside Memphis, Tennessee, with four indoor cats, seven barn cats, an ever-growing family of raccoons and one husband—not necessarily in order of importance. Carolyn, who has a master's degree in English, has won three Maggie Awards from the Georgia Romance Writers, and was twice a finalist for the Romance Writers of America RITA® Award. She has served as president of the River City Romance Writers, the Memphis chapter of Romance Writers of America and is a member of both Sisters in Crime and the Mystery Writers of America. When she's not writing, she rides dressage (badly) on a half-Clydesdale dressage horse and drives a half-Shire carriage mare.

Books by Carolyn McSparren

HARLEQUIN SUPERROMANCE

CHAPTER ONE

"GET YOUR SKINNY BUTT out here right now or I'm gonna start shootin'."

Liz Gibson snatched the cellular telephone off the table in front of her and spoke soothingly into it. "Relax, Bobby Joe. Everything's going to work out fine, if we all keep our cool here."

Four hours ago, when she'd first made contact with him, Bobby Joe Watson had been drunk as a skunk. He was obviously sobering up. Liz prayed he'd be more rational now, but the reality of his situation could hit him, and then…

While she spoke, Captain Leo started buckling the bottom strap on Liz's Kevlar vest. Next he picked up the black windbreaker with Shelby County Police Negotiator stenciled in white across the back. Liz slipped her free arm into the left sleeve, then switched the telephone to her left hand so she could shrug into the right.

"*Now*, woman. I been telling you I ain't lettin' nobody go until you come out here and get 'em personally."

"Bobby Joe, I'm just a grunt. I had to do some fast

talking to get my captain to let me come this far. He's only giving permission because you're an old friend."

"Friend, my ass. I'm startin' to lose my temper, Miss High-and-Mighty Senior Class President." His voice went low and guttural. "You all wouldn't want me to lose my temper, now, would you?"

Liz's stomach gave a lurch with the change in his tone. She caught her breath and said quickly, "I'm coming right this minute. Why don't you walk on out of the house with Sally Jean and Marlene? I promise nobody's going to hurt you."

"Yeah? Then how come I see a whole battalion of those TACT bastards poking automatic weapons out from behind half the trees in the front yard? Huh? You tell me that." His voice rose dangerously.

Liz heard the rising panic in his tone, and glanced at Captain Leo. He nodded. He'd heard it, too.

She forced herself to sound calm and relaxed. "Well, Lord, Bobby Joe, they're not about to shoot *me,* now are they? You'll be safe with me. Just put down your weapon and come on out."

"Listen, woman, I'm the one in control here. I tell *you* what to do, you don't tell me a goddamn thing, you hear? And ain't no bitch gonna kick me out of my own house what I paid rent on, try to divorce me and take my baby girl away from me, you got that? I have her now, and I ain't leaving."

"I know you love Sally Jean, and she loves you...." Liz used the child's name as often as possible. The little girl had to remain an individual in her father's eyes, not merely a possession. Liz hadn't dared mention his wife, Marlene, since their first contact. Her name sent Bobby Joe into paroxysms of cold rage.

"I send Sally Jean out, y'all won't never let me see her again."

"Of course you'll see Sally Jean again, Bobby Joe." *Through bars, if I have my way.* The judge who'd granted the man bond after he was arrested for landing both his wife and daughter in the hospital should be impeached.

Liz prayed Bobby Joe didn't realize how many additional felony charges he'd accrued with this home invasion and kidnapping. She prayed he wouldn't add murder to the list.

"You're Sally Jean's daddy. We have to start thinking what's best for her. Little girls think their daddies are heroes. Be her hero. You're a good daddy, Bobby Joe."

"Damn straight I am!"

In the background, Liz heard the muffled cries of a child, and a moment later, the sound of a palm striking flesh, followed by a howl of pain. "Hush up, Sally Jean," Bobby Joe snapped. "I'm busy here."

Some good daddy! This situation was more proof that restraining orders against abusive spouses didn't work. Men like Bobby Joe believed they *owned* their families. The most dangerous time came when wives finally broke free and started to turn their lives around. Men like Bobby Joe couldn't bear that. They wanted their families back under their thumbs. If they couldn't manage that, then they wanted them dead.

Thank God Marlene's next-door neighbor in this working-class Memphis neighborhood had seen Bobby Joe invade the little house, and had called the police. If officers had not been on the scene quickly, Bobby Joe might have taken both his wife and daughter at gunpoint and disappeared with them. With a squad car blocking the driveway, however, he had barricaded himself inside with an arsenal.

On some level he must know he couldn't stay there forever, and that the police would never simply let him walk away with his wife and child.

Liz wanted him to choose surrender rather than family annihilation. At this point, she thought he was considering her offer, and hoped fervently she was reading him right.

She closed her eyes tightly, hearing that slap. Not a sound she'd ever mistake. She'd heard it too many times, when the slap had come from her momma and the howl had risen inside herself. "Bobby Joe? Listen to me. I'll walk halfway up the driveway—"

"No! You come right up on the front porch. You hold your hands out to the side, away from you with your palms out, so I'll know you ain't carrying no gun. You ring the bell, then I'll open up and let 'em out. You got that?"

Captain Leo growled softly in the background

and whispered, "Wants another hostage. He'll try to drag you inside. Thinks having a cop at his mercy will give him more leverage."

Liz nodded. That might be a good sign. Bobby Joe wasn't the first hostage-taker to dream up that one. It meant he still hadn't decided whether to surrender, or to kill his wife and child—and then himself—rather than allow them a life without him.

She infused her voice with a trace of regret. "They won't let me do that, Bobby Joe. I'll have to wait in the driveway."

"No!"

"Bobby Joe, you got to give me something I can work with to get you out of this mess. A gesture of good faith. If you'd just come on out with them… Nobody's been hurt yet—"

"Oh, that right?" The man's laughter sent a chill up Liz's backbone. The phone went dead.

Liz froze, then turned to Captain Leo. He looked grim.

"I should have yanked you off this negotiation the minute that bastard recognized your voice, Liz. The taker is never supposed to know the negotiator. That's procedure."

"Captain, there were three thousand kids in my high school. I don't even remember Bobby Joe's face, much less his name. How could I possibly know he'd recognize my voice from way back then?"

"Obviously because you were already running your mouth." Leo looked closely at her. "You scared?"

For a moment Liz considered lying, then said, "I'm petrified. What if I blow it? There's an eight-year-old girl and a woman in that house with a control freak who gets his jollies putting them both in the hospital on a regular basis. And from what the neighbor said, he's got an arsenal."

"Unless he's got armor-piercing shells, he's not going through that Kevlar, Liz."

"I don't have any Kevlar between my eyes."

"You want to give it up?"

"No. I've got to try. Maybe he'll hold up his end of the bargain."

"If the TACT guys get a clear shot at him…"

"You know I'm not supposed to know that." She managed a grin and a thumbs-up, and opened the door of the mobile command post that had been set up on the country road at the end of Bobby Joe Watson's gravel drive. Suddenly that drive looked a million miles long.

The TACT team was in position, with weapons pointed at the silent cottage, its phones and electricity disabled.

The only communication Bobby Joe had with the outside world was through the phone they'd thrown him at the start of the siege. It was keyed to talk only to Liz's phone. She had no idea what the team's orders were. Her ignorance was critical. Her voice couldn't betray what she didn't know.

But it gave her an additional sense of unease. She could die just as easily from friendly fire as from

Bobby Joe Watson's rifle, if she accidentally "crossed the tube" and walked into the sniper's line of fire as he pulled the trigger.

She held the phone out in her left hand so Bobby Joe could see it. What he couldn't see was the microphone in her right ear that relayed instructions from Captain Leo.

Liz's heart banged against her ribs, and bile threatened to choke her. She badly needed to go to the bathroom. All those Kegel exercises she'd done had better pay off now, because she didn't have time to drop her drawers in the azalea bushes. Not in front of the TACT team or the television trucks. The latter might be out of range of bullets, but she definitely wasn't out of range of their long-distance lenses. She fought down a hysterical giggle.

She walked slowly up the drive into the lengthening shadows. She'd been negotiating with Bobby Joe for four hours now, ever since the neighbor had called 911 to report that he had come back home to convince Marlene not to divorce him.

That he'd recognized Liz's voice from high school had been bad luck, particularly when he'd refused to change negotiators. Personal history could have a deadly effect on a negotiation. Captain Leo had once allowed a taker's preacher to speak to him. After the minister called down the wrath of God on the guy and said he'd roast in hell for eternity, Captain Leo had physically yanked him away from the microphone. On that occasion, Liz had spent the next twenty-two hours trying to talk the taker into giving up. She had, but it had been close.

Never under ordinary circumstances would a negotiator have walked into plain view, Kevlar or not. She was supposed to be a faceless, nameless voice on a line. The sympathetic everyman, or in this case, everywoman.

But here she was, walking unarmed up a driveway toward an unstable man with a rifle. Liz regularly ran five miles with little effort, yet now she was panting after twenty yards. She could smell her own sweat mingled with the metallic stench of the Kevlar. The vest pressed on her shoulder blades. The steel pad in the center, over her heart, felt as if it weighed a hundred pounds. She shrugged, but didn't dare put her hands down to adjust the vest.

"Okay, Bobby Joe, I'm here. Send them out," she called.

For a long moment nothing happened, then the front door opened barely enough for the thin child to slip through. The door shut quickly behind her, but not before the fading light glinted off the barrel of a rifle.

Uncertain, the girl stood on the porch, her eyes on her ragged sneakers. Despite the cold, she wore only a thin T-shirt and grimy jeans two sizes too big. Her dirty face was streaked with tears.

"Come on, Sally Jean, honey," Liz said softly. "It's all right, baby girl. Just come on down the steps to Liz." She held out her arms. The child moved hesitantly down the porch steps.

Where was Marlene? Liz glanced at the door. She hadn't heard a word from the woman in over an hour.

She had a bad feeling about this. It was imperative that she get the kid to safety, then go back for Marlene. If she was alive.

The child looked up at her with terrified eyes and began to stumble toward her. Liz started to kneel to gather her up when she caught movement from the corner of her eye.

The door opened again. Marlene?

No! God. The rifle. Bobby Joe was going to shoot her. As she stared, openmouthed, the barrel of the gun swung across and down.

He was aiming at Sally Jean! His own daughter! He'd sworn he'd kill her before he'd let her go. Liz had failed. He'd chosen to kill them all rather than surrender.

Liz swept the child into her arms and spun to shield her with her own body.

Sally Jean screamed and fought, arms and legs flailing, as Liz ran crookedly toward the command post.

She felt the first impact in the middle of her back before she heard the soprano ping of the rifle shot.

As she fell forward, two other thuds hit her between the shoulder blades. Worse than a mule kick. Much worse.

No breath. She'd crush the child....

Another ping. Pain seared her hip.

And all hell broke loose. As she went down on top of Sally Jean, she heard the thuds of running boots, the shouts of the TACT squad, a barrage of gunfire.

Hands grabbed her under her armpits, swept the child away from her, dragged her toward the command post, hauled her up the steps and dropped her facedown on the floor.

Captain Leo was talking to someone. She heard his voice through a halo of pain. She managed to turn her head to stare up into the grizzled face of Bill Lansing, head of TACT.

"Is she okay?" Her own voice sounded strangled.

"The kid? Yeah."

"Am I dying?"

He laughed at her. Actually laughed, the bastard!

"Not unless one of your broken ribs punctured a lung." Then he was gone and Captain Leo took his place. Her leg felt warm and wet.

"Three in the back of the vest, Liz."

"I'm bleeding, I can feel it."

"Oh, yeah. That. Flesh wound. Graze. Couple of inches over and you'd have a brand-new asshole." He grasped her hand hard. "If you had to act like a goddamn hero, couldn't you have managed it without getting shot in the butt in front of a dozen television cameras?"

CHAPTER TWO

Six weeks later Liz shifted carefully on the wooden chair in the Cold Case interrogation room. Her rear end could still send a shock of pain through her if she moved the wrong way.

"Want to tell me about it?" Liz asked the obviously terrified young man who sat across the beat-up table. She could tell he longed to talk. He was barely out of his teens. He'd been seventeen when he'd shot one of his friends.

He'd been sitting in the "perp seat" for over two hours now. The front two legs had been shortened an inch and a half so that the chair canted slightly forward. Suspects were uncomfortable without knowing precisely why.

Liz kept her voice soft, gentle and understanding. One thing she'd learned from her negotiator's training was that the key to getting a suspect to confess or a taker to give up was to exude empathy.

She'd left Leroy alone for thirty minutes while he ate his burger and drank his cola. Through the two-way mirror she'd watched him finish the food, lay his head on the table and fall asleep.

"Gotcha!" she'd whispered. Suspects frequently fell asleep the moment they were left alone, as though suddenly released from the tension of trying to get away with whatever crime they'd committed. Now, seated once more on the other side of the table, she leaned forward and regarded him sadly.

His words tumbled out. "Man, I never mean to kill Skag," Leroy whined. "He my runnin' buddy. He just be in the way. It was a accident. See, I mean to shoot Marbles." He raised his eyes. He no longer looked frightened; he looked much put-upon. "Man, I ain't goin' to jail for no *accident.*"

He truly believed that because he'd shot his friend instead of his intended target, he shouldn't be treated as a killer. Unbelievable.

Twenty minutes later she left Leroy writing out his confession on a yellow legal pad, and stuck her head inside the door of the darkened room with the mirror. "So, Lieutenant Gavigan, how'd I do?" she asked the big man watching Leroy write.

He gave her a thumbs-up. "Not bad for your first solo homicide interrogation." He motioned her inside. She closed the door behind her.

She leaned her butt against the wall beside the mirror, but caught her breath and stood straight again when pain pierced her hip.

"Still smarts when you do that, huh?" Gavigan said.

"Yeah. It's been six weeks since I got wounded. When does it stop hurting?"

"Hey, I've never been shot. I hear it can take six months to a year. You'll probably have a groove in your rear end forever."

"How nice of you to mention that."

"Cop groupies love scars."

"They have male cop groupies, do they?" she asked.

"Sure. So, how do you like Cold Cases so far?"

How could she tell her new boss that she had been transferred to the tiny Cold Case squad not so much because she needed to recuperate from her wound, but because she needed time to recover from the entire experience? Waiting for her wound to be tended in the emergency room, she'd been told that Sally Jean had seen Bobby Joe kill her mother at least an hour before he let the child leave the house. Liz's physical wound was almost healed. The blow to her self-confidence might never heal.

She didn't think she'd ever get her nerve back. Or be confident that she could talk an armed taker into surrendering. She didn't trust her ability to read the taker's mind or voice level or body language correctly.

She'd been grateful the sheriff's department had basically created a job for her. They'd probably gone out of their way because the media insisted on calling her a hero—which she most definitely was not.

Cold Cases was theoretically a stopgap until she was fully recovered physically and ready to go back to Negotiations. She knew better. She had to make a success of the transfer to keep her career with the Shelby County Sheriff's Department on track.

She suspected Captain Leo had explained her loss of confidence to Lieutenant Gavigan, but he'd never said a word to her. "At least here the crimes were committed a long time ago," she said. "I'm not waiting for the other shoe to drop."

Like with Marlene.

"So, how'd you find him?" Gavigan hooked a thumb at the interrogation room.

"Did what Jack and Randy told me. Went back and reinterviewed all the witnesses. They were still scared, but not nearly as frightened as they were just after it happened. Several of them talked to me. They knew from the get-go who the shooter was. Once somebody pointed me toward Leroy's car, it was a piece of cake. The initial investigation never located the vehicle, but I guess after a while Leroy decided it was safe to bring it out of hiding. He was extremely upset when I had it impounded. Would you believe, we found a spent shell casing that matched one from the scene under the dashboard?"

Gavignan laughed. "Proves it pays to have your car detailed on a regular basis."

"I really think he's glad to get it off his chest. So, what's next?"

"Come into my office. This one's going to take a little explanation."

On her way to Gavigan's tiny office in the corner

of the bull pen Cold Cases shared with Homicide, Jack Samuels gave her a thumbs-up and Randy Railsback a prurient leer.

She threaded her way between the battered gray desks where the homicide detectives hung out, and glanced at the sign beside Gavigan's door that said, Bad Cop! No Doughnuts! She liked that better than the one that said Our Day Starts When Yours Ends.

Gavigan settled in the oversize chair behind his equally battered desk and motioned her to the chair in front. She lowered herself into it gingerly.

"Okay. So you cracked your first cold case. Big deal. That one was fairly easy. This is tougher. Give it two weeks. If you don't come up with a perp we can prosecute, put the box back in the stacks and go on to something else." He motioned to the credenza behind him. She turned and saw one of the gray cardboard deed boxes used to store everything connected to a case. "Get Jack and Randy to give you advice, but I'd like you to handle this one yourself."

"How old is this case, and why do I get the feeling I'm being set up?"

"Because you are. Frankly, I think this one has gone as far as it will ever go, but I've had a call from upstairs asking us to take another look." He grimaced. "As a favor to somebody important who shall remain nameless."

She felt a tingle down her spine. "Political?"

"A friend of the commissioner wants us to look into it. I'm not going to tell you anything else except that it's seven years old and a Shelby County homicide, or at least we think it's a homicide."

"Think? As in not sure?"

"Read the murder book. We had two of the best homicide detectives on it at the time. Both retired. One of them's dead. It's the kind of case where they knew in their gut what happened and who the doer was, but couldn't prove it. Seven years later, someone may be willing to talk, or you may find some forensics that we missed. Frankly, I doubt it, but as the new kid on the block, you're getting stuck with it. If you get nowhere, at least we can say we tried."

"I get it. CYA."

Gavigan grinned. "Right. Cover your ass. Think of this as a reward for finding Leroy."

"Oscar Wilde said no good deed goes unpunished."

"Not in this department," Gavigan said, and waved a hand toward the box, dismissing her.

CHAPTER THREE

JUD SLAUGHTER POURED himself two fingers of Jack Daniel's Black Label, dropped in a single cube of ice and waited until he'd settled into his elderly leather recliner in front of the fireplace to take a sip. If the November rain didn't slack off, the construction site would be twenty acres of slop.

Fifteen days from today was the seventh anniversary of Sylvia's death. It had been raining that night, too.

For seven years he'd held on to the fragile belief that Sylvia might be still alive somewhere, maybe amnesiac, but alive. Colleen swore her mother must be dead, for she would never have deserted her only daughter. Jud knew better. He'd simply never been able to figure out why Sylvia had left when she did.

He couldn't see her walking away from a hefty divorce settlement, which is what she would have received if they'd gone through with the split. She would have demanded custody of Colleen, too, although he knew damn well having a child underfoot was the last thing she would have wanted.

She'd have used Colleen as leverage, so Jud would

give her everything she asked for. Besides, her father, Herb, would never have understood Sylvia's abandoning his granddaughter. Being Daddy's girl was important to Sylvia. Herb was probably the only person in the world she actually cared about. She wanted his love, but she also wanted his respect.

Jud was taking a risk having Sylvia declared dead so that he could collect her insurance money. Even now, the cops might still charge him with her murder. Only the lack of a body had kept him from being arrested at the time she went missing.

For seven years he'd dreaded waking up to cops beating on his door, dragging him off in handcuffs in front of Colleen, because some hunter had discovered Sylvia's bones in the woods.

He was still eighty percent certain his wife had run away to start a new life.

The remaining twenty percent kept him looking over his shoulder.

The cops had never believed in the stranger-killer theory. The homicide detectives were old-school. Anything happens to the wife, the husband probably did it. Jud had had motive, no alibi and the best opportunity to kill her and hide her body. There had been no evidence of anyone else at the scene, and random killers didn't generally operate at night on a country road in a downpour.

He'd been forced to admit that when he was a boy, he'd hunted in the Putnam Woods Conservation Preserve, across the road from where Sylvia's car

had been found. He'd done so years before the owner
died and left it to the state as protected wildlife
habitat. Since then the trees had grown, and the
undergrowth and marshes had changed the woods,
but the fact that he'd once been familiar with it was
enough for the detectives. One more nail in his
coffin—or hers—as they'd told him repeatedly.

If she'd been dumped by someone unfamiliar with
the area, she'd have been found by now, even if
buried in a shallow grave. The detectives had warned
him that bodies always surfaced sooner or later.
They'd quickly declared him the only suspect, and
had stopped looking for anyone else.

Jud was so lost in his thoughts, recalling the past,
that he jumped when the telephone beside him rang.
He cleared his throat and answered it.

"Daddy?"

He smiled, although he knew Colleen couldn't
see him. "You got me, sweetheart."

"I just called to say good-night. Gran says she'll
pick me up after school tomorrow and take me to
soccer, then drop me by your office afterward."

"Thank her for me."

"I will. Good night, Daddy. Oh, Gran wants to talk
to you."

He sighed. He wasn't looking forward to this
conversation.

"Jud, honey?"

"Why are you whispering, Irene?"

"I don't want Herb or Colleen to hear me. That

man Jenkins from the insurance company came to see me this morning. Thank God Herb wasn't here. You're really going ahead with it?"

"Trip's already started the paperwork to have Sylvia declared dead. It's time, Irene. I'm sorry if it upsets everyone. I can use the money to send Colleen to a good college. As it is, I barely keep up with her school tuition. An Ivy League college is out of the question, even with a partial scholarship."

"I know it's hard for you, but I do not like that Jenkins fellow. He acts as though it's his own money. He as good as told me he was going to pull some strings and get the police to reopen the case."

Jud heard the question mark behind that sentence. His mother-in-law was really asking whether he had anything to worry about. She swore she believed him when he told her he'd had nothing to do with Sylvia's disappearance, but hearing Herb condemn him as a killer for seven years must have eroded her belief in his innocence at least a bit.

"It's going to be hard on Colleen," he said. "Everything dragged up all over again. When she was seven, she really didn't understand what a divorce would have meant to her. If they reopen the case, her schoolmates will probably dredge up the story of the disappearing mother and the murderous father. I wish I could keep her wrapped in cotton, but it's time to get it finished once and for all."

"I'll be here for Colleen, dear. And for you, too. I

know what Sylvia was really like, even if Colleen and Herb don't. I'll pray for you."

"Pray for all of us."

After he hung up, he leaned back in his chair, took a long drink of his bourbon and closed his eyes. He'd lived carefully for seven years. Now he was about to take the biggest risk of his life. Only time would tell whether he'd made the right decision.

LIZ CLIMBED OUT of her Honda in front of the Weichert and Slaughter construction trailer and stepped into a cold mud puddle. She hadn't seen it, given the late-afternoon shadows.

Great. You'd think a construction company would have enough leftover gravel to keep their parking area dry. Her boots were now covered with mud. Her black slacks were splashed, as well, and the darn things had to be dry-cleaned.

She left muddy footprints on the wooden stairs up to the trailer entrance, where an industrial rubber welcome mat lay. She scraped off as much muck as she could, and opened the door.

After staying up past midnight poring over the murder book, then spending most of today on the evidence box, Liz agreed with the two homicide detectives who had handled the case the first time. Jud Slaughter had gotten away with murder.

So far. That was about to change.

She'd hoped for a picture of Slaughter, but since he'd never been arrested, he hadn't been photographed. He'd volunteered his prints and DNA at the time, but the only description she had was that he was a big man.

The previous afternoon Randy Railsback had brought her a cup of coffee, plunked his skinny butt down on the chair beside her desk and asked her to dinner. To discuss the case. Right. If Randy Randy continued to hit on her during office hours she was going to hit him upside his expensively coiffed head.

Since Randy had been riding a squad car seven years earlier, he knew no more than she did about the case. Jack Samuels, however, had wandered over when he'd heard them talking. "Slaughter looked like a jock," he said. "Probably played college football. More than able to carry a hundred-twenty-pound corpse far back into those woods and dig a grave deep enough to keep the coyotes away. By now he's probably got a beer gut, no hair and an ulcer. Murder'll do that to you…if you have any conscience at all."

So Liz expected to find a big man gone to seed. The only person in the trailer had his back to her. Broad back, broad shoulders. He was wearing chinos, muddy work boots and a down jacket, although the room was comfortably warm. She couldn't tell about the gut.

He heard her come in, turned around and stood. "Hey, can I help you?" he asked.

No paunch! And not the least bit bald! No wonder Sylvia Slaughter had fallen for him. Most women would. He was not just big, he was immense, and good-looking in a craggy way. His nose had obviously been broken more than once. Jack said he'd played football, and Liz would bet he'd been a linebacker or a tackle. Running into him would be like hitting a marble column.

Yeah, he could carry a corpse a long way into the woods and dig a grave without breaking a sweat.

At five feet eleven inches, Liz didn't look up to many men, but she had to tilt her head way back to stare into his guileless gray eyes. He had more than an adequate amount of sandy hair falling across his forehead. She knew from the file that he'd be thirty-nine. He'd been thirty-two when Sylvia died—disappeared.

Drat the man, he probably looked better now, with his sun-brown face and crinkly eyes, than he had then. Liz made a mental note to check for mistresses and girlfriends. No way this guy would be celibate for seven years.

"Mr. Slaughter, I'm Liz Gibson." She showed him her shield, then shoved it back into the pocket of her blazer. "I'd like to talk to you about your wife."

The start of a smile froze on Slaughter's face. He sucked in a deep breath. "I wasn't expecting to have somebody like you show up on my doorstep for a couple of weeks."

"I beg your pardon? Why would you expect the police after seven years?"

He laughed, but there was no mirth in the sound. "Come on, Miz…Gibson, was it?"

She kept her face carefully blank. "Your wife's case has never been closed, Mr. Slaughter. We revisit all open, uh, cases from time to time." She'd nearly said "homicides." Bad move. She'd have to watch her tongue around this guy.

"So there's nothing suspicious about the timing? Give me a break."

"I'm sorry. I'm not with you."

"Look, Miz Gibson, I'm late for a meeting at the job site. Ride over with me, and we'll talk."

No way would she get into a car with this behemoth, be driven God knew where and left there while he met with one of his subcontractors. "This won't take but a few minutes."

He closed his eyes, whether in exasperation or acquiescence she couldn't tell. When he opened them, he reached into his pocket, dialed his cell phone, turned his back on her and spoke quietly to whoever was on the other end, asking to put off the meeting.

He had a pleasant baritone voice. On the surface, he seemed like a nice man. But then most of the people she'd talked down from hostage situations had sounded nice and rational, until they lost it over whatever crime they felt had been perpetrated against them. Then they turned rabid in a nanosecond. This man was as much a wife killer as Bobby Joe Watson. Like Bobby Joe, he had a daughter who needed protection.

This guy wouldn't get away with it.

He flipped the phone closed, stuck it into his

pocket, pointed to an old wooden kitchen chair beside his desk and shucked his jacket.

Oh, definitely no paunch. The front of the guy's plaid shirt slid straight under the waistband of his chinos, which slid straight down his flat belly until they hit a bulge at the crotch that looked proportional to the size of the man himself. She dragged her eyes back to his face and swallowed hard, then took the chair he offered her. He went around the desk and sat down.

"You can't tell me this visit isn't because of my petition to have Sylvia declared dead. I didn't think the police worked for insurance companies."

Damn! She'd been blindsided. But maybe Gavigan didn't know, either. She'd have to find out who had pushed the higher-ups to reopen the case. "After saying for seven years that your wife disappeared, you suddenly want to have her declared dead. What changed your mind? And why now?" No way would she let him know this was the first she'd heard of it.

"Should I call my lawyer?"

Liz smiled her most ingratiating smile. Of course he should call his lawyer before he said another word, but that was the last thing she wanted him to do. "That's your right, Mr. Slaughter. Do you need one at the moment? We're just chatting here."

He narrowed those gray eyes at her. They no longer seemed quite so guileless. In fact, they'd turned cold as glare ice. "Ask your questions. I'll answer them or not."

"Absolutely." She had to remind herself he'd been

through hours, days, weeks of interrogation. He knew the way things worked. But he'd been interrogated by a pair of old-line homicide bulls, never by a woman. "So, what *did* change your mind?"

"The law says that seven years is the legal waiting period to have someone declared dead. I'm sure you hear this a lot, but my family needs closure."

"That's the only reason? You have no new information?"

He sighed and rubbed his large tanned hand down his face. "As you know, Sylvia and I both had half-million-dollar whole life policies on one another. In Tennessee, murder kicks in the accidental death double indemnity clause. Meaning, instead of half a million, it pays out a million."

"You've been looking at a million dollars in insurance for seven years?"

"Money I could not in good conscience request, so long as I felt certain Sylvia was alive somewhere. Now that it is legally appropriate to claim it for my family, however, we should be the ones to benefit by investing it. Believe me, the insurance company has been making plenty on it for the last seven years and is no doubt loath to give it up."

"So you now believe your wife was murdered?"

"Let's say I'm not certain any longer that she's alive. None of the homicide investigators ever came up with evidence either way, although they continued to act as though they knew she was dead and I killed her. Sorry to say this, but once you people get an idea in your collective heads, it's not easy to get it out."

"Not without evidence to the contrary, it isn't," Liz said dryly. "When something bad happens to one spouse, the odds are extremely heavy that the surviving spouse is involved. The statistics would blow your mind."

"I'm not a statistic and I'm not a murderer. When I started trying to make up my mind whether to petition to have her declared dead, I finally hired my own private detective."

"Who?" There were a lot of good P.I.s in Memphis, but there were also some bums willing to take a client's money for precious little labor.

"Frank LaPorte. He's a retired cop. Handles mostly divorces and insurance claims. My business partner and I have used him to investigate a couple of worker's comp suits. Both times he's been able to disprove the disability claim. You shouldn't be able to mow your lawn or reroof your house when you're in bed with a bad back."

"I'll need to talk to him. What did he find?"

"He didn't have any better luck. Not surprising after this length of time. He did say it's not as easy disappearing into a new identity as it used to be before babies were given social security numbers in their first year, and birth certificates were collated with death certificates."

"Still, it can be done."

"With long-term planning. There's no evidence

that Sylvia had any intention of leaving when she did, nor that she had created a new identity."

"Then you truly believe she's dead?"

"I believe that if she didn't die at the time she disappeared, she must have died now."

"And you want that million dollars."

"Miz Gibson, I build mansions and starter castles for rich folks, but I'm not rich. Contractors live at the whim of the housing market. We have construction loans to service, subcontractors to pay and materials to buy long before a house is built, and we keep paying until the house is sold, hopefully for a profit. When the market tanks, a lot of us go bankrupt. Besides, I have a fourteen-year-old daughter. She should have the benefit of that money, as well as the income it generates. Invested well, it should pay for her college by the time she's eighteen, without using too much of the principal."

"You don't plan to take advantage of that money yourself?"

"If I'm lucky, I can survive without it, but good colleges are expensive and emergencies occur."

"So you started the process to have your wife declared dead."

"As I was legally entitled to do."

"Even if it puts you under suspicion again?"

"Miss Gibson, I was never *not* under suspicion, as you well know. This just puts me back in your cross-hairs. No doubt you've seen a copy of the paperwork. Has Jenkins been in touch with the police?"

She sat up. New name. "Jenkins? Should he have been?" Why tell Slaughter she had no idea who Jenkins was?

"My mother-in-law said he'd been to see her, and acted as though that money belonged to him and not the insurance company. He also said he was going to demand that the case be reopened."

"That information hasn't filtered down to my level yet," she said. Nor was it likely to. It seemed a good bet that this Jenkins guy had called in a favor from the higher-ups to get the case reopened, but she'd probably never know for certain.

She was about to launch into questions about the night Sylvia disappeared when the door to the trailer burst open and a girl exploded into the room.

At least Liz assumed it was a girl. She was as tall as Liz and wore an incredibly muddy soccer uniform. Her shoes, face and long blond hair were caked with the stuff. Liz had played soccer in high school, before she discovered she was better at volleyball. This girl looked as though she'd slid face-first across a muddy field not once, but several times. She probably had.

She was long-legged and coltish, with that elegantly slim frame that drove designers to turn thirteen-year-olds into the latest high fashion models. No woman stayed that sleek once she reached eighteen or nineteen. At thirty-two, Liz definitely hadn't.

"We won!" The girl flew across the room, arms outstretched.

"Whoa!" Slaughter laughed and held her at arm's length.

This must be Colleen.

"I'm glad you won, sweetheart, but I don't need half the soccer field all over this shirt." He grinned at his daughter, his face glowing with delight.

Liz's heart lurched. Could this guy really be a cold-blooded killer?

Yes indeed, he could. She'd known too many charming, lovable guys who disintegrated into dolts and oafs when the going got rough. Assuming they stuck around, which most of them didn't.

Still, watching the big man and his tall daughter, Liz found herself praying that he wasn't a killer, that she wouldn't take him away from this child, destroy that smile.

But if he was a killer, she'd damn well do what she had to.

At that moment, Colleen realized there was somebody else in the room. "Oh," she said, and turned to stare at Liz, assessing her from her muddy boots to the top of her head. She seemed to pay a great deal of attention to Liz's left hand. Looking for a ring? Seeing if Liz was a possible rival for her dad's attention?

Jud introduced them, but did not mention that Liz was a cop. She didn't, either, but said to Slaughter, "I can see you've got your hands full." She smiled at Colleen, who did not smile back. "How about we set up an appointment for tomorrow morning? What time would be convenient for you?"

The teen relaxed. She probably thought Liz was a prospective client.

A child who had lost one parent usually clung to the other and often acted as a protector—or a guard. Colleen had been seven when her mother disappeared, and wouldn't have comprehended that her father was suspected of killing her. At fourteen, however, she must worry constantly that if new evidence surfaced, her father might be snatched away from her, too.

She wouldn't be able to admit even to herself that she was afraid her father might have murdered her mother. Right now she seemed relaxed and happy, but she must be under an incredible strain. Liz would be willing to bet that both Colleen and her father tiptoed around the subject of Sylvia's disappearance. All teenagers carried a load of angst, but Colleen must be carrying more than her share. Kids with much less on their plates turned to drugs or alcohol or sex—acting out what they dared not express. Tough on the kid, but equally tough on Slaughter, particularly if he knew he was a killer.

Talk about a dysfunctional family! Liz felt sorry for both of them.

"I start early," Slaughter said. "I usually stop for breakfast around eight. Could you meet me at Lacy's Café? We could talk while we eat."

Actually, that would suit Liz just fine. She readily agreed, left Colleen to tell her father about the soccer game, climbed into her car and drove away.

At some point she'd have to interview the girl. By law Slaughter could elect to be with her during the interview, but kids never told the truth when their parents were listening to them. Was there any way to get her alone for an informal chat? Liz made a mental note to ask Jack Samuels what he'd recommend.

She wondered whether Randy Railsback would have more luck talking to Colleen. Much as she detested his macho-flirty attitude, she knew he could be charming and ingratiating, and might get more from the teen than Liz could. Obviously the girl regarded any female as a threat, not necessarily because of a dysfunctional attachment to her father, but because she considered him still married to her mother, and thus out of bounds.

Liz didn't have to deal with Colleen today. Better deal with Slaughter first.

She'd also have to get around to that Jenkins guy. Since he didn't seem anxious to pay Slaughter a flat million bucks, he must be keeping up the illusion that he believed Sylvia was still alive. He might, however, not believe that for a moment. He might even have evidence to support his view. Since a killer couldn't profit from his crime, Jenkins might be equally happy to see Jud convicted of killing his wife. Liz should find out if the money would go to Colleen if her dad went to prison for murder.

While waiting at a red light, she added the name Jenkins to the list of people in her notebook. She'd also have to talk to the P.I. Frank LaPorte, and the people Sylvia had worked with….

Liz realized suddenly she'd been driving without paying much attention to where she was going. Now, she stepped on the gas. She would have just enough time before the early November dark to check out the crime scene, even though any evidence was seven years gone.

Slaughter was dangerous. Maybe not to everyone, but definitely to her, embodying most of the qualities in a man that attracted her.

Good dark chocolate was equally attractive and just as bad for her.

She would have to get to know Jud Slaughter intimately. But not that intimately. One did not get involved with suspects.

Before she'd seen him, she'd been certain he was a killer. Those gray eyes had not changed her mind.

Had they?

CHAPTER FOUR

JUD LEFT COLLEEN IMMERSED in math homework at the table while he cleaned up the kitchen after dinner.

What would Liz Gibson ask him over breakfast? He found he was actually looking forward to seeing her again. That was crazy, considering their adversarial relationship.

Jud had no idea whether married detectives wore wedding rings on the job or not. He hoped Liz Gibson wasn't married, although there wasn't much he could do about that under the present circumstances. It was nice to meet a woman as tall as Liz, who looked cool enough to handle a gorilla on a rampage. He hated being around fragile little women. He was always afraid he'd break them.

That was one of the reasons he'd been attracted to Sylvia. She'd been so sure of herself, so confident. She hadn't looked or acted breakable.

Nor had she turned out to be. He didn't think a thermonuclear explosion could have shaken her, but he hadn't known that when he fell for her.

Seven years was a long time to be celibate. Jud had managed for three before he allowed himself to be swept into an affair with the wife of one of his clients. Separated, but still officially married, as he was. He wasn't particularly proud of himself, but they'd parted friends, when she went back to her husband.

Since then there'd been a couple of other women. He'd been up-front about the fact he still considered himself married and unavailable for anything except a casual relationship. Some women saw it as a challenge. He knew that on some level he was a catch, even with a teenage daughter as part of the package.

Suspicion of murder, however, was not an added inducement, particularly when the victim was his wife. Having a fling with the police detective who was trying to prove he was a killer was a very bad idea.

He should have petitioned for divorce years ago on the grounds of desertion, but he couldn't bring himself to do that to Colleen. He and Sylvia might have been dancing around divorce when she disappeared, but their daughter didn't know that. Once Sylvia vanished, Jud couldn't add divorce for desertion to the list of problems Colleen had to deal with. Better to wait the requisite seven years to be safe.

Those first years, he'd expected Sylvia to walk back in the front door as casually as though she had never left. That would be just like her.

But seven years? There was probably a reason that period had been chosen by law in the first place.

He watched Colleen poring over her books. Physically, she took after her mother. Her dark gold hair was streaked by the sun, where Sylvia's had been expensively streaked in a salon. The effect, however, was much the same. Colleen had her mom's elegant bone structure and natural grace. Not that you could tell after soccer practice.

Her personality wasn't much like Sylvia's, thank God. She was basically kind and loving, although at the moment she was going through a bad patch of teenage sulks and temper. His mother-in-law reminded him that these phases would pass, and sooner or later she'd grow into a fine adult. If he lasted that long.

Colleen usually looked and acted normal, but he knew how fragile she was inside. He and Irene worked diligently with her teachers, counselors and coaches to prop up her self-esteem. At age seven, children often fear anything bad that happens was somehow their fault. Colleen believed her mom had left because she herself failed her in some way.

The sad truth was that Sylvia had never wanted children, had wanted to abort the fetus she found she was carrying the year after Jud and she married. Only fear of her own father's wrath made her carry the child to term.

Maybe if they'd had a boy…

But seeing Colleen at fourteen, Sylvia would have considered the beautiful girl competition. On some level, he supposed, many women felt twinges of jealousy as they watched their daughters grow into young women, no matter how much they loved them.

Sylvia would have done everything she could to cut Colleen down to size. That was *not* normal.

In the countless counseling sessions he'd attended since Sylvia's disappearance, he'd learned that children, like cats, tended to be most devoted to people who were not attracted to them. They clung to the abusive parent.

Jud knew Colleen loved him, but she'd fought as fiercely as a seven-year-old could fight for her mother's love. She *had* to believe Sylvia was dead.

He still believed Sylvia was sitting pretty with a new life and a new identity. Maybe on the Riviera or the Costa Brava. Maybe in Canada or Brazil. He had no doubt she could come up with a stake or a sugar daddy.

The dirty casserole pan wouldn't fit into the dishwasher, and would never get clean without elbow grease, anyway. He set it in the sink and went to work on it with a scrubbing pad. The meal had turned out rather well for a first attempt at a new recipe. Shrimp and pesto and fettuccine noodles topped with cheese. He'd add it to his arsenal of one-dish recipes.

He'd always done the cooking, even when Sylvia was still with them. In the seven years since, he'd become pretty fair at it. He wished Colleen would show more interest in learning.

"I'll never be as good as you are, Daddy," she said whenever he tried to entice her into fixing dinner for them. Teenage shorthand for "I don't want to." He let her get away with it.

Shoot, he let her get away with nearly everything. So far she hadn't pushed him too far, but sooner or later she'd put him in a position where he'd have to lower the boom. He wouldn't be doing her any favors if he let her get into bad stuff. The world would not make allowances for her.

He prayed she'd stay a good kid, and that Irene would know how to deal with tantrums or boys or drugs or alcohol or tattoos or fast cars or Goths.

Colleen didn't realize it, but her life was much happier without her mother, just as his was.

But the policewoman could make both of their lives a living hell. He'd have to keep her away from his child.

"HEY, MA'AM, THAT'S NOT a good place to park."

Liz stood beside her unmarked car and looked around for the source of the voice. She saw an old man standing beside a small brick ranch house set back in the woods on her side of the road. She could barely glimpse the house through the closely planted pines. She leaned on her door and called, "May I park in your driveway? I'd very much like to speak to you if you've got a minute."

"Sure. Better move your car before somebody comes flying around that curve and creams you."

She moved the car. As she climbed out, the man walked over to her, removing his beat-up John Deere cap with the aplomb of a Victorian gentleman.

"Folks in the country drive twenty miles faster

than the road can handle." He grinned. "Can't tell you how many accidents I've seen on that curve in the forty years I been living out here."

She stuck out her hand and told him her name and her business.

She could feel the bones in his fingers, but the skin felt like well-tanned leather. His face looked like leather, as did the scalp that showed through his sparse white hair. He shoved his cap back on his head. "Name's Taylor Waldran, ma'am. Lord, don't tell me y'all are trying to find that woman's body again."

"Again?"

"Every couple of years some cop comes by to talk to me about what happened that night. I tell him the same thing. I have no idea. It was pouring rain. The wife and I stayed inside by the fireplace. Saw nothing, heard nothing. Didn't find out about the car being abandoned till the next morning." He waved a hand at his lawn and the pines. "The riders used our front lawn as the staging ground for the hunt."

"You said riders?"

"Yes'm. There's a bunch of riders brings their walking horses and hounds whenever somebody disappears in the woods, and Putnam's over there's been part of the Wolf River Conservancy for twenty years. At first they thought the woman might have wandered off and died of exposure or drowned in one of them marshes, but they never did find one single trace of her." He shook his head. "My Vachie kept the cookies coming and the coffeepot hot for three days."

"Could I speak to her?"

"No, ma'am. Gone these three years."

"I'm sorry for your loss."

"Thank you. Hard to be alone after fifty-three years. My grandkids want to move me to town into some kind of zero-lot-line old folks apartment, but I ain't havin' none of it."

An obese basset hound with a gray muzzle meandered off the front porch and slumped down beside Mr. Waldran's knee. The dog definitely looked more than seven years old. "That night the woman went missing, did your dog hear anything?"

"Maizie?" He laughed and reached down to scratch the basset's long ears. "She's been stone deaf for years and too lazy to hunt a cold biscuit."

"What about the hounds? Did they find any trace of her?"

"Ma'am, by the time they started looking, the rain had been pourin' down for hours. Any scent might 'a been there would 'a been long gone. On t'other hand, if he'd buried her, would 'a washed away the soil some, but didn't find no sign of a grave, either."

"Could she have walked away and abandoned her car?"

"In that weather? Had to be a mighty good reason to leave a perfectly good car sitting on the side of the road with the motor running, the door open and the dome light on."

"Could she have stopped to help someone and been abducted?"

"That's what they thought at first, but that husband o' hers swore she'd never do something that dumb. Besides, she carried a gun in the car. Had a permit and everything. It was still there. If she'd gotten out of the car, she'd 'a took that gun, if she had a lick o' sense."

"What did you think of the husband?"

"Seemed like a nice man. Real cut up. My Vachie tried to look after him some. 'Course, those detectives thought from the get-go he killed her."

"So they were just going through the motions on the search?"

"Oh, no, ma'am. They didn't let up for three solid days. Had them crime scene folks here, but wadn't nothing to find after that downpour. After a while I guess they just gave up."

Liz thanked Mr. Waldran and asked if she could leave her car while she walked across the road to look in the woods. He agreed and went back into his house. Maizie lumbered after him.

Contemplating the curve of the road, Liz was as surprised as Mr. Waldran that someone hadn't come around the corner and smacked into Sylvia's car all those years ago, especially since the driver's-side door had been open.

Though the rain had stopped earlier, mist still hung in the cold air, Liz noted with a shiver. A little more moisture and mud wouldn't make much difference at this point.

She walked across the road and stood on the

narrow grass shoulder to stare down into the water-filled ditch. If Sylvia needed help or refuge, surely she'd have headed up the driveway to the Waldran house. Mr. Waldran and his wife had both been investigated at the time, to make certain they hadn't kidnapped and done away with Sylvia.

Both had come up clean. He was a deacon of the Campbelltown Baptist Church. Pillars of the community, they'd raised four children and had a dozen grandchildren. Neither was senile or paranoid. There had been no sign that Sylvia had been in the house or the garage.

The obvious solution was that someone had stopped her on the road somehow, abducted her or killed her and hidden her body too well for it to be found, probably a long way from the scene.

She wouldn't have braked for someone she didn't know. She wouldn't have gotten into a car with a stranger. If she'd been accosted, she'd have used her gun to protect herself.

Her car had not been dented or disabled, proving she hadn't been rammed by another vehicle, and stopped to check the damage. Who else but her husband would even know she'd be alone on this road at night?

The one person she would have stopped for was big Jud Slaughter.

CHAPTER FIVE

"DADDY," COLLEEN SAID, "who was that lady, the one you arranged to have breakfast with? She's not one of your clients."

Jud turned his truck into the parking lot of Hamilton's Academy for Young Ladies and joined the line of SUVs, crew-cab pickups and fancy sedans also dropping off girls for school. He debated whether to tell her the truth and let her stew all day, or make up something he'd have to refute later. "How'd you know she's not a client?"

"Those slacks came from someplace like Target, for one thing. And ladies who can afford your houses always wear gynormous diamond rings and carry Coach handbags for every day. She's not married."

He glanced at his daughter in amazement. She was fourteen! How could she possibly identify where the woman's slacks came from, or be aware of purses and jewelry? "What do you study in that fancy school of yours?" He pulled into the unloading zone, stopped and turned in his seat.

"You always say it pays to know quality," she said with a cheeky smile. Leaning over, she gave him a kiss, slid out of the car, waved at a couple of other girls with long blond hair and ran up the stairs to the front door.

She'd forgotten to ask him again about Liz Gibson, but she'd remember sooner or later. He'd have to respond, but he'd have a better idea of how much he needed to tell her after breakfast.

When he walked into the diner, Liz was already sitting in a booth. She was reading the morning newspaper and drinking orange juice. He took a moment to assess her from the doorway.

Good-looking. Maybe late twenties, early thirties. Probably divorced, probably children. Well-spoken. He wondered how long she'd been a detective, because she obviously worked out. The homicide detectives who'd ridden roughshod over him seven years ago had not, but they'd been older. One dyed his hair blue-black, the other carried his paunch in front of him like a baby bump. Why were they not the ones reopening the investigation? Did they think he'd respond better to a woman?

In her case, they might be right. He'd liked her forthright hazel eyes, and the brown locks she pulled back in what his daughter called a scrunchie. Made him want to ease if off and find out what she looked like with her hair down. He'd also be willing to give his business partner, Trip Weichert, good odds that there wasn't a single drop of silicone in what Trip would call her "rack." Nice rack, too. Just about the right size to fit into the palms of his hands.

Altogether a very beddable specimen. If he were in the market, and if bedding a detective wasn't about the most dangerous notion he'd ever had.

She must have felt his eyes on her because she looked up, saw him, folded the paper and set it beside her cup. No welcoming smile, however. Very serious lady.

They greeted each other, but she didn't offer to shake hands. He sat opposite her, and before he spoke, Bella, his regular waitress, put a cup of coffee in front of him. "Morning, Jud. Your usual?" she said.

"Did you order?" he asked Liz.

"Yeah, she did," Bella answered, and turned back toward the kitchen.

"I don't think she approves of me," Liz murmured.

"She doesn't approve of anybody that hasn't been eating here for at least ten years."

Liz took a business card out of her pocket and shoved it across the table. "This is my extension and my cell phone. If you need to speak to me, don't hesitate to call."

"You mean if I want to confess?"

"I didn't say that. You might think of something you didn't tell the other detectives. So, shall we get down to it while we wait?"

Jud shrugged. "You've undoubtedly read the files. I don't have anything to tell you that wasn't in them."

"Humor me. For example, why was your wife driving home by herself at eight o'clock at night?"

"Sylvia was branch vice president of the Marquette National Bank. She usually worked late on Friday nights. The bank stays open until seven on Fridays, then she made certain whatever bankers do after hours got done."

"You don't know?"

"Not precisely, no. She liked working alone after everyone left. She wasn't a morning person, so she didn't go in to work early. She blamed it on her internal clock."

"Your daughter wasn't home?"

"She was spending the night with my in-laws. She frequently does that on Friday and Saturday nights. They live in Germantown." He grinned. "That means closer to malls and movies."

"She was only seven?"

"At that age she conned her grandmother into shopping and the latest Disney."

"I'm speaking to Mrs. Richardson later this morning."

That sounded vaguely like a threat. "Irene will tell you the same thing, Miz Gibson." But Herb wouldn't. She'd get a real earful if he was home.

Bella plopped a big glass of iced tea down in front of the detective and filled Jud's coffee mug. They waited until she was out of earshot again.

"Listen, do you mind if we switch to first names? Seems more informal," Liz said.

Jud was a bit surprised. "Sure. I'm Jud."

"And they call me Liz that do speak of me."

"Certainly not Liz the cursed?"

She laughed—the first time he'd heard her laugh. He loved it. A Shakespeare-quoting detective with a laugh like warm honey, and a smile that would melt icebergs in the Bering Strait. It definitely melted him, and warmed parts of his body that he'd rather keep dormant, thank you very much. He'd known she was dangerous, but not *this* dangerous.

"Certainly not the prettiest Liz in Christendom," she said.

"Who says?"

The silence was deafening, the look lasted too long and the connection was too sudden. She broke eye contact first, stirred two packets of artificial sweetener into her tea, squeezed the lemon and drank greedily. He did the same with his coffee and burned the roof of his mouth.

"Uh, what'd you fix?"

"I beg your pardon?" he asked.

"The file says you cooked dinner that night. What'd you fix?"

No one in all those hours of interrogation and interview had asked him that. "It was seven years ago."

"Come on, Jud, you might not remember what you had for dinner last night, but I'll bet you remember the menu that night."

As a matter of fact he did. The other detectives had asked him why he was the one doing the cooking, but not the menu. He took a breath as though trying to remember, then said, "I picked up a roast chicken at the grocery on the way home from the job I was working. And some fresh asparagus."

"Expensive in November."

He shrugged. "Sylvia liked it. I poached it in chicken stock until it was just crunchy, and thawed some brown rice in the microwave. I make it in big batches and freeze it in portions. Takes forty-five minutes to an hour to steam from scratch and only ten minutes to heat up in the microwave. That's it."

"What about rolls?"

He shook his head. "Two starches at one meal."

"Dessert?"

Again he shook his head. "Watching our weight. Sylvia never has a problem, but I have to be careful."

"To drink?"

"We'd opened a bottle of pinot grigio the night before and stashed the rest in the refrigerator. There was enough left for a couple of glasses each. I poured myself one when Sylvia called to tell me she was on her way."

"Then?"

"There was boxing on *Showtime*. I sat down to watch it. I'd been out on the site most of the day in the cold rain, so that one glass of wine put me right to sleep. The boxing must have been boring. I really don't remember who was fighting, but it wasn't a championship match or anything. When I finally woke up, I realized Sylvia wasn't home yet. It was nearly midnight."

"What did you do?"

"Tried her cell phone. No answer. There are a couple of places along that road where you can't get decent reception, particularly during bad weather. I figured she'd had a flat or something and couldn't reach me. I dashed some cold water on my face to wake up, grabbed my coat and headed out to find her."

Bella slapped down two plates in front of them. Jud's held at least three eggs, bacon and wheat toast. Liz's held a toasted English muffin.

Jud might worry about his waistline, although Liz couldn't see that he had any problems in that department. Obviously he wasn't bothered about cholesterol. She wished she'd indulged in at least an omelet or an order of bacon.

His answers had been interesting. He'd said Sylvia *has,* not *had.* Did he really believe she was still alive, or had he coached himself to use the present tense?

Liz would be willing to bet nobody had ever asked him what he'd cooked for dinner. The original detectives, Sherman and Lee, whose names had no doubt given rise to a million jokes during their partnership, were both middle-aged, had probably been horrified to find that Jud did the cooking for his family and had abandoned the subject.

He could have fixed the entire meal in ten minutes, leaving more than enough time to commit the killing and hide the body. The one call that had been logged from Sylvia's cell phone that night had originated from the tower closest to her office. In his original

interview, Jud had said that she called every night as
she was leaving to give him her ETA so he could get
dinner ready. She had not attempted to phone him
again, but that call alone would have told him ap-
proximately where her car would be and where he
could intercept her.

One of the most damning items against him was
that his partner, Trip Weichert, said he'd tried to
reach Jud at about ten and had gotten the answering
machine. Jud had said in his original statement he
must have slept through the call.

Maybe. Liz—who couldn't bear to let the answering machine pick up even if she knew the caller was
from a magazine subscription service—had never
slept through the ringing phone. He must really have
been dead to the world.

Or simply not there to pick up.

"So, Jud, between us, what do you think happened that night?" She leaned forward and gave
him her full attention.

He, on the other hand, leaned back and folded his
arms across his chest. She'd been taught to read
people's body language. His signified avoidance,
protecting himself, distancing himself. When he
spoke, however, he lowered his eyes and took a deep
breath, but did not look down and to the right. That
was a liar's look. Dead giveaway. Either he was
trying to tell the truth, or he'd practiced so long it had
become the truth to him.

"I think she had arranged for somebody to pick

her up, and left her car that way so we'd think she'd been abducted, and would stop looking for her quicker." He raised his eyes. "It worked."

"We couldn't find evidence of a pickup by any of the rental-car agencies or taxis, even the ones that will drive that far out," Liz responded. "With all the publicity at the time, surely any taxi or rental-car company would have come forward." She shrugged. "The alternative is a colleague, a friend or a lover. No evidence was ever found for any of those."

He started to say something, then stopped.

"If you know of any lover, or even a possible lover, I'd suggest you give me a name."

"I don't. To the best of my knowledge, Sylvia was not having an affair at the time she disappeared."

"Were you?"

"What? No, of course not."

"But you've had affairs since she disappeared." Liz made her comment a statement, not a question. She didn't know whether he'd slept around or not, but he would assume she'd traced his lovers. Or she hoped he would.

The man actually blushed. With shame or guilt?

"Lady, it's been seven years since my wife disappeared. What do you think?"

"I'd like to talk to the ladies."

"You find them, you talk to them. I'm not giving you any names. Believe me, there are damn few of them to find. What difference does it make, anyway?

I was a completely faithful husband until long after Sylvia disappeared."

It made a great deal of difference to Liz. She'd find those women and interview them—no, interrogate them, until they admitted their liaisons with Jud. Who knew what he might have let slip to a lover? "I don't need no stinkin' divorce," for example. She pushed her empty plate away. Jud pushed his plate back, as well, although most of his farmer's breakfast lay congealing on it.

So she'd rattled him.

"You're telling me you had a good marriage?"

"About average."

This time he did look down and to his right. He was lying.

"Money troubles?"

He dropped his fists onto the table on either side of his plate. Not exactly a slam, but close.

Good, he was losing his cool.

"Lady—uh, Liz, we moved into the new house in July, before she disappeared in November. Five months is not a long time to get the kinks out of a new house, not even one I designed and built. Colleen had just started second grade at her private school, with much longer travel time, plus after-school care until either I or her grandmother could pick her up.

"Sylvia had made vice president a year earlier and was working sixty hours a week or more. So was I, trying to get my construction business on a solid footing. We were all under a lot of stress. Sure, there were strains on the marriage, but I swear to God I never picked up on any signals that Sylvia was going to run away."

"I thought your business was having money problems."

"Half the time we're having short-term money problems. Trip and I knew we could weather them. We did, as you could see yesterday. We're going great guns. We were a little overextended, that's all."

"Nothing a million dollars wouldn't have cured," Liz said.

Without warning, he was furious. His skin grew mottled, his jaw set and his shoulders hunched. So he *did* have a temper. Not altogether Good Neighbor Sam, Mr. Easygoing.

"Miz Gibson, if I killed my wife for a million dollars, don't you think I would have arranged to have her body found so I could collect?"

"You're going to collect now."

He slid out of the booth and stood. He loomed over Liz, and for a moment she thought he might actually hit her with one of those huge fists.

He took a deep breath, however, and loosened both his shoulders and his hands. He sat back down and waggled a finger at Bella, who was watching them from behind the counter, for another cup of coffee. He pointed at Liz's tea. She shook her head.

Drat! Waiting for his coffee to be poured and for Bella to move out of earshot again gave him the breathing space he needed to get himself under control.

"Sorry. Sometimes all the suspicion gets to me." Good Neighbor Sam was back. He grinned at her sheepishly, and her heart turned over and went into overdrive. Uh-oh.

"Look, Liz, I'm going to say this one more time. I did not kill my wife. I did not hide her body. I do not know what happened that night. I would never have risked my own neck, my freedom and my daughter's happiness by depriving her of one parent, much less two. I won't help you railroad me into jail for a crime I didn't commit."

Liz nodded. "Okay. Now, let me give you my response." She wasn't telling him anything he didn't already know, but he hadn't heard it recently. Might shake him up a bit. "Sherman and Lee, the two original detectives on the case, firmly believed that you killed your wife and hid her body somewhere."

He started to speak, but she held up a finger to stop him. "I am not Sherman and Lee. I am starting from scratch. For every mystery murder case, there are ninety-nine straightforward killings where we know immediately who did what to whom.

"Our homicide squad had a solve rate of over ninety percent before all the stranger-on-stranger and gangbanger killings started. It's now down around eighty-four percent, which is better than most counties our size. Some cops just want to close the file, put somebody on trial whether they are convicted or not. I'm not like that, and I doubt Sherman and Lee were, either. If you are innocent, I'll prove that, if possible, and find the real bad guy.

"If you are guilty, however, I am your worst junkyard-dog nightmare. It doesn't matter that I like you and want to believe you. I won't feel a bit guilty if I decide to arrest you and deprive your daughter of her one remaining parent. You did that, not me."

He stared at her silently for a long moment, then he nodded. "Fair enough." He leaned forward and smiled that beatific smile that would melt a statue's heart. "So, you like me?"

Liz laughed so hard Bella came over to see if she needed a thwack on the back.

CHAPTER SIX

SYLVIA'S PARENTS, the Richardsons, lived in the less affluent section of Germantown. Their medium-size Georgian-style house was well-kept, but unremarkable.

The garden, however, was anything but unremarkable. Either the couple could afford a full-time gardener, or one of them worked continuously to manicure the lawn and the flower beds. Even in November, great clumps of gold and ochre chrysanthemums hadn't quite finished blooming, and the pansies glowed.

Interesting. They were planted in strict groups sorted by color. Somebody had a thing for order.

The trees hadn't been neglected, either. Liz wasn't very good on horticulture, but even she could identify the glowing red of dogwoods and Japanese maples that still hadn't lost their leaves. Each tree was carefully surrounded by a mulched circle planted with hostas and dwarf azaleas. There was no crab or orchard grass. Not one dandelion. This was property that would receive the yard of the month award more often than not. The gardener obviously had control issues. Whatever the rest of this person's life was like, he—or she—could impose his will on this little patch. Shrubs didn't talk back.

Liz wanted to see whether the backyard was as cultivated and staged, or whether the front yard—the one the neighbors saw—received all the attention.

She was reaching for the doorbell when a voice came over the intercom, startling her. "Miz Gibson?"

A female voice. Not young. "Mrs. Richardson?"

"I'm in my workshop out back. Come on around by the driveway and down the path past the fountain."

Liz walked around the house. At first glance the backyard looked no different, but then she realized the deep lot was bisected—quadrisected, really. The same precision governed the plantings around the house and deck.

Beyond the section of lawn on the right side was an equally neat vegetable garden. Turnip greens, cabbage, winter squash and cauliflower still remained in the beds.

The left-hand quarter, however, looked as though it be-longed to a completely different yard. She'd be willing to bet it belonged to a different gardener.

Although there were neat brick paths, instead of marching straight and intersecting at ninety-degree angles, they curved gently among deep beds of or-namental grasses and now-dying wildflowers. The paths met at an ornamental pond made to look like a natural pool fed by a small, mossy waterfall. When

Liz leaned over it, fat, parti-colored koi rose up to see if she had any nibbles for them.

The pool would be cool and shaded in the summer when the big oaks were in full leaf.

At the very back corner stood another building. Not a shed, but a good-size A-frame structure of dark green stained board and batten, with a window wall facing the backyard and up the driveway.

Liz made a mental note to see how long the Richardsons had lived here. This could not have been accomplished in a day or even a year.

"Down here, Miz Gibson." A tall woman in jeans and a hunter-green sweatshirt stepped from the side portico of the A-frame and motioned to Liz, then stood aside and let her enter ahead of her.

"In case you can't tell, I'm a weaver." Irene Richardson waved her hand at the room and laughed.

Diamond-shaped shelves built across the wall beside the door were stuffed with jewel-toned skeins of thick wool. A big bench loom faced the window wall at the front, and several pieces of equipment Liz assumed had to do with making yarn were positioned around the space. There was even an antique spinning wheel.

On the mantelpiece sat about twenty wooden candlesticks with tall ivory tapers in them. "They're made out of old-fashioned wool spindles," Irene said. "I collect them."

A scarred harvest table, several pine chairs and a tiny kitchen unit ran along the back wall. Above hung more shelves overflowing with what looked like craft books. A gas fireplace with fake logs burned cheerily in the far corner. A worn club chair and a Lincoln rocker sat on either side of the hearth.

A number of colorful wool rugs hung on the walls, and bright shawls were tossed casually over the furniture. There were no pictures; the weavings were art enough.

"Incredible room," Liz said. "Incredible yard, too. I'd love to see it in the spring."

"Come back in April. Herb is always delighted to show off his handiwork. We're on several garden tours every spring and summer, although I think it's even prettier in the fall, when the leaves turn, and before the summer flowers die."

"So he's the gardener, you're the weaver."

"Not quite. The little bit around the cottage is mine. Takes almost no maintenance, and I can usually con Herb into doing that for me. I loathe gardening, with its dirty fingernails, aching knees and sweat."

Liz wandered around, peering at the cloud-soft shawls draped over the chairs, and wondering whether Mrs. Richardson sold them. If so, whether she could afford to buy one. It wouldn't do to ask now, but after the case was closed, she might inquire about price. "When did you start weaving?"

"Six years ago." Mrs. Richardson sat in the rocker and motioned Liz to the club chair. "I either had to discover something to occupy my mind, or lose it.

Simple as that. I took a continuing-education course in weaving, and six years later, this is the result."

"Herb's the gardener?"

"He'd always gardened, but he went crazy after—you know. Same reason."

"So a year after."

"It took us both a year before we could do anything besides sit and stare at the walls and bug the police."

"After something like this happens, many couples split up. You're still together."

"That's debatable." Irene laughed, this time without mirth. Jud had laughed the same way. There wasn't much comedy in this family. "We have a granddaughter who needs us. Jud needs me, too."

"Just you?"

Irene sighed. Her shoulders sank, and for the first time, she looked her age. Liz had checked. She was sixty-two, her husband sixty-nine.

"I wanted to speak to you before Herb got hold of you. He's so angry. He thinks Jud…did something to Sylvia. He'll tell you a whole bunch of stuff that isn't true, although I'm sure he believes every word."

"You're certain none of it is true?"

"Oh, absolutely. Jud wouldn't hurt a fly, and believe me, Sylvia gave him plenty of motivation."

Aha.

"That boy was the best thing that ever happened to Sylvia, and he's blessed my life and Colleen's." Irene waved at the room. "He designed and built this cottage for me completely at his expense. He didn't even let me pay for the materials, although I'm sure he could have used the money."

Her attitude surprised Liz. Mothers didn't generally say negative things about their own children to the police.

"If Jud says he doesn't know where she is, then he doesn't know. Period."

"You think she deliberately disappeared?"

"Oh, yes. Wouldn't you like a cup of tea? I keep the electric kettle hot all the time these chilly days."

"If it's no trouble."

"None." Irene went to the small kitchenette, got a tall mug from the cupboard and turned to Liz. "China or Indian?"

"Indian, please."

"Lemon or milk?"

"Lemon, please, and one artificial sweetener, if you have it."

"I have it, all right. I don't use sugar. I already fight the battle of the old-lady bulge."

Looking at Irene's trim, upright figure, Liz figured she was winning that battle. When they were settled on either side of the fire, Liz asked again, "You really think she took off? Weird way to go about it."

"Sylvia avoided situations she didn't want to deal with. If she wasn't doing well in a subject in college, she'd drop it before she could fail. The day she met Jud, she broke her engagement to a young medical student without a word of warning."

"She must really have fallen for him." For the first time, Liz felt a kinship with the woman. Jud was easy to fall for.

"You have to admit, he's pretty spectacular." Irene laughed. "I thought she'd found someone she could find happiness with, but her discontent came from inside. Even Jud couldn't keep her satisfied for long. And she certainly made him miserable the last year or so."

"So he killed her."

"You think I'd love him the way I do if I thought for a single second that he'd hurt Sylvia?"

"Mrs. Richardson, nobody chooses to disappear that way. Car running on the side of the road, door open, lights on, handbag inside with cash and credit cards… She didn't even take money out of her checking or savings account. And how did she get away in a driving rainstorm in the middle of the night? That's not a disappearance. At the very least it's abduction, and given that nobody's found any evidence of abduction or any proof that she's alive, it's almost certainly murder. In my business we go by who had motive, means and opportunity. Slaughter had all three. So far as we know, he was the only person who did."

"He took two polygraphs after she disappeared, and passed them both."

"Polygraphs aren't admissible in evidence, Mrs. Richardson, because they can be fooled."

"Jud wouldn't know how to do that. Why on earth

you people continue to hound him I do not know. If she's dead, somebody else killed her. If she's alive, why haven't you found her?"

Because we haven't really looked. At least, not recently.

An hour later the two women were curled up with mugs of hot tea and had progressed to first names. Liz, however, didn't know much more than she had before. She was convinced that Irene was not telling her everything she knew or suspected, but Liz couldn't find any cracks in her story. She was getting ready to start over when the door opened so hard it slammed against the wall.

"Is this her?"

Both women jumped.

"Why didn't she tell me she was here? I looked out front and saw her car."

It had to be Herb. His well-worn jeans bore a knife-edge crease. His immaculate button-down oxford cloth shirt was so stiff with starch that Liz didn't see how he could raise his arms. Control issues. He was a small man with a tonsure of white hair, and the remnants of a gardener's tan—much darker on the lower half of his face. Liz immediately categorized him as a rooster ready to take on all comers.

She stood and extended her hand. "Liz Gibson, Mr. Richardson. Why don't you sit down and join us."

He blinked, narrowed his eyes and scanned her

from top to bottom, then glared at his wife. "What crap has Irene been feeding you?" He teetered on the balls of his feet.

I was wrong. Not a rooster. Jimmy Cagney in White Heat.

"Herbert Richardson, do not start," Irene said. "You are perfectly at liberty to join us, but you will not rant."

For an instant, it seemed he was going to slap his wife. Liz would have to intervene and arrest him, and she didn't want to do that. At least not before she'd pumped him dry of all that vitriol.

"Why the hell not? You're filling the woman's head with sweetness and light about that murdering monster who killed my child. I deserve equal time."

"Sit down, Mr. Richardson," Liz ordered. It came out tough, but it worked. Herb yanked a kitchen chair away from one of the worktables and sat bolt upright in it, with his small feet in their glaring white sneakers flat on the floor in front of him.

"So, what do you think happened to your daughter?" Liz asked.

"He tricked her into stopping on the road, yanked her out of her car, killed her, carried her somewhere and disposed of the body. Period, end of story. Why the hell you people haven't arrested his murdering ass I do not know."

"Mr. Richardson, let's say we arrest him. For that matter, let's say we'd arrested him seven years ago and put him on trial for murder. Which degree, by the way? Capital murder?"

"He deserves the needle."

Irene started to interrupt, but Liz raised a hand to forestall her. "Okay, we arrest him and put him on trial. He's passed two polygraphs—"

This time Herb started to interrupt. She stopped him, as well. "He has a million character witnesses, including his mother-in-law."

Herb glared again at his wife.

"He had no motive."

"The hell he hadn't!"

"Please, let me finish. No motive with evidence that would convince a jury. An insurance policy that he makes no attempt to claim. No forensic evidence that he was anywhere near that area on the night Sylvia disappeared. And finally, no body, despite an exhaustive search. If you were not personally involved, and if you were on that jury, would you have convicted him?" She forestalled Herb again. "The biggie is that if we had put him on trial and lost—and believe me, we would have lost—he couldn't ever be tried again. So long as he has never gone to trial, jeopardy exists for him. Acquit him, and he can walk out of the courtroom and write a bestseller about how he killed his wife. We wouldn't be able to touch him."

"I'd touch the bastard," Herb whispered.

"And you'd wind up in jail, where you could not be there for your wife or your granddaughter. Who wins under that scenario?"

"He's getting away with it anyway." Herb sounded

tired and defeated. The wind had gone out of his sails. He sat slumped in the chair, with his liver-spotted hands hanging between his knees.

"Who says?" Liz grinned at him. "I promise you, Mr. Richardson, if Jud Slaughter killed your daughter, I will get him with enough evidence to prosecute him and win."

"And if he didn't?" Irene interjected.

"I'll find the person who did."

"Big words, girlie," Herb said.

Liz sputtered into her teacup. "Girlie? Mr. Richardson, I haven't heard that word since my great-uncle used it when I was in the third grade. I am definitely not a girlie. I'm a detective and a good one. Forensics has come a long way in seven years, and so have computers. Give us a chance."

"You've had seven years of chances."

"Then give us the truth. You've never given us that."

CHAPTER SEVEN

HERB RICHARDSON DEMANDED that Liz speak to him alone on his own turf. His wife tried to forestall them, but soon gave up. As Liz followed Herb up to the deck at the back of the main house, she glanced back over her shoulder at the glass wall of the cottage. Irene was sitting in front of her loom, staring at them, with one of her heavy shuttles balanced in her hand, ready to throw across.

Once inside, Herb asked, "You want coffee? Irene drinks that green tea stuff. Me, I like good, strong, Southern coffee."

"No thanks." Liz took a seat at the polished farmer's table in the breakfast area of the spotless, if a bit aged, kitchen. She took out her tape recorder, laid it on the table and pointed to it with a question in her eyes.

"Sure. Record it all."

She hadn't taped her conversation with Irene, sensing that the woman would clam up if faced with a machine.

But Herb wanted his poison on record, in his own voice. Liz was happy to oblige.

"Listen, all that stuff Irene was telling you is bullshit."

"How do you know what she was saying?"

"She tells everybody. That Sylvia and Jud had a great marriage. He was a loyal husband and the perfect father. Good provider. Faithful. Even-tempered. Bullshit."

Whether what Herb was about to say was true or not, he obviously believed it. What was that thing reporters said? If your mother says she loves you, check it out?

"That marriage was a mistake from the get-go. Syl said she married him because she fell for his charm." Herb snorted. "That, and her girlfriends were getting married and she didn't want to be left behind. I guess she thought he was a catch. That he'd make a bunch of money fast. She'd have left him sooner, except she got pregnant. He wanted her to have an abortion, but she wouldn't do it. She wanted Colleen, even if he said it wasn't the right time. They couldn't afford it. Whatever. He puts on a good act, but he's never given a damn about that kid. Me 'n Irene raised her."

Interesting. Colleen had been seven when Sylvia disappeared, but Herb didn't say "raised her since her mother was killed." How much attention had Sylvia and Jud actually paid to their child in those first seven years?

"He said he'd kill her if she tried to leave him. She did and he did."

Whoa. First time she'd heard that.

"She tried a couple of times before, but he'd find her, beat her up."

Double whoa.

"Did she have him arrested?"

"Nah, she wouldn't. She didn't even tell Irene he hit her. But when he started in on Colleen, she finally told him it was over."

"When was that?"

"She told me a week before she went missing. She was going to take Colleen and go to one of those battered-women's shelters. Then she was going for full custody and half the marital assets. He couldn't have that, so he killed her before she could leave."

"Did the police check the shelters?"

"Sure did. Nobody saw or heard from her, but then they wouldn't. She'd never have told anybody ahead of time. Sure as shootin' not *him*." Herb leaned forward. Liz was starting to feel queasy. If what he'd said was true, she'd been dead wrong about Jud, and so had Irene.

"You saw the bruises?"

"I saw them, all right. At first she said she was just clumsy, said she'd run into a cabinet door in the kitchen, fallen over a pile of lumber on one of those construction sites, but she finally admitted to me he got mad over the money they were spending on the new house and Colleen's school, blamed her and beat the crap out of her, but never when anybody was around to see. And he kept the bruises where she could cover 'em up."

"Drunk?"

"Yeah. Beer and wine mostly. He'd watch sports on TV and get so drunk he'd fall asleep in his chair and not come to bed at all half the time."

As he had purportedly done the night Sylvia disappeared. But he'd said he'd only had part of a single glass of wine.

"What about infidelity?"

"She said whatever time he didn't spend watching sports, he spent watching Internet porn. He spent the money they needed to pay the bills on those pay-for-view sites."

"How about affairs?"

"Sylvia said she thought he slept around, but she couldn't give me any names. I know he's been a'whorin' since he killed her, though."

"Any names?"

"Ask Irene. She may know. Not that she'd tell you."

"You said he was worried about money?"

"Heck, Sylvia wanted to quit that job at the bank and stay home, be a full-time mother to Colleen, like I always told her she needed to do. But he wouldn't let her. She had the health insurance and the steady salary. He had construction loans and building that house."

"About the house…"

"Sylvia didn't care about that house. He said it would be a showcase for his business. Out there in the middle of nowhere. Wouldn't surprise me any if he'd been plannin' to kill her since before they started building."

After almost an hour of listening to his ranting and repetition, Liz thanked Herb and left by the front door. She realized someone was sitting in the passenger seat of her car, then saw it was Irene. She slid in. "Hey. Can I drop you somewhere?"

The older woman reached over and laid her hand on Liz's arm. "He's wrong about Jud. None of those things he said were true."

"He saw the bruises."

"Jud didn't give them to her. He was the one trying to save the marriage."

"You're saying both your husband and your daughter lied?"

"Herb believed her, but then he always believed her."

"You don't?"

"She was given to exaggeration." Irene opened the car door and slipped out. "And she always knew how to push her daddy's buttons. Do your own checking."

Liz drove away as the woman walked back down her driveway toward her weaving sanctuary. Obviously, the only way that pair could live together was not to live together. Liz wondered how Colleen dealt with the dynamic in that household.

CHAPTER EIGHT

COLLEEN KISSED HER DAD'S cheek, grabbed her backpack and ran up the driveway to the Richardson house. Jud saw the drape in the living room move; Herb was staring out at him. Jud always felt as if he had a target painted on his back when his father-in-law was around. Irene had finally made clear to Herb that either he kept his mouth shut about Jud's supposed transgressions when Colleen was present, or he wouldn't be allowed near his granddaughter. So far he seemed to be complying.

The minute Liz Gibson had driven away, Irene had called Jud to report on the meeting and to warn him that the detective had spent time alone in the house with Herb.

Jud knew what Herb would have told her. He understood the man's need to blame him, and even felt sympathy for him, but was sick and tired of having to deal with Herb's litany of viciousness, when he had no way to fight back.

What Liz thought mattered, and not only because she could have him arrested for murder. Jud wanted her to think well of him.

Actually, he wanted her to swoon into his arms, except she didn't seem like the swooning kind. She'd be more likely to throw a choke hold on him.

She definitely turned him on, but then she'd turn on most men. Even the momentary fantasy of taking her to bed caused his body to react. He felt that underneath the tough exterior lurked a soft and sexy lady. She gave off an indefinable air that said Woman with a capital *W*.

He wasn't likely to so much as kiss her while she still suspected him of murder.

That gave him another reason to find out once and for all what had happened to Sylvia. The woman was an incubus. Even though he'd not laid eyes on her for seven years, she still sucked the joy out of his life.

Suddenly he felt he had to talk to Liz. He pulled out the card she had given him, dialed her extension at the squad room, got her voice mail, left a message for her to call him, hung up and checked his watch. Six o'clock. She'd be headed home, if she wasn't running errands or going out. She probably had a date. Hell, she might be engaged, or living with someone.

That thought bothered him more than it should. He couldn't figure out how she'd managed to get to him so quickly or so thoroughly. Maybe because she seemed so different from most of the women he met. They often seemed absorbed in externals like matching the color of their bedroom walls to the color of their poodle. Liz was real. She was a challenge worth the risk.

Her home phone was unlisted, but he had her cell number and got her address on the Internet. He started to dial, then clicked the off button. Not good enough. He wanted to see her face-to-face. Make her look into his eyes when he swore he was innocent.

He grabbed his jacket and headed for the door. From the other desk, Trip said, "Hey, where you going in such a hurry? Hot date?"

"I wish. See you tomorrow."

"How about we go somewhere? Order a big steak. Totsy's having a couple of her girlfriends over to watch some tearjerker on the satellite."

"Sorry. Another time."

"Hey, that woman detective called. Wants to come by and see me tomorrow morning." Trip looked uncomfortable.

"Tell her the truth. All of it." Jud shut the door behind him, leaped down the steps, climbed into his truck and peeled out of the parking lot. His tires spun mud behind him like a rooster tail.

This was crazy. Liz would probably think he was stalking her, or getting ready to add her to his string of serial killings. She might shoot him. He seldom acted on impulse, and never over a woman. Sylvia had pursued *him*. He still didn't quite know why. He'd been flattered. She was beautiful and smart. It had been like being hit on by Christie Brinkley. He didn't realize until after he'd married her that he'd actually been hit on by Jaws.

The drive from the construction site to Liz's neighborhood took more than half an hour. He used it to try to talk himself out of what he was doing, and had almost succeeded as he pulled to the curb in front of her house.

Liz lived in a small 1920s-era cottage close to the Pink Palace Museum off of Poplar in East Memphis. He knew the neighborhood and the houses well. Most had hardwood floors, built-in bookcases and a fireplace in the living room, a separate dining room, three bedrooms, two baths, small closets and a galley kitchen. Most had been renovated with added-on dens, master suites, updated kitchens and rear decks. He'd done a number of the renos himself when he was getting started, although he hadn't worked on Liz's house.

Her Honda sat in the driveway and not in the single-car garage. The porch light was on, and he could see lights behind the plantation shutters that covered the windows. She was home, but there might be a live-in lover or roommate's car in the garage. A dark SUV sat at the curb. Her date's?

This had been a crazy idea. Jud ought to drive right on by without stopping. As he started to step on the gas, the front door opened. Hands on her hips, Liz stood under the porch light facing a man no taller than she. Jud lowered his window so he could hear their conversation. He needed to know their relationship before he blundered in.

"Go home, Steve. Sleep it off before your shift starts," Liz said.

"Come on, one drink?" The man leaned forward and she leaned back. He sounded as though he'd already had a few. He reached for her.

She put both hands in the middle of his chest and shoved. He staggered, and barely caught one of the columns that supported the small front porch, saving himself from falling down the steps.

"Hey, is that any way to treat your husband?"

"Ex-husband. Shoo."

"I miss your sweet ass, and that isn't the only part—"

Jud stepped out of the car. "Miz Gibson?" He started up the front walk.

"Jud?" Liz shaded her eyes against the porch light.

The man turned and stared. "You datin' the Incredible Hulk?"

"Bye, Steve. Go sit in your car and call a cab. You're well over the limit for DUI."

"Am not," he said. "You think any of my brother officers would stop this ole SUV? Not likely." He went carefully down the steps and the walk. "Hey, Godzilla, you take care of my lady, ya hear?" He waved a hand over his shoulder, climbed into his vehicle and slowly drove away.

"He's right, you know," Liz said. "The blue lights won't stop him, although they'll follow him home to see he doesn't cream a pedestrian or another car." She seemed to remember Jud. "Why are you here? I didn't need saving. Steve started tying one on every six months or so after we divorced. He usually winds up here, feeling lonely and amorous. He always apologizes afterward."

"I take it he didn't want the divorce."

"It was mutual. We fell in love at the police academy, married too young, and our priorities changed. He's happy riding a squad car for twenty years. I'm not."

She hugged her arms across her chest and shivered. She had not asked Jud in. "What *are* you doing here?"

"I'm sorry. I shouldn't have come." He started down the steps.

"Wait. You drove all this way and now you're going to leave before you've said your piece?" She opened the door wide. He followed her inside.

"Coffee?" she asked. "A drink?"

"The cops wouldn't be so charitable to me if I got stopped on a DUI. I wouldn't mind a soda if you have one."

"Sure. Regular or diet?"

He grinned. "Diet. Still watching the waistline." He felt something touch his leg and looked down on a huge black cat that eddied around his ankles, tail twitching. He bent down to scratch its ears. "Hey, buddy." The cat arched its back and purred.

"That's Poirot. Have a seat."

This was a woman's room. It didn't have chintz and ruffles, but the walls were a soft peach. He shuddered. He hated peach. An Oriental rug in shades of peach and green lay on the floor, and the beige upholstered sofa and chairs were accompanied by gleaming side tables and other antiques.

He was surprised at how feminine the place looked. He had pictured her living with stark Scandinavian furniture and lots of glass and steel. Maybe even exercise equipment in the living room.

Liz brought him a tall glass of soda with a cocktail napkin wrapped around its bottom. She set her own glass of soda on a coaster on the coffee table in front of her. "So?"

His throat and mouth felt too dry to speak, so he gulped his drink, then half choked before he got his mouth under control. He couldn't tell her that he'd come because he wanted to see her again, to check if the sparks he'd felt at breakfast were really there.

He'd avoided looking at her when he came in, but now he did, and realized her brown hair fell loose around her shoulders just the way he'd pictured it. She wore a pale green T-shirt and a pair of threadbare jeans that she probably had to lie down to zip. All the planes and angles of her face were softened, and she smelled faintly of wildflowers and autumn wind.

He clutched his glass with both hands to avoid leaping over the coffee table and taking her in his arms.

And probably getting his neck broken.

"I came to tell you that Herb wasn't telling you the truth."

She raised her eyebrows. "How do you know what Herb told me?"

"He tells everybody pretty much the same stuff. Irene called me after you left to say you'd spent an hour with him. I can almost quote him word for word."

"Why would he lie?"

"I didn't say he lied. He truly believes everything Sylvia told him. She was the liar."

"Again, why?"

"I've wrestled with that for years. She was his little girl. If she told him the moon was made out of marzipan, he'd have believed her." Jud took another drink. "I also think she was building a divorce case."

Liz sat back. "You said you had a good marriage."

He twisted the glass in his big hands. "I lied."

"Really."

"We'd been talking about divorce for a long time."

"How long?"

He shrugged. "Since Colleen was born."

"After Sylvia wouldn't have the abortion you wanted?"

"What?" Jud gaped at her. "Herb told you *that?*"

"Answer the question." Liz watched his body language. He seemed genuinely stunned. So he hadn't known everything Herb would say. But the older man had been right about the bad marriage. Was he right about the abuse?

Jud set his glass down on a nearby coaster and took a deep breath. "I was not the one who wanted an abortion. Sylvia did."

"Why?"

"She said being pregnant would make her look and feel gross, and she was terrified of the actual process of giving birth. She also said having a baby would put her on the mommy track and interfere with her career. I promised her I'd make arrangements to look after the baby somehow. Even then I had to threaten to tell Herb and Irene she was pregnant long before she wanted to. Once Herb knew, she didn't dare have an abortion. That's one thing he would never have forgiven, even if she blamed it on me."

"She could have lied, said she had a spontaneous miscarriage."

"She was afraid I'd find out and tell her parents." Jud looked at Liz, and for the first time, she saw cold rage in his eyes. "I would have, believe me." He picked up his glass and finished the cola. His knuckles were white, and for a moment Liz was afraid he'd squeeze the glass until it broke.

The man in front of her would be capable of murder to protect someone he loved. As he loved his child. "So what about the bruises and the black eye?"

"Herb exaggerates. Probably because Sylvia did. It's damn dangerous around a construction site. We knock into stuff all the time. She told me she walked into a guy carrying a stack of studs, and blackened her eye while she was helping to supervise the construction on our house. Why would I doubt her?" He pulled back his sleeve to reveal a scrape and multi-colored bruise on his forearm. "See what I mean? I never touched her in anger. After Colleen was born, I seldom touched her."

"Whose choice?"

"Mutual. I hate to say this, but she was capable of bruising herself to look good to Herb and make him a better witness for her if we went to trial over the divorce. If there was one thing Sylvia was good at, it was thinking ahead." He sounded bitter.

"So the hookers and the Internet porn were substitutes?"

"Excuse me?" He looked at her sharply. "Herb's upped the ante, apparently. I know enough about hookers and the Internet to know those sites cost money. I barely had enough to keep up with the construction loans on the houses we were building. Sylvia's salary was paying most of the day-to-day expenses for the family."

"How'd she feel about that?"

"Pissed, but she wanted our house, even if we couldn't fully furnish it right away. She said it was an investment in our future. A showplace to bring clients. As it turned out, she was right."

"But she didn't benefit."

"She was going to. In the three months before she disappeared, Trip and I signed contracts for three mansions in our first development. We were golden."

"But the police said you were on the verge of bankruptcy."

"Home construction companies look bankrupt on paper half the time because of the lag time between contract and payment. Did your detective buddies bring in a forensic accountant who would have known what he was looking at?"

Liz knew they had not, probably because of budget restraints. Those guys cost a fortune. The homicide detectives no doubt felt they knew enough on their own to read the records.

"Trip borrowed some money from his parents until the down payments cleared on the construction, then we paid them back in full six months after Sylvia disappeared. If you like, I can show you our tax return from the following year, when we actually made money."

"Didn't her salary stop when she disappeared?"

"After her vacation and sick leave pay ran out. Colleen and I barely scraped by for a while, but we managed."

"What about *your* family?

He shook his head. "My mother died when I was a teenager, and my father a year after I graduated from college. They never had much money. I used what little I inherited to set up with Trip in the first place."

"Did you consider borrowing from Sylvia's family?"

He snorted. "You're kidding, right? Irene had to fight to keep Herb from filing for custody of Colleen after Sylvia disappeared. He'd have loved to starve me into submission." Jud narrowed his eyes. "You know all this. You've read the files, or I assume you have."

"The first rule of the Cold Case squad is to go over everything from scratch. Face-to-face. So far as you're concerned, I don't know anything."

He stood. "I shouldn't have come." He sounded exhausted. "I thought we'd connected. I guess I was wrong. You're as convinced as those other guys that I killed my wife."

She intercepted him, grabbed his arm and felt his heavy muscle tense under her fingers. "I want to believe you, but you've already admitted you lied to me. If you do it again, I swear I'll arrest you for felonious stupidity."

When he turned to her, she realized how close he was and how far back she had to tilt her head to look into his face. Uh-oh. Big mistake. Those blue-gray eyes bored into hers and suddenly her tongue wouldn't work, her heart began to race and she felt as though her blood pressure was careening off the charts. He was too close.

And then he was closer. She didn't remember lacing her fingers behind his neck, but she felt his arms around her waist, his body leaning over her, lifting her as those giant hands drew her against him.

He kissed her urgently. Mouth met mouth, tongue met tongue without hesitation or pretense.

She fought to remain rational while waves of unreasoning heat and longing rolled through her.

He killed his wife, he killed his wife, he killed his wife.

Did he?

She broke the kiss, shoved him away. His chest rose and fell as though he were suffocating, and those eyes, those marvelous eyes, had lost focus.

"Stop," she demanded. "Stop right there."

He moved back a pace. "I'm—"

"If you say you're sorry, I will slug you," she snarled.

He grinned. "I'm not sorry, but I'm willing to admit that may have been a tactical error."

"On both our parts." She turned from him and sucked in a couple of deep breaths, then turned back. "You didn't kill your wife, did you?"

"What?" He shook his head in confusion. "No, I didn't." He chuckled. "Hell, if I'd known that was all it took, I'd have kissed the heck out of Sherman and Lee."

"I doubt that would have helped your case. But let's get back to your wife. I get the feeling you might toss her out of a second-story window in rage or accidentally break her neck. Then, I think you'd call 911 and wait until the ambulance and the cops arrived. That's what usually happens, you know. The police come in, find the DB, turn to the person standing there, say 'you want to tell me about it?' and ninety-nine times out of a hundred, they do. You'd be one of those ninety-nine."

"You're saying I'm dumb?"

"No, I'm saying that you're a good citizen who would be horrified to have committed violence, and a very large man who has learned to monitor his size, to be very careful not to hurt anyone."

"You're one of those profilers, aren't you?" he asked. He tilted his head down to stare at her.

Backing up carefully, she settled in the rocking chair beside the fireplace and tried desperately to relax. "I'm not a profiler. At least not in the sense you mean." She pointed to the sofa. "Sit."

He complied.

"I'm trained as a hostage negotiator. I've just joined Cold Cases." She crossed her arms over her still-tender breasts and looked away from him. "I'm trained to read voices, body language, choice of words. If I do it right, everybody lives."

"And if you do it wrong?"

She shivered. "People die." She still couldn't meet his eyes, but felt hers fill with tears. She could not—would not—cry in front of him. She sniffed and forced herself to look at him. "Anybody can kill, given the right circumstances. You could, I could. Even your daughter could."

He started to protest, but she held up a hand to stop him. "It's true. All I'm saying is that the way I read you, you might kill to protect your family, maybe even your career, but you'd kill in the heat of anger, not with cold-blooded premeditation. Afterward, you'd be filled with remorse, and probably incapable of any further action. You would not set up some kind of elaborate body dump. And you would sure as shooting not work out an involved murder mystery that leaves you as the prime suspect. That dumb you are *not*."

"Thank you. I think." He leaned forward and

dropped his hands between his knees. "So why'd you quit?"

"Quit what?"

"Negotiating. The police department must have a good deal of money invested in you. How come they let you go over to Cold Cases?"

"Go home." She stood and walked to the door, carefully avoiding coming within arm's length of him.

He followed her, just as deliberately staying out of touching range.

She opened the door and moved aside.

"You're not going to answer me, are you?" he asked.

"Nope." She held up her hands. "Go away. Do not touch. I won't make that mistake twice."

He walked down the porch steps and called over his shoulder, "Who said it was a mistake?"

She shut the door on him, then leaned against it. "It was a mistake all right," she whispered. "A big mistake."

She bent down to pick up Poirot, who immediately turned over to lie in her arms like a baby, his furry belly exposed. He was purring like a chain saw.

"I've already proved my instincts are not infallible, cat. I could be wrong about him. I need evidence one way or the other. Evidence that will stand up in court."

She heard Jud's car start and drive away, then

dropped Poirot on the sofa. "What really happened to Sylvia? How on earth am I going to find out when I don't know who she really was?"

CHAPTER NINE

"So, MR. WEICHERT, shall we get right down to it?" Liz sat across from Trip Weichert with a steaming cup of coffee that she did not want resting in front of her. She had considered asking him to meet somewhere neutral, or even down at the station, rather than in his office. She'd known that the familiar surroundings of his construction office would give him a natural advantage. Finally, she'd decided that if he felt comfortable, he might loosen up and reveal something he didn't intend to. The framed law degree on the wall over his head told her he might not answer any questions at all, but she had to try.

"I don't know what I can tell you that I haven't already told half a dozen other detectives."

"Where's Mr. Slaughter this morning?"

"At his daughter's school watching a soccer practice. Those girls are deadly. They go at it no matter how cold or miserable it is."

"Tell me about Mr. Slaughter's wife."

"Beautiful woman. Intelligent. Charming. Excellent financial sense. She was vice president of a bank, you know."

"You liked her?"

"We didn't see each other that often." His eyes flicked down and to the right.

Behind him, an old train clock clicked off the seconds steadily. Liz let the moment drag. Most people couldn't handle silence.

"I'm not saying we avoided each other," Trip said after a long moment. "She and Jud came over to barbecues and cookouts at our house. Our daughters are friends. My wife's a great cook and loves to entertain. I do the ribs. Best in town, if I do say so myself." He caught himself, obviously aware that he was babbling.

"Did they reciprocate?"

He shrugged. "Totsy's a stay-at-home wife and mother. Sylvia really didn't have time to entertain, what with her job and building the new house and all."

A cell phone rang. Both Trip and Liz reached for jacket pockets, but then Liz realized the ring tone wasn't hers.

Trip swung his chair around so that the high back was between them. "Weichert here." He listened. "I know, but… I don't even have to talk… Okay, if you say so." He clicked off and turned around. "That was Jud. As a lawyer, I do not believe in answering non-specific questions from the police. For some reason, he thinks you may have a more open mind than previous detectives." Trip squinted at her. "I wonder why."

Liz felt herself blush. His inference that she was

using feminine wiles on Jud was too close to the truth for comfort. But he'd used his own wiles on her, hadn't he? "I am only interested in getting to the truth, Mr. Weichert."

"If you say so." Outside, a truck rumbled by. Weichert glanced at it and stood up. "Come on. I have to check on that concrete delivery. You want to talk, you come with me."

He was shorter than Liz and had the beginnings of a paunch, but she had to stretch to keep up with his lope, then wait as he talked to the driver and turned him over to a man who must be the foreman.

The five houses in this development stood around a big cul-de-sac and would be huge when finished. Starter castles, Jud had called them. "We're pouring a garage floor," Trip said when he got back to her. "Been too wet the last couple of days." Instead of returning to the trailer, he sat on a pile of lumber. "Okay, so Jud wants me to tell you everything. First time he introduced me to Sylvia, I thought he was the luckiest guy alive." Trip shook his head. "Poor bastard."

"What changed your mind?"

"I got to know her."

"Give me a for-instance."

"Doesn't sound like much now, but she had a way of making other people feel like crap, under the guise of being helpful."

"You?"

"I can take care of myself." He started back down the newly paved road toward the construction trailer.

Liz caught up with him as he entered the office again.

"Who, then?"

He shrugged once more.

She reached across his desk and turned a framed photo around. "Nice family. The girl looks about the same age as Colleen."

"They go to the same school."

"Did Sylvia help *her?*" No doubt this was Weichert's daughter. She was chubby, cheerful, with unruly dark hair and a happy smile.

"Sylvia offered to design a diet so she could drop thirty pounds."

"Thirty pounds?" Liz looked at the picture closely. "That's ridiculous."

"She nearly stopped eating and started throwing up. Took us a couple of months to get her back. Totsy wanted to kill Sylvia." He realized what he'd said and blanched. "I didn't mean…"

"People say things like that all the time, Mr. Weichert. Don't worry about it." But Liz planned to worry about it. Next stop, Totsy Weichert. Weird name. *Family nickname, probably.* "Did she and Mr. Slaughter have a happy marriage?" She knew the answer to that one, but wanted to see what Weichert would say.

He dropped his gaze.

Then he took a deep breath and looked her straight in the eye. "They were talking divorce."

"Grounds?"

"Officially, irreconcilable differences. Unofficially, serial adultery."

"Whose part?" Liz asked.

"Hers. Excuse the pop psychology, but I think she needed to prove her power over men."

"Did she seduce you?"

He sat up straight. Color suffused his face. "I'm a happily married man, Miz Gibson."

"She was a beautiful woman. Must have been flattering," Liz said.

"Listen, I didn't sleep with her." He stood up and walked to the door. "I've got to get back to work."

Liz nodded and followed him. He held the door open for her. As she started down the steps, he said to her back, "Nobody killed her. She walked out and set Jud up to take the fall. She's down in Rio or up in Canada. You'll never find her. Leave us alone." He slammed the door.

TOTSY WEICHERT STOOD no more than five-two in her Nikes. She wore jeans that stretched across her ample rump and an oversize sweatshirt that said Queen of the Kitchen on the front. The house smelled of apple cider. It was comfortable, a little battered, with stacks of books and magazines on every flat surface.

She and Liz sat at the kitchen table over spiced tea.

"Jud called me. He said to tell you the truth. Here goes. I have never felt sorrier for anybody than I did for Sylvia."

Liz sputtered, set her cup down and wiped her mouth.

"She was a like a child who says, 'If I can't have your toy, I'll break it.'"

"Your husband said she tried to seduce him."

"Actually, she probably did, although he won't admit it. I can't see him being that upset over a seduction that didn't come off."

"You don't mind?"

Totsy's cup clunked against the table. "Certainly I mind. Not so much the physical part of it, but because it made a liar out of my husband. That was Sylvia all over. Put you in a position where you betrayed the people you cared about. She'd have loved to see me file for divorce."

"Blackmail?"

"Wouldn't put it past her. She had to get money from somewhere, to run away."

"So you think she ran away?"

"There's an old Victorian term—I was an English major at Ole Miss. Ever heard of a bolter?"

"I'm not sure in what context."

"Women that ran away from their husbands for no good reason, or their children or their responsibilities whenever things got tough were referred to as 'bolters.' I'll bet this was not the first time Sylvia bolted."

"You said you were sorry for her. You're the first person I've talked to who has said that."

"She kept trying to love, but I don't think she was

capable of it. I don't know why. Maybe because she didn't realize that real love takes real work. She wanted somebody or something to *make* her happy. When they didn't, her instinct was to run away and try again. I don't think she wanted to believe that others could feel what she couldn't. Don't get me wrong. You might have liked her a great deal when you first met her."

"I doubt that."

"I did, and I'm a fairly good judge of character. She could be hysterically funny. Only later, you'd realize how malicious she was. And she was truly beautiful." Totsy looked down at her jeans wistfully. "I gave up on beauty years ago. I never wanted to stand out. Sylvia did. She was a born exhibitionist."

Driving away, Liz considered what she'd heard. Might be childhood sexual abuse... Did being Daddy's girl mean more than she'd thought? Did Sylvia disappear not to get away from her husband and child, but to get away from her father?

CHAPTER TEN

LIZ BOUGHT A CHEESEBURGER, fries and a diet soda from a drive-through and ate in the car as she toured the neighborhood to study the houses Jud had built and was building.

His early homes, closer to Germantown or Collierville, were fairly modest, but as the Weichert and Slaughter reputation grew and the market got richer, they'd moved on to developing estate-size lots with mansions along winding country roads. Conventional, but with interesting uses of brick and stonework. Who could afford them?

She decided to see what sort of mansion Jud had built for his own family. She had a map of the route Sylvia had taken from her bank to her house, and Liz had been to the crime scene, but she still got lost twice before she found the narrow gravel road on which Jud's house was situated.

The area was still pretty much wilderness. Eight years earlier it must have seemed like a national forest.

Liz was definitely a city gal. The sunken lane between the giant oaks and closely growing pines seemed vaguely threatening. The leaves had fallen from the deciduous trees, but in summer the road would be in perpetual shadow.

She imagined driving home after dark night after night. No streetlights. Alone. No wonder Sylvia carried a gun and called her husband before she left work.

Liz drove around a ninety-degree curve and up an incline. The mailbox at the top read simply Slaughter. No fence, no gate. The access road dead-ended in more woods a quarter of a mile away. No other houses lay beyond it.

She made a left turn up the driveway, which was blacktopped, unlike the access road. The solid wall of trees fell away, the sun reappeared and the drive curved across a couple of acres of brown November lawn dotted with big old oaks and hemlocks.

This was no starter castle, but a modern jewel box, with lots of glass, balconies and a high beige metal roof. Big but not humongous, it was timber framed, unusual in this part of the South. Not at all like the other houses built by Weichert and Slaughter.

No curtains graced the windows, upstairs or down, that she could see. At night it must seem like being onstage, while the audience sat in the dark forest and watched every move you made.

Liz shivered. Like most cops, she always fought for the seat in a restaurant with its back to the wall and a view of the entire room. She had no idea where she could stand in this house that wouldn't feel as though she were waiting for a sniper to pick her off. She'd probably find herself cowering behind the furniture.

Jud had designed the house for Sylvia, but was this the house she'd *wanted?* It was extraordinary, but Liz didn't think she could ever live in such a place.

The woman must have been supremely confident, or simply oblivious to the world around her. Maybe she couldn't take living in a fishbowl any longer and had bolted—to use Totsy's word.

Jud's truck was not in the driveway, and the house both felt and looked unoccupied. Liz parked in front, climbed out, walked up the stone path to the front door and rang the doorbell. Chimes sounded inside, but no one responded.

Even the front door was glass. She shaded her eyes and peered in. Ahead rose a staircase, but she couldn't see into the living areas.

She considered walking the perimeter and peering in, but the landscaped plantings around the house were thick and wet, and would drench her clothes in no time.

She wouldn't have been surprised if a bear or a panther charged out of the woods. Just the thought made her look over her shoulder.

She was really attracted to Jud. That kiss had only confirmed the fact. But although the man who'd designed and built this house might be a genius, his taste in homes was definitely different from hers. She preferred her neat cottage, where she could drive to the supermarket in three minutes flat.

As she opened her car door, she heard an engine and turned to see Jud's crew-cab truck pulling in. He drove around a corner and out of sight, probably to a garage behind the house. Liz had seen the outlines of two people in the vehicle. Jud and Colleen, probably. She assumed he'd come through the house and let her in, so she walked back up to the front door and waited.

A few moments later, he opened the door for her. "Hey," he said. "I wasn't expecting you."

"I probably should have phoned ahead. May I come in?"

"Sure. Colleen," he called over his shoulder, "we have company. Come say hello."

The girl wore a school uniform—a plaid pleated skirt and a white sweater—but was in stocking feet. There must be a mudroom by the garage door, Liz surmised.

The floor of the house was concrete that had been scored and painted to look like dark red quarry tile. Very practical and relatively inexpensive. Easy to keep clean with a mop.

"Hey," Colleen said without warmth, then ran up the stairs and disappeared. A moment later a door slammed.

"Homework." Jud shrugged. Then he smiled that glorious smile and reached for Liz.

She ducked. "Remember, we said that was a mistake."

"We were wrong."

"Interesting house," she stated, changing the subject as she backed away.

"Uh-oh. People either love it or hate it. You must be one of the haters."

"What was Sylvia?"

"She loved it. She picked out the land and half designed it. I'm the one who wanted timber framing. She loved all the glass. Said it made her feel like she was onstage."

"She *liked* that?"

He walked over to the wall of windows that rose all the way to the roof peak two stories up. "Yeah. When Colleen was away at a sleepover or at her grandparents', sometimes Sylvia'd walk around down here naked."

"Really."

"She said she liked to give the deer a thrill." He flipped a switch. The window became marginally darker. "If you went outside now, you wouldn't be able to see in. All the windows in the house are like that. Saves on air-conditioning in the summer, as well as providing privacy. Very ecologically sound. This is a green home."

And no doubt very expensive.

"It's the same principle as the two-way mirror you cops use when you grill suspects."

"We do not grill suspects!" Liz grimaced. "Well, maybe a little, but we have to leave our rubber hoses outside these days. Did she flip the switches?"

He shook his head slowly. "Almost never. She didn't like *me* to, either."

"Could a stalker or Peeping Tom have followed her home from the bank and watched her?"

"I doubt it. Getting through those woods between the lawn and the road isn't easy even in winter, when the honeysuckle's dormant. In summer, you'd be eaten alive by chiggers and poison ivy, if you weren't bitten by a copperhead. There are motion-sensor lights along the driveway. Sometimes the deer set them off."

Now Liz knew she *really* wouldn't like living out here.

"Can I get you something to drink?" he asked. A well-fitted bar sat in an alcove at the back of the room beside the large fieldstone fireplace.

Liz shook her head. There was no evidence of pets. If she lived in this house, her first purchase would be an attack-trained bull mastiff. Her second would be a yappy little terrier of some kind. One to alert, one to protect.

She sat on one of the black leather sofas that flanked the fireplace. "You didn't tell me your wife was unfaithful."

He hitched a hip over the arm of the sofa opposite, so he was higher than her and in a position to bolt. Interesting. "You didn't ask."

"Did you know?"

"Maybe not all of them."

"Trip Weichert?"

Jud sat down across from her, leaned back and closed his eyes. "She loved telling me that. I warned her that if she told Totsy I'd kill her."

He realized what he'd said and was about to clarify when Liz waved her hand. "Did she? Tell Totsy, I mean."

"Trip told her first."

"But not that he'd actually slept with her, only that she'd *tried* to seduce him," Liz said.

"Totsy knows Trip."

"So Sylvia frequently discussed her affairs?"

"Of course not. She told me about Trip to prove that my best friend would betray me for her."

"Would he kill her?"

Jud jerked his head. "No way. She didn't have anything else to hold over his head. Besides, their... thing was over months before she disappeared."

"So, how'd she do it?"

"Huh?"

"You keep saying she disappeared, but not how. In seven years you must have worked out a theory."

He went to the bar and pulled a long-neck beer from the small refrigerator. "Want one?"

He was stalling for time. Deciding what to tell her...if anything, Liz decided.

She shook her head, watching the way his hands twisted the cap off the bottle. This was no time to remember the feel of those hands on her skin. She jerked herself back to the present as he began to speak.

"The first couple of years I thought of precious

little else. A million different scenarios. I always came back to the same one. She arranged for somebody to pick her up at her car and drop her off somewhere."

"You don't think she was kidnapped?"

"Not like that."

"Then where did he take her? Surely whoever helped her would come forward sooner or later. Didn't you offer a reward?"

"Ten thousand dollars. Nobody ever tried to claim it except a couple of semiprofessional crackpots. She was even on that missing person's TV show. Nothing turned up." He leaned back and tilted the bottle, took a long pull and set it on the glass side table.

"Did you ever consider she might have been kidnapped somewhere else, and the scene set where the police found her car?" Liz asked.

For the first time, he shared a spark of real interest. "Go on."

"Someone could've stopped her with a log across your road between here and the highway. She gets out of her car to see if she can inch by. She feels safe on that road."

"Nobody else lived along it then, although there are a couple of other houses between us and the highway now."

"One person grabs her and either drugs her or manhandles her into another car or van," Liz continued. "The other drives her car back down to where it was found, turns it around so it's facing the right way, leaves the keys in the ignition and the driver's door open, gets in the van, stops to remove the log and drives away." The rain would have washed any tire tracks away.

"Then why no ransom request? The FBI tapped our phone."

"Routine procedures. It's called a 'trap and trace,' and I'll bet they covered not only your landline and cell phones, but Trip's and Sylvia's parents', as well."

"For three weeks. Then they disappeared one morning with a shrug and a kiss my ass."

"I'm sorry to say this, but they had decided she was dead, probably in the course of the kidnapping or shortly thereafter. If she'd seen one of her attackers, recognized somebody, say a customer from her bank, they wouldn't let her live. I'm only surprised they didn't try to ransom her even so. The kidnappers could have bluffed."

"The FBI told me that if anybody called, I was to ask to speak to her."

"That's what they call a POL—proof of life. Somebody made a movie about that a while back. No POL, no negotiations."

"You said you were a negotiator. You ever involved in something like that?"

"The FBI has its own negotiators. They do not play well with others." She stood and walked toward the front door. He followed. "Did they ever look for evidence along your road?" she asked. "A fresh tree down, maybe, and shoved to the shoulder?"

"Not that night, but if anyone had moved a limb off the road and onto the shoulder, no one would notice it. We lose branches all the time in bad weather. I've cleared several that have fallen across the road. The Tennessee Department of Transportation handles the big ones, but not that night. It was pouring rain. The ditches at the side were full and running fast."

"I wonder if that's what they were waiting for," she said under her breath.

She felt eyes on her and turned to see Colleen sitting on the top step. Liz tried to recall if either she or Jud had said anything that might alert the girl to the chemistry between them. She didn't think so. "You have anything to add, Colleen?" she asked.

"What are you doing up there, honey?" Jud called. "Come on down."

Without a word, the girl fled out of sight down the hall. A second later the door slammed again.

"Sorry," Jud said.

"She doesn't like me."

"She's scared of you."

"There have been other cops. Was she scared of them, too?"

He smiled and ran his finger down Liz's cheek. "She's not scared of you as a cop." He brushed a loose strand of hair back from her forehead. "I liked you with your hair down."

Her nerve endings tingled again and she felt

herself leaning toward him, ready to fall into his arms.

She caught herself. "Touch me again, buster, and I'll shoot you."

She pulled open the heavy front door, marched down the stairs, climbed into her car and only then took time to catch her breath, before driving away.

Glancing back once, she saw Jud standing on the steps with his hands in his pockets and a quizzical smile on his face.

Thank God Colleen had been there, otherwise who knew what would have happened? Maybe one of them would have hit the switch to darken every one of those windows, and then…

Liz was dying to stop and unhook her bra. At the moment it felt like a steel breastplate against her nipples. She lowered the window and let the cold, damp air blow against her face. Might bring her a little sanity.

She wasn't some fourteen-year-old kid with raging hormones. But she had a terrible suspicion that one more kiss from Jud Slaughter would be all she'd need to fly right off the cliff and keep soaring.

CHAPTER ELEVEN

"I'M BEGINNING TO THINK Jud Slaughter may not have done it."

Lieutenant Gavigan looked up from the stack of reports on his desk and motioned Liz into his office. "Sit. How come?"

"Not his style," she said.

"Great. I can see us introducing that into evidence."

"He's not sly, and he's not devious. Sylvia was. Wherever she is now, she planned her disappearance."

"How?"

"I don't know yet. I'm just getting started on that. I'm headed out to talk to her boss at the bank. The woman had no friends, that I've found. I'm hoping her colleagues will be able to tell me things."

"All the other detectives who worked the case were certain he killed her, starting with Sherman and Lee. After less than a week, you think maybe he didn't? Forgive me if I don't support you enthusiastically."

"You don't have to support me at all," Liz said. "Until I can show you how she did it and, hopefully, find her alive and kicking in Acapulco or Capri."

"Necessitating a trip to one of those places?" Gavigan chuckled. "Not in the budget."

"I didn't mean that literally. I'm driving over to Arkansas to talk to Dick Sherman. I need to hear why he and Lee were so certain Jud killed Sylvia."

"Jud and Sylvia?"

Liz felt herself blushing. "I couldn't keep calling them Mr. and Mrs. Slaughter, could I? I also think there may be a history of child abuse."

Gavigan leaned forward. "Slaughter's molesting his daughter?"

"Good Lord, no. I meant Sylvia may have been abused by her ever-loving daddy, if not physically, then psychologically."

"What makes you think that?"

"Everyone agrees she was beautiful. I mean, be*u*tful. But she was constantly currying favor with her father and she seemed devoted to making everybody else miserable. She was an exhibitionist, and a serial slut."

"Reason for the husband to get rid of her."

"Absolutely. If we'd found her bludgeoned to death in his living room, I'd swear he killed her. But not this. According to his business partner, he'd asked her for a divorce."

"Killed her to save money, then."

Liz shook her head. "The money was mostly hers, anyway. He'd probably have made out better than she did in a divorce settlement. And he didn't ask for the insurance payment."

"So why disappear?"

"One of the people I talked to described her as a bolter. People do repeat themselves."

"I still think he's guilty, but I gave you two weeks to run with it. You using your own car to drive to Arkansas?"

Liz nodded. "I'll keep my mileage."

"No side trips. We don't have the money."

"WHEN YOU CALLED, I dragged out my old case notes," Dick Sherman said. "Not that I don't remember every word of them. You always recall the ones that get away."

Liz leaned back against the shabby sofa in the small living room and sipped the hot mulled cider he'd offered her. Outside, the rain threatened to turn to sleet. Inside, a fire burned cheerfully, while a large ginger cat slept curled on a pillow that showed signs of serving as a scratching post. "Maybe this time we'll find out for sure what happened."

"We already know for sure. He did it."

"I was at one of his job sites yesterday while they were pouring concrete," Liz said. "There's no mention that you looked for Sylvia's body in any of the foundations of the houses he was building at the time."

"It had been too cold and wet to pour concrete for a week before she disappeared, and three days after," Sherman stated. "Otherwise we'd have brought in an army of jackhammers." He chortled. "He and his partner would have loved that. Don't they say Hoffa's buried under an apartment building in Jersey?"

Liz tried to keep her eyes off his way-too-black dyed hair, part of which was probably a way-too-black toupee. "I heard Yankee Stadium."

"Perfect place to hide a body." Sherman leaned back in his leather recliner and took a pull on his cider. Liz had checked, to find that he'd been retired four years now, but he still had the bearing of a cop.

She was torn between wanting to just let him talk, and needing to get back across the Mississippi River before the bridges iced over.

"The unsolved ones that still bother me are those where I knew in my gut who did the deed, but couldn't prove it."

"You were certain, then?"

"Wasn't no other solution."

"Stranger abduction? Genuine disappearance?"

"How? There was no evidence of any stranger either on the car or at the scene, and believe me, we searched. Slaughter's prints were all over the car. His DNA, too."

"It was his wife's car. Of course his prints would be on it. No blood, though."

"That's what his lawyer said. We asked him why his prints would be all over the tailgate. Know what he said? He'd taken her Christmas presents out for her a couple of days earlier."

"Where were the presents?"

"There were packages in the house under the

bed. Nothing she couldn't have carried herself easily enough."

"You think her body was in the back of her van. How do you get around the need for a second car?"

"Somebody picked him up, maybe helped him stash the body, then drove him home."

"Any idea who?"

Sherman shook his head. "Mistress? If so, we never found her. At first we thought Weichert, but there's a record that he called Slaughter's house at ten-thirty and got the answering machine. He was home with his family all night. Solid alibi."

"Slaughter says he was asleep in front of the television."

Sherman snorted derisively. "Nobody sleeps that hard."

"Unless he's drunk or drugged."

"He says he had one glass of wine," the ex-cop said. "You've read the reports. Everybody else had a firm alibi."

Everybody you knew about. "He passed a lie-detector test."

Sherman snorted again. "Gimme enough antihistamine, I'll pass any damn test you give me. Plenty of other ways, too."

The ginger cat stretched, rolled over to toast its other side and went back to sleep. "Why are you so certain she didn't just disappear?" Liz asked. She set her empty mug on a stack of *Field and Stream* magazines on the table beside her.

"If she was gonna disappear, she'd have left her car in the long-term parking lot at the airport, taken a plane under another name and paid cash."

"Maybe she figured that's the first place you'd look. And what about needing photo ID?"

"Shoot, you can do one of them licenses good enough to pass on any color printer. They had color printers at that bank even back then, and she stayed alone after hours plenty of times. Thing is, women that bug out always take their good jewelry and maybe a couple of shots of their families with them. She didn't."

"What happened to the car?"

"Damned if I know. Could still be in the impound lot."

"After seven years?"

"Probably went in one of those police auctions, if he didn't want it back. No way to trace it now."

"So why do you really believe Slaughter is guilty?" Liz asked.

"Two reasons. First, in the three years before I retired, nobody used her credit cards or withdrew money from her accounts. That means she's dead. Second—and this is the biggie. Nobody's that easy-going. They're on the verge of divorce, and he's fixing dinner for her? Doesn't happen."

"You're still positive it wasn't a stranger?"

"Absolutely. They wouldn't have left the car like that. They'd have done something with it to give themselves as much time as possible to get away.

Slaughter's the only man I've ever met that could probably carry *me* a couple of miles without breaking a sweat, and I weigh twice what she weighed. Even if we never found a woman, her dad swears Slaughter had at least one mistress, maybe more, and a hellacious temper."

Liz leaned foward. "You believe Daddy?"

Sherman shrugged. "Maybe, maybe not. But the husband does not compute. He may look like a big teddy bear, but consider where he's got to in business. He's a smart, tough guy. Smart enough to set the whole thing up and then laugh at us."

Driving away into the early darkness, still mercifully free of sleet, Liz decided it was the "laughing at us" part that had convinced Sherman and Lee. They trusted their guts, even in the absence of evidence. In most cases she'd trust their guts, as well, but this time they'd taken the easy way out, because Jud's size and intelligence intimidated them.

Heck, his size would intimidate the Statue of Liberty.

CHAPTER TWELVE

SHE DECIDED TO USE her personal cell phone rather than the one the department furnished. What she was about to do was against regulations. As the new kid in Cold Cases, she didn't want to put Gavigan in a position where he'd have to reprimand her, or worse, take her off the case and give it to Randy Randy. She dialed, waited while the cell phone rang.

"Pick up," she whispered. She would not leave a message on Jud's phone, and she didn't think he'd recognize her cell-phone number.

She was about to hang up, when he finally answered. "Slaughter!" he snapped, sounding breathless and annoyed.

"Whoa! Did I call at a bad time?"

"Liz?" His tone warmed immediately. "Look, can I call you back? One of my men just slid a road grader into a ditch."

"One second only. I don't know what your babysitting arrangements are, but could you possibly run into me at the grocery store in Oakland at five?"

"Tonight?" He hesitated. "Shoot, why not. We'll

either have the darn thing out of the mud before then or not until morning. What department?"

"At the little coffee shop in the back."

"Yeah, but I have to be home before six to fix dinner for Colleen."

Liz hung up. The way his tone had moderated the instant he'd heard her voice—and recognized it—made her heart speed up. She sank back against the headrest of her car and closed her eyes. "I am doing what I think is appropriate for the case. I am not losing my professional objectivity." *The heck I'm not.*

That gave her three hours. She checked in with the office, gave them her updated schedule, turned down a dinner invitation from Randy Randy and drove north along the route Sylvia would have taken every morning to her bank.

Again, she hadn't called ahead, but Rainer Iams, the branch manager, Sylvia's boss, agreed to see her, and took her to a small conference room.

"Coffee?" he offered. He was a handsome, fiftyish man, in good shape, with a great deal of beautifully cut silver-gray hair. His dark gray suit had been tailored for his broad shoulders, and disguised his thickening waist. His handshake was firm, his brown eyes twinkled and his smile had that "trust me, would I steer you wrong?" charm.

How did that line from the crocodile poem go? "And welcomes little fishies in with gently smiling jaws."

Liz went over the same questions about Sylvia's disappearance. It was becoming boring, hearing the same answers. "Was there any evidence of malfeasance?" she asked.

"Was she embezzling, you mean?" He chuckled. "Anytime something like this happens, the auditors come in and go over everything, including the inventory of paper clips. Not a penny missing. She certainly hadn't been squirreling away funds from the bank. She was an excellent employee. On the way up the career ladder. I was mentoring her to take over her own branch, probably within six months."

"Did she have problems with any of the other employees or clients?"

She caught his look, down and to the right. *Here comes a lie.*

"She worked herself harder than she worked her staff, but they all liked and respected her."

"Any special friends?"

"She was all business. Didn't believe in fraternizing with the tellers."

"And with you?"

Again that sideways glance. *Another lie coming up.*

"We were colleagues, and as I say, I mentored her."

"She was a beautiful woman, and you're a very attractive man. I'm surprised you didn't at least do a little flirting. Like at the Christmas party."

His blush caused the blood vessels beneath his facial skin to show up like a roadmap. "What are you suggesting?"

She raised her hands. "We know she was getting ready to divorce her husband, and frankly, Mr. Iams, several people have told us you were probably the cause."

"Listen," he said, and leaned forward. His eyes no longer looked merry, and the crocodile's jaws no longer smiled gently. "I'm married. I have two kids in the University of Tennessee and a third in private school. I would never be unfaithful to my wife, and certainly not with Sylvia Slaughter."

Liz opened her eyes wide. "Why not Sylvia? If you considered infidelity, I mean, not that you'd act on it."

He dropped his voice to a whisper. "Any man would be safer taking a saber-toothed tiger to bed."

"My word! I've heard she could be…difficult." Liz sounded sympathetic even to herself. She nearly reached across the table and laid her hand on his, then decided that would be going too far.

"Oh, damn." He drove his fingers through his immaculate hair and left it standing straight up on top like a Kewpie doll's. "I'm going to tell you the whole truth."

In Liz's experience, that phrase invariably preceded a big fat lie.

"I almost went too far once after a bank function in Nashville. I was drunk and thought she was, too." He curled his lip. "She never mentioned it again, but every once in a while when she wanted to know something I didn't think she needed to know, she'd give me this knowing little smirk and touch me, you know, that too-friendly way. And she'd mention Margaret—that's my wife. I was mentoring her to get her own bank, all right. I wanted her out of this one."

"But you never actually slept with her?"

"Haven't you been listening, Detective Gibson?"

"Still, you didn't like her."

His eyes snapped open. "Now, see here, I didn't have anything to do with her disappearance."

"Not even to pick her up and drive her to the airport when she asked you? To get rid of her?"

"And keep my mouth shut for seven years? Ridiculous. Now, if you'll excuse me, I have some mortgages to look over." He didn't see her out, but looked down at his desk with fierce concentration. Liz would have taken a hefty bet that he had no idea what he was staring at.

Back in her car and on her way to interview Jud's private detective, Frank LaPorte, she realized one comment in all that nattering might lead to something. Iams had said, "When she wanted to know something I didn't think she needed to know." Small Southern banks that served large agribusiness concerns run by good ole boys frequently went the extra mile to keep their customers solvent.

A man couldn't make a crop if he couldn't buy seed. Some farmers said they were solvent one day a year—the day they received the subsidy check from the government and the payment from the cotton or soybean wholesaler, and paid off their crop loans for the year. The next day and the next crop loan put them back in debt.

If Iams skated too close to the wind, or received kickbacks from his farmer friends, Sylvia might have threatened to blow the whistle unless he cut her in. Blackmail money wouldn't have showed up as embezzlement from the bank, but blackmail was an excellent motive for murder.

There wasn't much chance Liz could subpoena Iams's bank records without more probable cause than she had. Judges didn't like fishing expeditions.

SHE WAS SO BUSY going over her notes that she didn't realize Jud had arrived at the café in Oakland until his shadow fell across the table. When she looked up into his gray eyes, her heart gave the kind of lurch it had as a teenager when the captain of the football team smiled at her in the lunchroom. That particular crush had petered out. With luck, her feelings for Jud would go the same way.

Not that Jud was smiling. He loomed over her, pulled out one of the metal chairs and sat down. It protested but did not break. His chinos were mud-splattered, and his eyes looked exhausted. She longed to put her arms around him…. *Stick to business.*

"What I'm doing could get me in big trouble," she said.

"And that would be?" *Now* he smiled. Just what she needed to keep her focused.

At least here she couldn't leap across the table and into his arms for another one of those incendiary kisses. "Unless we prove what really happened to Sylvia, you'll always be under suspicion, even if we never find a body."

That sobered him. He nodded. "I've been living with that for seven years. It's not news."

"Help me find the truth."

He narrowed his eyes. "Why should I trust you?"

"I've already said I had doubts about the official line."

"But you're not one hundred percent convinced I'm innocent, are you?"

That was the problem. She wasn't. Could he possibly be conning her? She refused to answer him directly. "You want that million dollars, don't you? And you probably inherit whatever money your wife had in the bank, and the stock market, too, don't you?"

"I have no idea. I can't legally open her will."

"But you know you get the insurance money."

He nodded slowly.

"If she's dead and you didn't kill her, then somebody else did. If she's alive, then we need to find her so you can divorce her. If you really are innocent, then you should want to know the truth."

"That's a lot of if's." He leaned back, and the chair groaned. He stared at her for nearly a minute in silence. "What about Colleen?"

"What about her?"

"If we find her mother ran away, she'll always believe she is to blame."

"You don't think she already thinks that? That's why she says her mother must be dead. She can't get past what she can't face. You can't, either."

"She tells people her mother's dead," Jud said. "But I don't think she fully believes it. Without real evidence to the contrary, she'll always keep hoping her mother will walk in the door again."

"What about you?"

He stared at the table without speaking for a moment, then raised his eyes to Liz's. "My mind knows that after all this time she must be dead, but every time I answer the telephone or the doorbell, some small part of me wonders for a second if it'll be Sylvia. If we had proof Sylvia was dead, Colleen would grieve, but at least we'd all know."

He sat there, musing. Finally, he said, "What would I have to do?"

"For starters, keep your mouth shut. This is totally against procedure. One does not investigate a probable homicide with the prime suspect as a sidekick. Nobody must know we're doing this, and I mean nobody. Not Trip, not Colleen, not Irene, and definitely not Herb."

"What else?"

"I want to go over the area that was searched after she disappeared. I have a couple of ideas."

"Such as?"

"I think the weather was important. It hadn't

rained for almost a month. Then we got our usual late-November frog-strangler, with enough wind to tear the remaining leaves off the trees. Any evidence would have been covered up, blown or washed away. A week earlier that would not have been the case. I think she waited for that first big storm. Maybe she had to work so fast that at the end she made a mistake and left some evidence."

"Which won't exist after seven years."

Liz shrugged. "Won't know until we look."

"We can't get back in those woods on foot in this weather. We'll need an ATV. Trip has one I can borrow." Jud's eyes were showing some animation now.

"Don't tell him why you need it."

"He knows I don't hunt any longer, but I do go prospecting for possible land acquisitions. He might suspect, but he won't ask and I won't tell. When?"

"Tomorrow morning?"

"Yeah, if we can make it eleven o'clock or so. I'll call Trip tonight, check in at the job site, then pick you up with the ATV on its trailer. Just tell me where. I suggest the parking lot at St. Stephen's. People drop their cars there to carpool all the time. Another vehicle won't be remarkable. Dress in layers and wear waterproof boots, preferably to your knee. Hat and gloves. I'll bring the vests."

"What vests?"

He chuckled. "You *are* a city girl. It's deer-hunting season. Unless you want to come home with a hole in your chest and strapped to somebody's front fender, you better be wearing an orange vest."

He picked up her empty foam coffee cup and tossed it expertly into the garbage can. "Feels good to be doing something beside watching the clock tick. What else do you want?"

"Come with me to see your detective."

He was suspicious again. "Why do you need me?"

"I called Mr. LaPorte this afternoon to check my appointment. He blew me off. He won't see me without your written permission, and even then he won't be happy about it. He's a detective, not a lawyer, so he can't invoke attorney-client privilege, but he can put a bunch of roadblocks in my way. With you along, I'm sure he'll cooperate."

"I can give you his reports."

"Face-to-face is better."

Jud thought for a minute. "Sure. Make the appointment. Maybe late tomorrow afternoon. I do have a job, you know."

"So do I, and I am putting it on the line for this. Don't you forget it."

CHAPTER THIRTEEN

"YOU'RE KIDDING, RIGHT?" Liz looked at the muddy four-wheeled ATV strapped to the flatbed trailer behind Jud's SUV. "There's barely room for you, much less me."

"We'll fit you in somehow. Come on." He opened the door of the SUV for her. "I checked out inconspicuous places to park along that road on my way here. I assume you don't want me to park in that old man's driveway again and have him ask questions."

She shook her head.

"There's the remains of a road from when they logged pines on this land. It won't be passable by the SUV for any distance, but we can at least get off the road where we can't be seen. Here." He reached behind the seat and handed her a neon-orange vest and baseball cap. "Put them on. I wasn't kidding about deer season. This land is posted, but some folks don't pay a lick of attention to the signs." He grinned. "Us included."

If he hadn't pointed them out to her before he turned in, Liz wouldn't have noticed the ruts that must have constituted a road at some point. They bumped along until they were well back into the trees, then he stopped, and showed her how to help him unstrap the ATV and back it down the ramp.

"How do you know about this road?" she asked as they worked.

"They wouldn't let me take part in the search, but I didn't leave the area until the horses and ATVs gave up. This was the only easy way in they found. I remember it, although it's a damn sight more overgrown and rutted now than it was, and I don't know how far back it goes."

He situated the ATV so he'd have room to maneuver around the SUV once they started.

"M'lady, your carriage awaits," he said, climbing aboard and pointing to the other seat. "Squeeze in." He started the engine. The growl in the midst of the quiet woods made her jump. No wonder hunters said the things scared deer for miles around.

It was definitely a squeeze. She could feel the muscles of his shoulder and arm even through two down jackets. Glancing at him, she realized he wore a broad grin. She snuggled her hip closer to his and felt not a cell phone, but a gun. A big automatic by the feel of it. She had her Sig Nine, of course: she never went anywhere without it. But she hadn't expected *him* to be armed.

They bounced along the narrow lane surrounded by second-growth hardwoods and loblolly pines. When she looked behind, she could barely see the track, much less the SUV. A couple of steps into the trees, even in winter when the leaves had fallen, and anyone might get lost. Was that what had happened to Sylvia?

Was Liz crazy, coming out here alone with this guy? Nobody knew where she was or who she was with; her car was ten miles away in an anonymous parking lot. If she was wrong about Jud's innocence, he'd already hidden one body in this area so well it hadn't been found in seven years.

"Whoo-ee! Hang on!" Jud slid around a curve and into a patch of watery mud at least twenty feet long. The windshield deflected most of the slop, but she was still sprayed with dirty water.

"Slow down!" she squealed. "You love this, don't you? You lunatic!"

He slowed instantly. "Sorry. I guess I do. It's a guy thing. Hey, what's that? See? Way back there on the left." He stopped, pulled out a pair of binoculars and fiddled with the focus.

She hadn't even thought to bring binoculars. Some detective. "What is it?"

"A shed or old barn, maybe. I don't remember it, but I never hunted this part of the woods when I was a kid." It seemed to be on its last legs, but still standing. "The search team is bound to have checked it out when they were hunting for Sylvia."

"And we're going to check it out again now." Liz slid from the ATV and landed ankle deep in icy water. "Oh, shoot!"

He came around the front, wrapped one arm around her and swung her easily out of the puddle and onto the grass verge. "City girl, city girl," he chanted. "Come on, city girl, let's see what you're made of." He started in the direction of the building, stooped to pick up a broken branch and used it to brush vines and limbs out of his way. She followed carefully in his footsteps. She couldn't get used to the ease with which he could lift her. It was disquieting that he made her feel so feminine and so vulnerable.

"Been some kind of trail here," he said. "Not for a long time, though. But it might have been passable on foot seven years ago."

"Slow down, Paul Bunyan," she gasped.

"I thought you cops were in such great shape," he said over his shoulder.

"I am in superb shape, thank you, but not when I've got twenty pounds of mud on each foot." She stared at the shack. It couldn't really be called a barn. "What is this place?"

"Probably storage for hay back when they logged with mules and draft horses. Looks to be in pretty good shape for the shape it's in. The doors are still on their hinges."

The searchers must have torn this old place apart looking for Sylvia's body seven years ago. Still, when Jud reached to open a door, Liz held her breath. "Big enough to hide a car?" she asked.

"You might have been able to drive a car up here during the drought," he said. "These doors are wide enough. But you'd never have been able to drive it out during that rainstorm. Besides, we found Sylvia's car, remember. We only had the two."

"What happened to her car?"

"I sold it to a wholesaler for pennies on the dollar. Never wanted to see it again once the police released it." He ran his hand over one of the door hinges. "This metal isn't rusty. Stainless steel. Much younger than the building."

Liz felt a stab of excitement. There was no reason to think a steel hinge had anything to do with Sylvia, but any oddity was worth pursuing. "Open it."

The doors had sunk together at the center, but were not secured by a padlock or even a hasp. The left side squealed when Jud lifted it free of the mud and pulled it toward him. She kicked the leaves built up against the sill out of his way.

Out of the shadows, a silent white shape flew straight at Liz. She ducked, threw up her hands and flattened herself against Jud's back with a scream. She felt the wind in her hair as it floated no more than a foot above her head and into the trees.

He turned and grasped her in his arms and she clung to him. Liz didn't believe in ghosts, but at that moment, she would have believed the white thing was Sylvia's spirit trapped for seven years inside that barn.

"Hey, it's okay," Jud whispered, and stroked her hair. "We disturbed us a big old barn owl."

"What?"

"She's pissed to have to vacate in the daytime.

Babies ought to be fledged and on their own by now, but I'll bet she's got a nest in the rafters." He tilted Liz's chin up. "Not a ghost."

The man could read her mind. She hated that. The next moment, when he lowered his face and touched her lips with his, she realized she could read his, as well. Heat radiated up from her center as she leaned against him, wishing that even in this cold, she could feel his skin against hers. He tasted like cinnamon, and surrounded her with the scent of aroused male.

"Please," she whispered. "We can't…."

He stepped back. "Not in forty-degree weather and muddy parkas, we can't. That, however, can be changed."

"Let's just check out this shed." She pulled her flashlight from the inside pocket of her parka and moved past him. She did not want to be the first to enter that darkness, but she had to. After all, she was the cop.

The inside was surprisingly dry except around the sides. The metal roof had remained intact although it gapped at the edges. At the back, twenty or thirty bales of dusty hay were heaped, although they might have been piled there thirty or forty years ago. A dozen or so had tumbled from one of the stacks and lay on the clay floor.

Liz jumped when she heard what sounded like castanets. Jud shone his light up into the rafters and laughed. "Not fully fledged yet, I guess."

Three owlets with white moon faces clicked their beaks in rage as they peered down from a neat nest high in the rafters. Jud moved the beam away. "Go back to sleep, guys. Dream of all those fat field mice Momma's going to bring home to you."

Ignoring the furious owlets now that she knew what they were, Liz began to quarter the interior in a tight grid, training her light just ahead of her feet. Under the nest the floor was littered with small bones, fur and owl pellets. "There are a couple of faint boot prints," she said. "Surely they can't be from seven years ago."

"Could be if nobody's been inside this place since the search. It's dusty, but dry and out of the wind."

"Too big to belong to a woman," Liz stated. She took out her digital camera and took several flash shots, enraging the owlets all over again. "They sound like the second act of *Carmen*," she said. "I never knew they did that."

"It's a warning. Those beaks can chop off a finger."

"Can you help me shift the bales that have fallen? The boot prints disappear under them." She reached for the nearest one and tried to lift it by the rusty wire wrapped around it. It didn't budge. "These things must weigh a hundred pounds each," she said.

He lifted the bale she'd been struggling with and tossed it casually onto the stack in the corner, then proceeded to do the same with the rest of them.

"I knew I brought you along for a reason," she said.

"Over and above my sexy smile?"

She ignored him, got down on her hands and knees and aimed her light along the floor. "The closer we are to the ground, the easier it is to spot irregularities," she said. "Watch where you step."

"I'm sure they searched behind those bales," he said, and sank to his haunches beside her.

"That must be why the prints disappear behind the fallen stack." She slowly raked her light along the floor from left to right and back again, a couple of inches forward each time. He started to move, but she lifted a hand. "Wait. What's that line in the dirt?"

"Snake track, probably."

She rocked back.

"It won't bother you now. Too cold for snakes. It's denned up someplace this late in the year."

"Don't snakes wriggle? That mark is straight. And there's another one right beside it. See, they cross. Narrow. Tire marks." She looked over at him. "Bicycle tires. Got to be." She started to take photos. "Somebody stashed a bicycle in here at some point." She sank onto her heels. "Damn. That's how she did it."

"No way tire marks would last seven years, Liz. Probably some camper getting out of the rain left the boot tracks and the bicycle tracks this summer. You can't date dirt."

"No, but sometimes you can date tires. I brought some of that goo they use to make molds, but I left it back at the ATV in my satchel."

"Let's go get it."

"I really ought to stay here. Maintain the chain of evidence, now that we may actually have some." She batted her eyelashes at him in a parody of the helpless female. "Could you go back for it?"

He sighed. "What does it look like?"

"Just bring the whole pack. I've got a couple of bottles of water. We can use that to mix it up."

"No problem." He disappeared through the door.

The owlets had stopped snicking their beaks, but continued to peer at her over the rim of their nest with round, insane eyes. Liz sat back on her haunches, suddenly feeling very alone. She was gaining grudging respect for Sylvia. The woman might be a crook, but if so, she was a gutsy one.

Liz actually wanted to be alone, at least for the time it would take Jud to get to the ATV and back. Carefully avoiding the tracks, she followed them to the stack of bales. Her gut told her Sylvia was the owner of the bicycle. She could easily have ridden it here during dry weather and stashed it until she needed it to get away.

If she knew of the existence of the shed. If she possessed a bicycle. If she could ride one at all, much less down a dark country road in a storm.

Liz ran her hand over the bale at handlebar height and felt a slight indentation just where the end of a handlebar might have pressed into the hay. The barn had stayed frozen in time. Had Sylvia left something that indicated she'd been here? A calling card would be nice, or one of those old "Kilroy was here" messages, except saying "Sylvia was here."

Grateful for her thick gloves, Liz ran her hand over the top of the bale and brushed aside the owl pellets. Sylvia would have been in a rush. She probably hadn't considered the additional time it would take to walk back here after dark in a rainstorm, get the bike, walk back to the road and ride off.

How could she be certain Jud wouldn't come hunting for her, when he couldn't get her on her cell phone after half an hour? She couldn't have known he wouldn't wake up for hours.

Or could she? He'd had a glass of wine from a bottle that had been opened the evening before. Had Sylvia drugged him, to give her time to get away? At this point, Liz believed she was capable of that sort of planning.

Praying that a snake had not chosen the space between the bales for a winter den, Liz slid her hand down one side and felt nothing. She tried the other, probing carefully with her gloved fingers.

And touched—what? It felt metallic. She withdrew her hand without moving the object, then took her camera out and photographed the bale and its neighbors from every angle. She'd wait until Jud came back to fish out whatever the object was, so that she'd have a witness to where and how she'd found it.

"SHOULDN'T YOU CALL IN some CSI types to make that tire mold?" Jud asked.

She looked up at him. "We don't need to bother them. This is public land, after all, so I shouldn't need a search warrant. Even at this temperature, this mold should be set in five minutes. Now, watch me while I check something." She went back to the bale and stuck her hand in the slit, grasped the metal object, pulled it out and stared at it. "What is it? Some kind of hay thing?" She held it out. "Don't touch."

"Where did you grow up? That's a plain old-fashioned bicycle clip. Goes around the bottom of your pants so they don't get stuck in the chain."

"So there was a bicycle here. Yes!"

"I keep telling you, Sylvia didn't own a bicycle. Both Colleen and I have bikes now, but not then. She was too little, I was too busy and Sylvia wasn't interested."

"Could she have bought one you didn't know about?"

"The woman was an accountant. She kept every slip of paper she ever generated. The police went through everything."

"You're sure they didn't find a receipt for a bicycle?"

"Nope. They brought the papers back because I needed them for taxes. I never looked at them after my business manager returned them to me after he filed."

"Where are they now?"

"At the house with all the other old files."

"If she was smart, she paid cash and didn't keep the receipt. But she may not have thought anybody would ever make a connection. Maybe, just maybe, she made a tiny little mistake." Liz carefully dislodged the tire mold, wrapped it in her extra T-shirt and put it into her pack. "I am freezing! Can we go to your house? I want to look at those receipts."

CHAPTER FOURTEEN

GETTING THE ATV LOADED onto the flatbed was much more difficult than getting it off. It was slick with mud. The tires kept sliding off the ramp.

"This thing weighs a ton," Liz said. "Can't you just drive it up onto the trailer?"

"You'll have to do the driving while I guide."

"No way!"

"Then shove. We're almost there."

She leaned against the rear end of the ATV and pushed. Without warning, it broke free of the mud and rolled onto the trailer.

Liz's feet slipped out from under her, she overbalanced and fell facedown into mud soup. "Damnation!" She sputtered, started to wipe off her face and realized her gloves were even muddier than her cheeks.

She felt strong hands grip her waist. Jud lifted her by her middle like a suitcase and swung her to her feet. She glared at him over her shoulder and glimped the curve at the corner of his mouth. He was laughing!

Not stopping to think, she reached back with her left foot, caught him behind his ankle and yanked.

Jud's feet flew out from under him.

He went down with a satisfying splat, creating a small muddy wave. "Hey! No fair!"

She realized as he twisted her and yanked her down on top of him that he was a darn sight faster than a man his size ought to be.

"Lady, that was pure malice."

"You laughed at me, you jerk."

He wrapped his arms around her. She struggled to get at least one hand free to push him away.

He laughed again. A moment later she was laughing, too, so hard she could feel tears making tracks down the already hardening mud that covered her cheeks. A moment later the laughter died.

She felt her heart thud. This time she was the one who initiated the kiss. He didn't seem to care about the mud on her lips as he lifted his face to meet hers. Even through all the clothes, the wet and the dirt, she felt his body harden, felt hers respond, felt her hips move against him.

His gloved hands reached beneath her parka, ran up her spine and then down to cup her against him.

"Crazy," he said against her lips.

She drove her fingers through his muddy hair, tasted his tongue, longed to feel him skin to skin, inside her, filling her, weighing her down with that massive body of his.

"I can't," she whispered, even as her body insisted she must. "Not with you. And not like this."

"I want you," he whispered back, holding her face between his big hands.

She disengaged herself and rolled away from him to pull herself up by gripping the edge of the trailer ramp.

He sat up. "Tell me you don't want me. Say the words."

"You know I can't," she said, without looking at him.

"Can't want me, or can't say so?"

"Both." She took a deep breath, straightened her shoulders and turned to him with a grin. "Besides, this mud is probably crawling with bacteria, and it's freezing. I don't necessarily require champagne and roses, but clean, dry and warm would be nice."

He stood up in one easy movement. His face was clouded, but a moment later he smiled down at her. "Man, talk about a high-maintenance woman."

"Believe it." She opened the passenger door of the SUV and looked at the nice, clean upholstery. Well, moderately clean, at any rate. "We'll mess up the seats."

"They've had worse than this on them. Climb in."

"My car seats certainly haven't."

"My house is closer than your car, anyway. I'll drop the ATV and trailer at home, you can have a shower and I'll clean your parka before I drive you back to your car."

"I don't think that's a good idea."

He slid a hand across her thigh. She jumped, but didn't move away. "We have two guest baths with locks on the doors." He glanced at her. "Of course, you can always share mine."

"Thanks. One of the guest showers will do nicely. But a shower won't solve the what-to-wear problem. I always keep a change of clothes in my car, so if you'll drive me back there…"

"Shower first. I'll toss your stuff into the washer with mine. You can borrow one of my sweatshirts and a pair of pants while they wash and dry. I'll fix us a sandwich, then I'll drive you back."

She checked her watch. It was barely noon, but her stomach was rumbling. "Okay. But no funny business. I mean it. You're still officially a suspect."

"No problem. How about unofficially?" When he realized she didn't intend to answer, he backed carefully down the narrow road, skillfully guiding the trailer around curves until they reached the pavement. He had to wait while a couple of pickups drove by, then he backed out and turned toward home.

They drove in silence for a while until Liz said, "I'm a little surprised at your house. I would have expected you to build yourself one of those starter castles."

"You've stumbled on my secret passion. At first that's what Sylvia envisioned, but I dissuaded her. Shoot, there were only the three of us, and our money is generally tied up in building loans for our developments. I wanted a chance to build an eco-friendly, energy-conserving living space, as self-contained and nondestructive to the environment as possible." He turned down the gravel road leading to his property. "While your clothes are drying, I'll give you the grand tour."

Liz couldn't help being impressed. She still thought the house was weird, but at least he was trying to do something good, as opposed to ostentatious. They dropped their dirty boots and outerwear in the mudroom. "Most of it'll shake off when it's dry," he said.

He led her upstairs by way of a narrow back staircase, got her situated in one of the guest rooms and handed her an enormous terry-cloth robe.

"Let me have your clothes," he said. "I'll be back in a minute."

He returned with an oversize gray sweatshirt, gray sweatpants and heavy gray athletic socks, which he exchanged for her jeans and turtleneck. She didn't offer him her bra and panties. They weren't muddy or wet, and somehow the thought of being entirely naked under the robe bothered her in ways she didn't want to think about.

"I hope you don't mind," he said, "but the sweatpants belonged to Sylvia. The shirt is mine, but my pants would look like elephant drawers on you."

"Probably keep falling off, too."

"Say, I hadn't thought of that. Want to swap?" He reached for his waistband.

She grabbed his arm to stop him. "Whoa! I'll keep these, thank you." She frowned down at the pants draped over her arm. "You've kept her clothes?"

Jud sighed. "Irene and I tried to get rid of them a couple of times, but Colleen won't let me give away anything. Sylvia's room is just the way she left it, down to half-empty perfume bottles and used lipsticks. My cleaning service dusts and vacuumns every week, but otherwise it's in a time warp."

"Actually, you'd be amazed at how many people leave everything untouched after someone disappears or dies." Liz shrugged. "Jack Samuels, one of my colleagues in Cold Cases, says he's been in bedrooms that look like Miss Haversham's after the wedding feast." Then it hit her. "You had separate bedrooms?"

He dropped his eyes. Wouldn't most men want their wives beside them at night? Had he given in gracefully, or did he fight?

"I moved into the big guest room and left her the master suite when Colleen was just a baby. Sylvia said I snored, and she needed her rest."

"Do you snore?" Liz didn't realize the implication of her question until he raised his eyebrows and grinned at her.

"Want to find out?"

"Not today, thank you." She turned toward the bathroom door and stopped with her hand on the knob. "How will Colleen feel if she sees me wearing these?"

"Let's hope she doesn't." He paused on the way out and said, "Come downstairs to the kitchen when you're ready. I'll go put our clothes in the wash, drop the trailer and ATV, shower and change and see what I can find for lunch." He hesitated another moment. "I could reschedule all that if you'd like somebody to scrub your back."

"What I would like and what I'm going to do are entirely different things."

He flashed that lopsided grin and shrugged. "Oh well, it was worth a shot."

Liz luxuriated in the hot water that coursed down her body and warmed her frozen toes. The shower was furnished with bath gelée, shampoo and conditioner, so she could wash the mud out of her hair. She dried it with the hair dryer that hung beside the bathroom mirror. No man would think of those items, so either Colleen or Irene must have made arrangements for the comfort of guests. The toiletries were not seven years old.

Jud had said Sylvia's room was caught in a time warp. The other detectives had no doubt been through it a dozen times over the years, but they were men. If she could check it out, Liz might spot something they'd overlooked. It was amazing to have if not the actual crime scene, then the victim's room preserved as it had been.

Liz did the best she could with the small amount of makeup she kept in her tote bag, slipped on the sweatpants, which were long enough but a tad tight around the hips, and pulled on the sweatshirt. She'd always preferred them oversize, but this was ridiculous! The socks were too big, as well, but they were warm and dry. She straightened everything, left the robe hanging on the back of the bathroom door, rearranged the towels and went downstairs to find the kitchen.

Jud stood over the stove. His sweatshirt stretched over his biceps and chest, and barely reached below his waist.

He was whistling "I Can't Get No Satisfaction" and doing something with a skillet on a restaurant-size gas range. When he heard her he stopped whistling and turned, spatula in hand. "Hope you don't have anything against cheese and bacon," he said. "Toasted cheese is my comfort food of choice."

"One of mine, too," she said, and sat on a tall stool by the center island. "Can I do anything?"

"Check the washer. It's back there. Everything ought to be ready to go into the dryer. After lunch, you can take your stuff upstairs and change."

She came back a couple of minutes later to find he'd served the sandwiches and poured a couple of diet sodas. "Only one sandwich for you, too?" she asked.

"Yeah. I'd like four of five, but I'd regret it."

"Tell me about your house," she suggested as they started to eat.

"It's one of the reasons I want the insurance money," he said. "Besides for Colleen's college fund. Contractors aren't rich—at least Trip and I aren't. We build fancy houses, but that does not equate to personal wealth, not even in a bull market, which this is definitely not. Land values have shot up, and so have all the permits and service on construction loans. I know there's nothing wrong with building luxury homes, but we can't go on ignoring global warming or middle-class people who can't afford a half-million-dollar mortgage."

His eyes shone with enthusiasm. Liz hadn't ever seen him so fired up before. "In the Southwest and West there's a lot more interest in going green than here. They've got houses built of hay bales with stucco over them, and sod roofs with wildflowers growing on top. Try doing that around here and see if you can get a building permit. Timber framing is about as far-out as I could get away with." He waved his hand in the air. "It's a god-awful part of the world for either sun or wind energy. You can't count on either one. But you can work with them if you use backup power."

"I saw the solar panels on the roof."

"Yeah. With a generator that runs on propane for when the power lines are hit by an ice storm. A couple of years before we moved out here, the little house we were living in was without power for two weeks."

"I remember that storm. Mine was out ten days."

"Anyway, we've used recycled and recyclable materials wherever we could. We water the lawn and shrubs from cisterns that catch rainwater runoff from the roof, and we have a septic tank and our own well. The floors are concrete slab, painted and scored to look like quarry tile. The lights are low-energy.

"Most of the windows face south. In the summer the sun is high enough that it doesn't penetrate under the eaves. We manage to stay cool and cut down on air-conditioning. But in the winter, it's low enough to give us both light and heat."

"You designed the house?"

"Sure did." His voice swelled with pride. "But it's eight years old, and a lot has happened in the green world since then. I want to build some affordable, attractive, economical green houses that people will be glad to buy and live in."

"Why can't you?"

"Nobody's interested. Not the banks, not the mortgage companies and certainly not private investors. Maybe if I had five or six up and ready to show so that people weren't afraid they'd lose their investment if they had to sell them later... But that takes money. Money that building all the starter castles in the world won't provide. Not anytime soon."

"Would a million dollars finance you?"

"Shoot, half a million would get us launched, as well as provide for Colleen's college fund."

"Weichert is part of this?"

"He think I'm nuts. He agrees with the concept, all right, but he thinks this area is twenty years away from giving a hoot about global warming or building green. Architects and subdivision covenants want conventional construction, and in this area, that means brick and stone. Trip may be right, but I've got to try."

"So you're on your own."

"He'd do everything he could to bail me out if I got my tail in a crack, but he's got three kids to my one, and a wife who doesn't work outside the home. I'd go bankrupt before I'd ask him for a dime."

"What about Irene and Herb?"

"You're kidding, right? Actually, Irene has her own money and would help me out. Again, I can't ask her. She already does so much, looking after Colleen, buying her clothes—girl stuff I have no idea about." He finished his sandwich in two bites, drank his diet cola, then put his dishes and hers in the dishwasher. He turned and propped himself against the kitchen counter, folded his arms and waggled his eyebrows. "So, Colleen's car pool isn't due home from school for a good three hours. Plenty of time…"

"Plenty of time for you to find Sylvia's receipts from the year she went missing, and for me to take a look at her room."

"Don't you need a warrant?"

"Not if you give me permission."

"What do I get out of it?"

Liz stood up and pulled the too-tight sweatpants above her navel. "You do not get arrested for assaulting a police officer, for starters."

He opened his hands and gave her an innocent look. "Hey, as I remember it, you assaulted *me*."

"Yeah, but I'll be writing the report. Come along, sport. Even if I were eager to indulge in fun and games, I wouldn't be able to concentrate while I'm listening for the sound of a car door."

She took the stairs two at a time. He followed with a sigh. "You are no fun."

"Believe it. Where do you keep your receipts?"

"The room over the garage. It's not used for anything else, so it's kind of a catchall."

"Can you locate the receipts for the right year?"

"Sure. It may take me a little while, but I'll find them." He stopped and opened a door, then stepped aside. "Sylvia's room."

"I'll put everything back the way I found it."

"Good. Thanks."

She stood in the doorway and waited until he'd gone down the hall and around a corner toward the garage room. Then she went back to the room, dug a pair of latex gloves out of her tote and returned. Liz didn't want to leave any evidence of her presence in this room.

She stepped in and left the door open behind her. By rights she should have another detective with her, but with so few of them on the squad and so many cases, they were invariably on their own. At least with the door open it would be more difficult for anyone to accuse her of planting evidence.

What that evidence might be after all this time, Lord only knew.

The only thing that surprised her about the room was the color. It had elaborate flocked peach wallpaper, deep-piled peach carpet and a satin bed canopy. All were so close to the color of her own living room that Liz made a mental note to call her painter the minute she got home. Sylvia's peach cave suddenly seemed to give off the odor of overripe fruit.

The furniture was expensive and copied from Louis XIV—white, cold, with lots of curlicues. Not Liz's idea of comfortable. Maybe Sylvia's business environment had been so dry and sparse that she wanted this nest of hers to be the opposite—ultra-luxurious and ultrafancy.

Was he invited into this room, this bed? Or did Sylvia slip across the hall to join him?

They'd been married over eight years when she left—seven years after she became a mother. Significant? Had it taken that long for her to get sufficiently fed up, and to plan the perfect escape?

Liz made a mental note to ask Jud on the drive back how he had met Sylvia and how they'd decided they were compatible enough to want to spend the rest of their lives together. On the surface they seemed to have precious little in common.

She knew well how easily two people could mistake passion for love. Heck, she'd done it herself. But although Steve had sworn he didn't want to give up on the marriage, both of them had known within two years they weren't meant to spend their lives together. For one thing, Steve drank too much, too often. Besides, he was content to ride a squad car until he made his thirty, while she planned to build a career as a detective. He swore he wasn't jealous of her drive, but deep down he was.

"Early divorces, dear," her mother had said when Liz had told her the marriage was over. "Always best. Don't wait until there are children involved. Then you must deal with each other forever, and the children suffer. Get a divorce when you're childless and too poor to have money to fight over. You can go your separate ways and never see one another again."

Liz and Steve still saw one another and remained friends, despite his occasional maudlin calls at her house, but the rest was true. They hadn't even owned a cat or dog when they separated—two people who had discovered they no longer walked in step. Was that why Sylvia and Jud had slept in separate rooms? How could Sylvia give up closeness with a hunk like him?

Jud was certainly adorable. In college and after he must have had to beat the girls off with a stick when he walked across campus. The only thing Liz could figure was that Sylvia was so beautiful he couldn't believe his luck when she'd come on to him. She must have seen him as the best bet for upward mobility available at the time.

Maybe Sylvia always considered Jud a stepping stone. Having Colleen must have annoyed her; she wouldn't have been able to walk away clean. Unless she disappeared into a new life.

Liz knew she was being hard on a woman who might have been murdered, but everything she'd heard about Sylvia led her to believe that Jud's wife had the instincts of the average wolverine.

Liz snapped the cuff of her glove in irritation and walked over to the elaborate dressing table, skirted with heavy peach silk that fell in thick folds to the floor. As Jud had said, several gold lipsticks with brand names she herself could never afford lay casually beside a lamb's-wool powder puff and a silver-backed comb and brush set.

She hadn't found a jewelry box yet. She went to what she assumed was the bathroom door and opened it. More peach. The space was luxurious. A Roman emperor would have felt right at home here.

She recrossed the bedroom to double doors that must open to the closet.

It was the size of Liz's master bedroom and completely fitted by one of those fancy closet designers. Immaculate. With enough shoes to make Imelda Marcos jealous. Liz checked the labels on a couple of jackets. Not exactly Chanel, but definitely upscale. The sweaters neatly folded on the shelves were cashmere. A built-in jewelry cabinet held gold chains and earrings. Simple, elegant and expensive. So were the handbags.

They weren't in the thousand-buck range, but definitely in the several-hundred. Apparently, once Jud got going on construction, he'd made enough money to support his family, and Sylvia used most of her income on herself. He'd already said that Irene bought most of Colleen's clothes.

Why would any woman walk out and leave all this stuff? Wouldn't she at least take her gold jewelry, if for no other reason than she might need to hock it at some point?

Every scrap of paper had been removed from the room during the first investigation, but had led nowhere. Maybe Liz could locate something everyone else had missed.

She got down on her hands and knees, pushed aside the silk drapery that covered the dressing table, stuck her head under, then twisted to look at the bottom. Something small might have gotten lodged behind one of the drawers.

"What are you doing?"

Liz reared up so fast she banged her head on the underside of the dressing table and saw stars.

"Who are you? Get out of here or I'll call the cops! Daddy! Daddy!"

Surely it wasn't time for Colleen to be home from school. Liz backed out, sat on her heels, then stood up. She held her hands out in a gesture of peace.

The girl stood at the open door, her book bag at her feet, fists at her sides, her face splotchy with rage and fear.

"Hi," Liz said. Boy, talk about lame.

"You! You're that cop! You've got no right…." Her eyes darted to Liz's clothes. She must have recognized Jud's sweatshirt. Or at least Liz thought she did.

The girl screamed at her. "You're wearing my

mother's pants! Nobody touches her things but *me!*"
She started toward Liz with her arms outstretched,
fingers curved into claws.

"It's all right. I'm only borrowing them for a
little while."

"You'll stretch them," Colleen sobbed. She
glanced at the dressing table. "You'll break something!" It was a howl of primeval rage. Liz knew that
sound from her years as a negotiator. It usually
happened just before somebody got badly hurt.

"Get *out!*" The girl reached down, picked up her
book bag, lunged forward and swung it straight at
Liz's head.

Liz put up her arm and caught the brunt of the
blow between her wrist and elbow. She heard the
thud and felt the pain just before the teen drew back
for a second shot.

Liz grabbed the bag, twisted it free and tossed it
behind her, where the girl couldn't get to it without
going through her. That was not going to happen.
She managed to get her hands up to protect her face
from those fingernails, grasped Colleen's wrists and
held her, while the teen kicked at her viciously and
screamed obscenities that Liz certainly hadn't
known at that age.

"Stop that," Liz said. She kept her voice level. She
couldn't very well deck a fourteen-year-old, even one
as tall and strong as Colleen, but she might have to.
At least her gun was in her tote bag and out of sight.

Jud appeared at the door, obviously out of breath.

"Colleen, Colleen, for God's sake!" He rushed to his daughter, wrapped his arms around her and swung her off her feet and away from Liz. The girl continued to kick and flail.

He dropped her onto the bed, but she bounced up. "She—"

"Enough." Jud sounded remarkably calm.

Colleen glared at him, then flung herself facedown onto the pillows and sobbed, "These are Mom's. You can't let her…"

He turned to Liz. "I'm so sorry. I knew she'd be upset if she found you in here, but I didn't expect her home for another couple of hours." He turned to Colleen. "Why are you? Home, that is?"

Through her sobs and gulps, she choked out, "Soccer practice got canceled. Coach has the flu. Why is *she* here? In Mom's room? How could you let her wear Mom's clothes?" She lifted her head and glared at her father. "Why does she even need other clothes?" She sat up and glanced from one to the other. "Daddy?"

"Mine got wet and muddy," Liz said. "Your father lent me these while mine were in the wash."

"Daddy, you shouldn't have. You know nobody touches Mom's stuff but me. Nobody. Not till she comes home." Colleen was no longer sobbing, but tears continued to stream down her cheeks, and her jaw trembled.

Despite their earlier encounter, Liz wished she could put her arms around the girl's shoulders. She

was obviously angry and frightened, clinging desperately to her last shreds of hope that she hadn't
been abandoned forever. Underlying it all was
probably a terrible sense of guilt that she was the
cause of her mother's leaving.

"I'm sorry, Colleen," Liz said.

"Sweetheart, I gave her Sylvia's sweatpants
because mine wouldn't fit her. But they're just a pair
of pants, period." He shook his head sadly and
yanked open the closet door. "It's about time we
stopped all this nonsense and got rid of all this…this
stuff!"

"Nooo!" Colleen leaped off the bed and flew to
him. "Please, Daddy, no! She'll need them when she
comes home."

"You said you think she's dead," Liz said gently.

"She's not! Somebody kidnapped her. She wouldn't
leave me. I'd know if she was dead. I'd feel it."

"Then why say she's dead?"

The girl's legs gave way and she sank back onto the
bed. Probably without realizing she was doing it, she
picked up the big square pillow and hugged it to
herself. "Everybody laughs at me, okay?" Then she
added, so softly that Liz had to strain to hear, "They
say she left to get away from me. She didn't, Daddy,
did she?"

"Of course not, honey," Jud stated. "Your mother
loved you."

"Loves me, you mean." Colleen's voice hardened,
but she continued to hold the pillow against her

stomach as though it could protect her from body blows. "When she comes home she's going to find all her stuff exactly where she left it. I won't let you get rid of it."

"All right. I won't get rid of it now, but one day soon we'll have to go through it all. We can't leave this room this way forever."

"We won't have to," Colleen said blithely. She lifted her shoulders and gave Liz a cool glare. "My mother is coming home to be with my dad. They're still married, you know. Deal with it."

"And you need to know that assaulting a police officer can get you serious time in juvenile detention," Jud said. "I suggest you apologize to Detective Gibson and ask her for mercy."

"No."

Jud took in a lungful of air as if about to read her the riot act.

Liz stopped him. "It's okay. Colleen was surprised, that's all. She thought I was a burglar."

The teen kept her mouth shut.

"In any case, you will not threaten or attack anyone ever again," Jud said. "Now go to your room and stay there until I say different. And I am locking this room. That is, if Detective Gibson is through searching it."

"For the moment, thank you, Mr. Slaughter. Now, if my clothes are dry, I need to get back to my car."

"Colleen, do your homework in your room. No Internet, no games, no television, no phone, cell or otherwise. When I get back, we're having a serious talk."

His daughter grabbed her book bag, then ran out of the room, down the hall and into her room, slamming the door behind her.

Jud closed the closet and sank onto the bed. "God, what am I going to do?"

"Nobody likes being chastised in front of strangers, Jud. Definitely not teenagers. You don't actually think she's going to stay off the phone and the computer while you're gone, do you? All her friends will hear about how horrible we both are before we even make it to your car."

"She doesn't have a computer in her room and mine is password protected. I monitor what she does and where she goes on it."

Liz wondered just how secret Jud's password actually was. What if Colleen had cracked the code? Could she actually be in contact with her mother? From the way she acted, Liz didn't think so, but made another mental note to ask Lieutenant Gavigan. She might be able to get another search warrant, or Jud might give her permission to check it out. At the moment, she had too much else on her plate.

"She's usually pretty good about obeying me," he said sadly.

"Jud, she's fourteen and she's miserable. Have you talked to her teachers lately to see if the other kids are really making fun of her about her mother?"

"I guess not recently. Irene says mood swings are just part of growing up." He ran his hand over his head. "Sometimes I don't know who she is any longer, and I'm sure not handling this well, am I?"

"Is she seeing anyone?"

"She's fourteen. She doesn't have a boyfriend."

"I was thinking more of a psychologist. You do realize that if there had been a gun available, or if she'd gotten hold of mine, she might well have shot me?"

"No way."

"Way. It happens. Weapon plus rage equals blood. The perpetrator may be horrified a second after pulling the trigger, but can't reverse the action. Murder is the only crime that can't be undone. She needs counseling. And she *doesn't* need to see me, obviously. I'll change downstairs."

CHAPTER FIFTEEN

DRESSED IN HER OWN clothes, carrying her tote and wearing the boots that Jud had cleaned, Liz met him in the garage.

"These are the receipts from the year Sylvia went missing." He slid a large cardboard deed box onto the backseat, held the truck door open for her, then climbed in and started the engine.

On the drive back, they were silent at first, both obviously unwilling to talk about the scene with Colleen. Finally, Liz asked, "How did you and Sylvia wind up together?"

He shrugged. "You can't understand what she was like when I met her. She was so beautiful, so warm, so smart and funny. She dumped the guy she was dating, a guy who was going to be a doctor, for Pete's sake, for me. I was knocked out that she'd do that. She said she didn't want to support any man through medical school, internship and residency, then have him waltz off with a nurse." Jud glanced over at Liz.

There was no mention of not loving the med student or of falling in love with Jud.

"I had a lot of great plans. She was going to push

me into the big time. I think she had visions of turning me into Donald Trump by the time I was thirty-five." He shrugged. "I was a big disappointment."

"Did she mind having to work?"

"No, that's the one thing she didn't mind. To Sylvia getting rich was a game. She loved playing it. Money was how you kept score, and I didn't meet her financial projections, especially after I got her pregnant. She never forgave me for that."

"Poor Colleen."

"She doesn't know."

"Of course she knows. Mothers can't fake that sort of thing. There's even a diagnosis for it—attachment disorder. I came across it all the time in hostage negotiations. This is a hard question, but think before you answer. Did you ever consider Sylvia might have been sexually abused as a child?"

He nearly drove the SUV into the ditch. "What? You mean Herb? Some funny uncle? God, no. One of the few things she really enjoyed was good, uncomplicated sex."

Liz blinked. She'd assumed Sylvia was as cynical about that as about the rest of her life.

"Let me rephrase that," Jud said. "I'm telling you stuff I probably shouldn't, but under the circumstances…" He took a deep breath. "It wasn't so much sex she enjoyed as the control she could exert over men that way. And she loved having orgasms."

"And you could give them to her."

"Well, yeah." He cut his eyes toward Liz and smiled. "I don't guess this is the most appropriate time to suggest a demonstration?"

"No." Although she was thinking precisely that. How could she sit here talking about a man's ex or dead or absent wife's orgasms, and still want to make love to him?

"Was she pregnant before you got married?"

He shook his head. "No. We had a formal wedding. Trip was my best man. Not much of a wedding party. As you can probably guess, Sylvia didn't have many close girlfriends, although she was in a sorority in college. She thought it made for good contacts."

"So, how did it—Colleen—happen? Do you know?"

He turned left into the church parking lot and drove to the back corner where Liz had parked her car. He pulled up beside it and cut the engine. "She didn't want to take the pill. Said it made her fat, so we used condoms."

"Not the most reliable form of birth control."

"Obviously. After Colleen was born, Sylvia got an IUD. She wanted me to get a vasectomy, but I refused, although I knew she would never agree to have another baby, no matter how much I wanted one."

So even then he'd had an inkling that the marriage wouldn't last.

He turned in his seat so that he faced Liz across

the broad console. "Do you have to write all this in your report?"

"Don't worry. I won't mention Colleen."

"How about my sex life?"

"Only if it becomes germane. Did you keep having…I mean…"

"Did we sleep together after Colleen was born and I moved into the guest room?"

Liz felt a blush spread up her face. These were pertinent questions in a murder investigation. Randy Randy would have asked them without a thought. But Randy Randy wasn't emotionally involved with the prime suspect.

Jud reached across and took her hand. "I could say no, but that would be a lie. I said she enjoyed sex. So do I. I stopped enjoying it with her. She had plenty of other partners willing to fulfill her needs. I know men are only supposed to be interested in the physical side, but that's not me. I haven't really wanted anyone since. Until now."

He tugged Liz across the console and into his arms. She came willingly, and kissed him as deeply as he kissed her.

Moments later, she pulled away. "You have to get home to your daughter."

"She'll be fine." He ran his hand along Liz's rib cage.

"No. She needs you. Besides, we're sitting in the middle of a church parking lot at two o'clock in the afternoon. Can we put off meeting with your P.I.

until tomorrow? I've got to go down to the office and write reports, and I'd like to go through those receipts before we meet him."

Jud sighed. "I'll call him and reschedule. It's Saturday, but I doubt he'll mind."

She slid back to her own side of the truck, got out and picked up the deed box from the backseat. "I'm going to go over these at my place this evening."

"Can you call me if you find anything?"

"I'll see. Go home."

Clutching the box to her chest so that her nipples didn't show so blatantly through her sweater, she watched him drive away. Part of her longed to have him turn around and sweep her away with him like the robber bridegroom.

The rational part knew his daughter did indeed need him, while Liz needed to go back to being a detective.

Even if she solved every aspect of this nasty little puzzle, she and Jud could never be together until his daughter was able to come to terms with the loss of her mother. His first duty had to be to his child. A child who wanted nothing to do with Liz.

Not for the first time, she was glad she and Steve hadn't had a baby together. She'd seen too many second marriages break up over stepchildren. She might feel sorry for Colleen, might try to help her if she could, but no way was she going to come between father and daughter.

No. She had to maintain her professional approach. Her duty was not to Jud, but to the truth. In a sense, she was the only advocate Sylvia had.

CHAPTER SIXTEEN

"WELL, HELLO, PRETTY LADY. Where you been hiding?" Randy Randy sauntered over and sat on the edge of her desk.

Liz pasted a smile on her face. "I couldn't stay away from you any longer."

"I knew it. My charm's finally getting to you." He leaned forward. "So how's about we ditch this place for a drink and an early dinner?"

"Sorry. I've got reports to catch up on."

"Ah, come on." He reached over and touched her arm. She winced, saw his eyes widen. Before she could stop him, he pushed up the sleeve of her sweater.

"Who the hell did that? Hey, Jack, look at this. Who hit you?"

"Nobody hit me. I ran into a door." Colleen's book bag hadn't broken her arm, but it had left one hell of a bruise. She hadn't looked at it, but now that she saw the purple oblong, she felt a twinge. Her forearm would hurt like hell by morning.

"Did that SOB Slaughter hit you? I hope he's rotting in a jail cell as we speak."

"That particular SOB didn't touch me."

"Don't bother with the old door thing."

"Okay. I slipped in the mud and went down against the bumper of my car. Satisfied?" Not bad for a quick story. She *had* slipped, and the bruise did sort of bear a resemblance to a bumper. She didn't want either man to know she'd been injured by a fourteen-year-old kid, even one as big and angry as Colleen Slaughter. Liz pointed to her feet. "See? Muddy boots. Bug off, you guys. I'm busy."

"Okay, Liz," Jack said. "The lieutenant wants to see you the minute you come in."

"Right," she said as she continued typing. "In a minute."

"Right now means right now," said a gruff voice behind her.

She caught her breath. "Yes, sir. I was trying to finish a report to give you."

Gavigan held his door open for her, followed her in and sank into his chair. "So tell me instead."

"I'm about convinced Sylvia Slaughter disappeared on her own, and I think I've figured out at least a part of how she did it."

Gavigan listened, and looked carefully at the bicycle tire impression. "After seven years? How can you prove any of that?"

"Bound to be a database of tires that includes motorcycles and bicycles. Maybe we'll get lucky and find that tread was discontinued seven years ago."

"Proving a bicycle with that tread was in that shed

seven years ago." Gavigan spread his hands. "First question. Why disappear? Second question. Where did she go? Third question. What did she use for money?"

"Fourth question," Liz continued. "Where is she now?"

"You got it. I've given you free rein on this one…."

"Because you thought I wouldn't get any further than anyone else."

He looked abashed. "Yeah. Call it your initiation. And you haven't. Bring me proof. Then I'll listen to you."

"Can I check Slaughter's computer?"

"No judge would give you a warrant. Ask him, since he's being cooperative. Maybe the kid's been communicating with her mother all along."

As Liz rose and turned to go out, Gavigan said, "Give me your report and your logs before you leave tonight. If you intend to get paid, I've got to have proof you haven't been sitting in a movie theater or at home reading a book."

Liz knew he was only half joking, and felt her temper rise. She quelled it, smiled and said, "Yes, sir."

She went back to her desk. Annoyed, she sat down hard and gasped. She hadn't paid much attention to her rump recently. She'd fallen on her face in the mud, but Jud hadn't hit her scar when he'd held her against him. Or if he had, she'd been too involved with him to notice. Now it was reminding her that it was not completely healed.

Another reason not to go to bed with Jud Slaughter. Her rear end was not pretty at the moment.

Randy Randy called from across the room, "How'd your little closed-door one-on-one with the lieutenant go?" He wiggled his eyebrows.

"You let the lieutenant hear you say something like that and you'll be the city's most experienced crossing guard," she retorted.

CHAPTER SEVENTEEN

SHE NUKED A DIET MEAL then carried it and the deed box to her tiny dining room. At least it wasn't peach. When she'd walked through her front door, she'd looked at what she had begun to consider "Sylvia peach" and had felt slightly nauseated.

Sylvia had organized receipts alphabetically by date and stapled them together in two sets—taxable and business. Liz had no idea what she was looking for—other than something that would connect Sylvia to a bicycle—but she didn't intend to miss so much as an oil change.

Going over every charge on every bill would take half the night. She'd already had her one break, the tire tread. And her one big idea. Now she was back to scut work.

Poirot hopped up on the table, sat in the middle of the automobile receipts and washed his paws. Liz shoved him off. "Sorry, sweetie. Mommy's busy."

Mommy. How could Sylvia have produced a baby daughter and not fallen in love with her the moment she saw her? How could she walk away from Colleen without looking back? Granted, Colleen at fourteen was not very likable, but then what teenager was? And she'd been only seven when her mother left.

What kind of child would the mixture of Liz's genes with Jud Slaughter's make?

She smacked herself on the head. Where had that thought come from? If he should turn out to be guilty despite all her instincts, and if, God forbid, she were to get pregnant, his defense lawyer would have a field day, her career would be shot and she'd spend the rest of her life taking their child to visit Daddy in the big house.

She couldn't get pregnant if she didn't sleep with him. Her aunt always used to say, "Keep both feet on the floor." Unfortunately, whenever Liz saw Jud, she seemed to float about four feet above the ground. Not a good thing. She downed a diet soda and went back to work.

Three hours later she stared at the organized list of receipts she'd found filed under "Xmas Presents." Her eyes felt as though they'd been hit with pepper spray. Despite endless cups of tea and another diet soda, her mouth felt dry, and when she looked down at her hands, she realized they were shaking.

The clock read eleven forty-five, too late to call Jud's house. He and Colleen would probably be asleep. But Liz didn't want to wait. If he kept his cell phone on his bedside table, where she kept hers, maybe she could take the chance.

He picked up just as the phone started to roll over to voice mail.

"Huh?" he said sleepily. Then an instant later he was wide-awake. "Liz? What's wrong?"

"Not wrong." She picked up the receipt. "Did you, Colleen or any of your friends receive a bicycle for Christmas after Sylvia disappeared?"

"I already told you. No."

"Could it have been hidden somewhere else, say at Irene and Herb's, to be given to Colleen on Christmas morning?"

"They would have said something."

"No bicycle helmet, either?"

"What's this about? Don't tell me you found a receipt for a bicycle."

"One of the receipts in the stack marked X-mas Presents has a receipt from the Happy Peddler for one girl's bicycle, twenty-six inch, and one bicycle helmet."

"You're kidding."

"Nope. She paid cash and took delivery at the time of purchase."

"Sylvia never paid cash for anything."

"Could she have gotten a bicycle into her car?"

"Yeah. It was a Windstar. I definitely never saw a bicycle."

"The date reads November 1. She disappeared the Friday before Thanksgiving. Now that I have the name of a store, I can check the type of tires they would have used on that model."

"Why bother with a helmet? I had to keep at her

about wearing her seat belt and making certain Colleen did."

"She knew she'd disappear on a dark, rainy night on a country road. It's hard to identify someone wearing a helmet unless you get a good look at them."

"Taking one hell of a chance that somebody would remember a cyclist."

"Maybe somebody did. I'll call Mr. Waldran and ask if he saw someone on a bicycle that night." She leaned back and yawned. The cat placed his front paws on her shoulders and touched her nose, the signal that it was past time to go to bed. "One thing I don't understand. If she was so careful, why would she leave that receipt for anyone to find?"

"Damned if I know. I guess she figured nobody would make the connection. She was right, wasn't she? The cops were so sure I was a killer, they didn't bother looking for other clues. And throwing away a receipt, especially one for cash, would have been agony for Sylvia."

"I've been over and over her bank statements. I can't find any unusual withdrawals. All the other receipts for Christmas presents were charged to credit cards. Did somebody give her the money, or did she have another bank account you don't know about?"

"Sherman and Lee didn't find evidence of one. Our lockbox is joint. Her salary and bonuses were accounted for in our regular bank statements. She had a small brokerage account and an even smaller money market account, but neither one's been touched since she disappeared."

"Who pays the taxes?"

"We haven't filed jointly since she left, so I guess nobody has. My accountant says because I can't access the money, I'm not liable. If she shows up now, I guess she'll incur penalties, but you'd have to ask a CPA."

"Those accounts might have grown significantly in seven years." So, he would not only collect the insurance money if Sylvia was declared dead, he'd probably inherit whatever was in those other accounts, as well. A further motive for him to kill her. "Would your P.I. know about those other accounts?"

"He didn't mention them in his reports to me, but they weren't part of what I asked him to do. I changed the appointment to ten o'clock tomorrow morning, by the way. Okay with you?"

"Fine. I'll meet you there."

"Liz, thank you. I'm not used to having anyone believe me. You're the first person who's ever tried to find out what really happened. Can I buy you breakfast tomorrow morning? I drive morning car pool to soccer practice, but I can meet you at Lacy's about eight-thirty, then we can take my truck to LaPorte's office. I want to see you."

She wanted to see him, too. Just the prospect of watching that big, lithe body of his stride into the restaurant excited her. She took a deep breath and attempted to sound professional. "Of course. See you then. I'll bring the receipt. Bye." She started to hang up.

"Liz?"

"Yes?"

"You ever indulge in phone sex?" She could hear his chuckle.

"No. Good night." She hung up.

And darn near called him right back. She took a deep breath. She still had the *Y*s and *Z*s to go through.

CHAPTER EIGHTEEN

LIZ STIRRED SWEETENER AND lemon into her tea. The waitress had brought it without asking. Good memory. Her smile was reserved, however.

"Did Sylvia travel for her job?" Liz asked when they were alone again.

"In spurts. Sometimes she'd go off to meetings a week at a time, over three or four months, then nothing for half a year."

"What about the last six months before she disappeared?"

"She went to several meetings."

"Where?"

"You'd have to ask Iams, her boss. Once to Nashville, I think. Once to some fancy hotel in the desert. Yeah—once to San Francisco."

"Did she bring presents back for Colleen?" Liz prayed she had. She remembered waiting for her mother to return from business trips, and dreaming about the gift she'd bring. Her mother never forgot. Kids measured their importance by small things like that.

Jud sighed. "If she remembered at all, she picked

up something in the airport on her way home. You can always tell. Airports all have the same stuffed toys and children's books."

"I'm sure Colleen didn't care where the present came from, so long as she got one."

"I finally loaded up a file drawer in the construction trailer with enough goodies so that Colleen wouldn't know when Sylvia forgot her."

Poor child. "Did Sylvia pay her own travel expenses?"

"The bank paid. She filled out forms for reimbursement for whatever she used her own credit cards on. We had to keep the business funds separate from household expenses and from her business expenses, for the IRS."

Liz felt her pulse speed up. "I wonder if the bank would have the travel vouchers after all this time. And if that dreadful Rainer Iams would let me see them without a warrant."

"Iams wouldn't let you see last year's Christmas card without a warrant."

Jud sounded too casual to know about Sylvia's fling with Iams. Or maybe he didn't care.

"I'd be willing to bet she had a new identity set up that would let her slip into a new city, possibly someplace she'd visited recently," Liz said.

After breakfast, she and Jud took separate vehicles to Frank LaPorte's office. She needed to do some things on her own after the meeting, and Jud had to check in at his construction sites.

LaPorte's office was located in midtown in one of the small, older office buildings housing financial planners, small accounting firms and the like.

As they walked toward the entrance, a man was getting into a beat-up black pickup in the parking lot. As he backed out, Liz said, "That guy's nearly as big as you are."

"But not as cute." Jud reached for her, but she ducked under his arm.

"Right. We're fifteen minutes early."

"We could waste that fifteen minutes in the elevator," he murmured.

"No, we could not. Come on."

LaPorte's office was on the fourth floor, the top. None of the other offices appeared to be open, given that it was Saturday, but at the far end of the hall, the door Jud was heading for—to LaPorte's suite— stood ajar, and light shone into the corridor.

"See, he's waiting for us." As they reached it, Jud called, "Frank, it's Jud Slaughter and Detective Gibson."

"Stop!" Liz grabbed Jud's arm, yanked him back into the hall, shoved him against the wall, then pulled out her service pistol. This morning she'd worn it on her belt where it belonged.

"What?"

She looked around the door frame, her Heckler & Koch held two-handed against her chest, muzzle up. "Wait here."

She expected him to argue. Instead, he did as she

asked. Most men wouldn't have. He rose even higher in her estimation.

She slid around the door. The suite was divided into two small rooms, a front space for a receptionist, a single office beyond with its door open and lights on. Even from behind Jud's shoulder Liz had spotted the mess—papers strewn everywhere, a chair on its side. She picked her way across the floor and checked the inner office. It was, if anything, a bigger mess.

She smelled the blood from the doorway. Fresh blood had no odor, but took on the scent of rusty iron in a few minutes. She'd always had a sensitive nose, and had learned what old blood smelled like when she'd been shot and had lain on that gurney on her face while her rear end seeped.

She spotted the man's feet first, sticking out from under a heavy file cabinet. The drawers had apparently been pulled all the way out to make it easier to dump them. That had overbalanced the cabinet and dropped it on the prone figure on the floor. "Jud, help!"

An instant later he was beside her. A moment more and he'd righted the cabinet and shoved the drawers closed. "It's Frank," he said as he dropped to his knees.

Liz placed her fingers against the man's throat. "He's alive, but his pulse is thready. Call 911. Tell them to send an ambulance." Jud reached for the telephone on the desk, but she stopped him. "Use your cell. We don't want to mess up any fingerprints." Jud's fingerprints would be on the file cabinet. That couldn't be helped, but it might lead to suspicion that he'd been the one to dump it in the first place.

She took a packet of tissues from her shoulder bag and wadded them against the wound on the back of LaPorte's head. He'd been hit where the bone was thick, but he wasn't a young man.

"He must have pulled the cabinet over on himself," Jud said, after he clicked off his phone and sank onto his haunches beside her.

She rolled her eyes. "You don't believe that. Neither do I." She could already hear a siren in the distance. "Who knew about our meeting this morning?"

"Nobody."

"It's Saturday. Probably the intruder didn't expect LaPorte to come into the office. He must have disturbed whoever was trashing the place, and been bashed for his trouble."

"Hello?"

Liz looked up to see a pair of EMTs standing in the doorway. "That was quick."

"We try." The first paramedic grinned at her and moved into the room, while his buddy brought in a gurney.

She and Jud stood out of the way while they worked.

"You call the cops?" one of them asked as they finished strapping LaPorte to the stretcher. The sheet mounded over his belly like a snowy mountain. His face was white and his breath shallow, but at least he was breathing.

"I *am* a cop." Liz showed them her badge.

"You know what happened? He hit him?" He gestured at Jud.

She shook her head. "He was with me when we found him. I'll report this. You taking him to Med Center Trauma?"

"Right. He needs to be scanned. I don't know whether his skull is fractured, but he's bound to have a doozy of a concussion. Name?"

Liz gave them the information, then watched them trundle LaPorte into the elevator, leaving only enough room for one EMT. The other took the stairs.

"I have to call this in," Liz said, and reached for her cell phone. "The attack isn't necessarily about this case...."

"But the timing's suspicious," Jud finished. He looked around the room as she talked to her office.

"Who knew about your hiring LaPorte?" she asked Jud afterward.

"Everybody who knew Sylvia, I guess. Frank interviewed them all. But that was months ago, when I was deciding whether to go for a declaration of death or a divorce."

"And now, after seven years, the police are nosing around again. Maybe considering other suspects, other solutions. Somebody got scared."

"Of what?"

"Sixty-four-thousand-dollar question… Cold Cases doesn't usually work weekends, so my guys probably aren't available, but they'll send somebody," she said. "It'll take them at least twenty minutes. Don't touch anything. Just stand there with your hands in your pockets. Better yet, go out into the hall."

"No. I can help you look."

"For what?"

"The files on Sylvia, obviously."

"Go wait in the hall. Please."

He gave her a narrow glance, but went.

The instant he was out of sight, she took a pair of thin latex gloves from her pocket, slipped them on and turned to the laptop on LaPorte's desk. Both it and the laser printer beside it were on. There was already a CD in the slot. She clicked on it, and found a number of files had been copied. She sent a complete list of files to the printer and slipped the copy into her pocket. The CD was evidence. It could have the fingerprints of the person who had attacked LaPorte on it.

He probably wouldn't have maintained Jud's files on his laptop. So the guy had most likely been searching.

Had he found them? Liz had no idea. Old files might be stored in another location.

She walked into the hall, to find Jud staring out the window with his hands in his pockets. She touched his shoulder. "Are you okay?"

He turned to her and wrapped his arms around her. "I thought the guy was supposed to ask the girl that."

"I'm a tough girl and you are a sensitive guy. Deal with it." She stroked his back and hugged him close.

"I consider him a friend," Jud said. "You think he'll be okay?"

"Sure he will," Liz stated. She let Jud go and stepped back. "Is he married?"

"Divorced, I think. I went to his house one time. He doesn't live too far from you."

"Then we need to get someone over there as quickly as possible."

"You think whoever did this might trash his house, too?"

"If he didn't find what he was looking for here."

"I'll go." Jud started for the elevator.

"Stop. We have to wait for the police."

"We may already be too late."

"Not necessarily." She dialed another number on her cell phone. "Hey, Steve, you on duty?" She listened, told him the situation and asked him to have someone check LaPorte's house. "Address?" She looked up at Jud.

"It's in the phone book. I don't know the number offhand, but it's on Jefferson, this side of McLean."

"You get that? Call me. Thanks." She hung up.

"Your ex?" Jud asked. "The one I saw at your house?"

"He's a good cop when he's sober, which is most

of the time. Want to bet that Mr. Big in the parking lot was our assailant? You didn't recognize him, by any chance?"

Jud shook his head. "Never saw him before, and except for his size, wouldn't recognize him again. I could have taken him."

Liz rolled her eyes. "Mr. Macho. You might have gotten us both shot."

"LaPorte is an ex-cop, and no lightweight. He wouldn't have had a chance against a guy as big as that, but he put up a fight."

"There ought to be a weapon somewhere. Surely he pulled it out when he realized somebody was in his office."

They both began to look.

"The guy must have taken it away from him. Probably kept it." Jud began to quarter the office. A moment later he pointed. "Or not." A small automatic lay on the floor under an overturned end table.

"Walther PPK," she said. "We'll have to check it against LaPorte's registration, but the big guy we saw looks more like a magnum sort."

"Mr. Big must have taken the gun away from him, smacked him with something that knocked him out, and dropped the file cabinet on him."

"Then he either found what he was hunting for or he panicked and got the hell out of Dodge," Liz said. "A few minutes earlier, we might have run into him up here instead of in the parking lot."

"And been in big trouble," Jud muttered.

"Hey, you said you could take him." She grinned and punched him on the shoulder.

"Well, well, well, what have we here?" Randy Randy Railsback sauntered into the office.

Liz heard him snap on his latex gloves as she turned to confront him. "Since when do you work Saturdays?"

"Catching up on some paperwork, heard the call and came along. So, what gives?"

She told him, and also told him, against her better judgment, that she and Jud had been together since early that morning, and that they had run into the guy who might have done the deed on their way into the building.

"Right," Randy said. He didn't sound convinced, but the smirk he gave Liz made her want to slap him. "So how early is early? Like, before midnight?"

"Say, buddy…" Jud started toward him, but Liz held up her hand.

"Like eight this morning. We met for breakfast. Plenty of witnesses. I told you, we ran into the guy who probably did it. The attack just happened, and none of the other offices are open yet."

"And you know he was in this office how, exactly?"

"Where else would he have come from?"

"He could be an accountant or a day trader checking his computer."

"Look," Liz said. "I'll come down and do an Identi-Kit. If he's ever been in the system, I'll find him. In the meantime, Mr. Slaughter has to go check on his daughter, don't you, Mr. Slaughter?"

Jud took the hint. Randy didn't want to let him go, but Liz insisted that she could alibi him, and knew everything he might say, anyway.

He left to check on LaPorte's house. If he ran into Steve, she hoped he wouldn't be mistaken for the burglar himself.

"So, my lovely," Randy said, easing his hip onto the receptionist's desk, "how long you been sleeping with our suspect?"

CHAPTER NINETEEN

LIZ SAID THROUGH GRITTED teeth, "I am not sleeping with the suspect." She would if circumstances were different, but had no intention of telling Randy Randy that. "Besides, I don't think he is a suspect. I've got more than half an idea how his wife disappeared. What I don't know is why."

"Sex, money, revenge," Randy said. "Not necessarily in that order."

"You might be right." She dropped to her knees, picked up papers and stacked them loosely on the receptionist's desk. "She didn't need to put Jud in the crosshairs for murdering her. That was gratuitous nastiness." Liz sat back on her heels. "From what I've heard from everyone except her father, she could be real nasty."

Randy was hunkered down, picking up papers, as well. "Good reason for Slaughter to off her."

She'd never had a chance to see Randy actually working before. He cut through the bull and he seemed to know what he was doing. "I'm going to start on LaPorte's office," she said. "There's a CD in the laptop. May have fingerprints on it." No sense in telling him she had a copy of the list of files, until she'd checked what they were. She carefully kept her eyes straight forward and her body language honest.

"Yeah. We can go over the papers when they're in some sort of order."

Her cell phone vibrated. When she clicked it, she heard Steve's voice. "You were right. Some guy was getting out of a black pickup in front of LaPorte's house. When he saw us, he drove off."

Not Jud, then. His truck was white. "You get the license number?"

"Carefully covered with mud. Big man. Wearing a hoodie. Your knight in shining armor appeared while we were checking locks. Something going on I should know about there?"

"No, Steve, and thanks."

"We'll drive by, keep checking on the place. The guy probably won't come back."

"You never know." She clicked off and told Randy, "Somebody just showed up at LaPorte's house. Sounds like the big guy Jud and I ran into downstairs. I'll go down to the Med, see if LaPorte's awake, maybe obtain his permission to search his house. Get his keys. That way we won't need a warrant."

"No, I'll do that," Randy said.

"But—"

"You need to keep your distance. You're getting too close to Slaughter. Trace the money, find whoever helped the wife escape, if they did. But stay away from the suspect."

"Now, listen…"

"I'm serious." Then he grinned at her. "If you won't fall for me, don't fall for this guy."

She nodded. He was right. She was losing objectivity. She wanted Jud to be blameless, but he was just as likely to have hired somebody to take care of LaPorte and his records as anyone else, and he knew the time of their appointment.

He had access to a large labor pool of big, tough guys. If Liz and he hadn't arrived fifteen minutes early, Mr. Big would have been gone. She tried to recall whether Jud had attempted to delay them. Not that she remembered, but she was getting too distracted by him. She wanted to spend as much time as possible with him, even with a restaurant table between them.

How sick was that?

BEFORE SHE WENT DOWN TO the office, she drove by the Happy Peddler Bicycle Shop. The manager was in, but when she asked him whether anyone on staff might remember a cash customer from the first of November seven years ago, he laughed at her.

"Nobody but me's been here that long, and I'm only here because I own the place. And we sell a *lot* of bicycles."

"Could you look up your records? I need to know what kind of tires a bike purchased that day had." She handed him the receipt.

He barely glanced at it. "That model has used the same tires for several years."

Liz caught her breath. "Could I possibly see what the tread looks like?"

He grimaced and glanced around, probably hoping to find a customer he could blow her off for, but the store was empty except for a couple of lanky clerks lounging behind the cash register.

"It's important."

"Yeah, yeah. You're lucky I file copies of old specification sheets. Look around while I hunt." He gave her the once-over. "You seem like you could handle a mountain bike. Lots of clubs around. Camping out. Trekking. Great people. Lots of guys your age." He called, "Sam, come show the lady our mountain bikes."

Liz made nice with long, skinny Sam while her mind kept up a litany of *Please, please, please let it be the right tire.*

She let out her breath when the owner returned and held up a photo for her—a bit wrinkled around the edges but in color and completely recognizable. "Yes." she whispered, then leaned over and kissed him. "Can I keep this? I'll give you a receipt and sign for it."

"Sure. I got others."

"Here, please write your name, the name of the business and today's date across it." Chain of evidence had been drilled into her head since her first day at the academy.

Since officially she wasn't on duty, she drove home, shucked her bag and looked over the files she'd copied in LaPorte's office. The only relevant

file names looked like bills to Jud. Jud would certainly have copies of the P.I.'s reports themselves, so
what was the big guy hunting for?

She called Randy Randy on his cell.

"LaPorte's still unconscious," he told her, "but
they think he'll be okay. I left somebody sitting on
him in case he wakes up. Whoever konked him
might decide to finish him off to avoid any risk of
identification. The Med will call if there's any
change. Don't bother to come down for the Identi-
kit. There's nobody here to do it until Monday."

"Thank God. I am so tired."

"I give great back rubs."

"You know, Randy, just when I think you may be
an all-right guy, you prove me wrong. Thanks for
today. Now go home."

"Spoilsport. Stay away from Slaughter, or I'll
have to rat you out to Gavigan for your own good.
I mean it."

"There's nothing going on. But if you cause
trouble for me with the lieutenant you will never
bed another female in your lifetime. I mean it."

She hung up, then called Jud to tell him what she'd
found. "I don't suppose you can come by?" she asked.
"I need to see your copies of LaPorte's notes to you."

"Not a lot in them. As much as I would like to
come over, I'm babysitting Colleen and a couple of
her girlfriends. She's watching me like a cat at a
mouse hole. I keep expecting her to barge into the
bathroom to make certain I'm there."

"I'm sorry."

"She's been uptight the few times I've dated since Sylvia left, but this is the worst it's been. I guess she realizes how I feel about you."

"And how do you feel?" Liz cleared her throat and tried to sound natural instead of like a groupie at a rock concert. "We've never gone on a date."

"Don't play games, and don't tell me you don't know. I've known there was something between us since the day you stormed into my office, ready to chew my head off."

"Hardly a turn-on."

"I thought you were cute."

She choked. "Cute? I have never been cute in my life. Formidable, maybe. Professionally astute, perhaps. A superb hostage negotiator, definitely. At least I used to be. But cute? Hah!"

Cradling her cell phone, she wandered into the bedroom, kicked off her shoes and stretched out against the pillows. Poirot jumped up and curled up beside her. She stroked him gently.

"How'd you ever get into the negotiation business, anyway?" Jud asked.

"Long story."

"Since I am a prisoner in my own house, surrounded by teenage girls who would take your head off if you attempted to rescue me, I've got nothing but time."

"I was raised in a funeral home."

"I beg your pardon?"

"My dad died in a training accident. He was a marine. My mother went off the deep end for a while, so my aunt and uncle looked after me. He managed the biggest funeral home in town, and my aunt played the organ and sang at funerals. One of my earliest memories is being picked up in a chauffeured limousine. I didn't know it normally carried families to the cemetery."

"How'd you handle it?"

"I loved it. They lived upstairs in a fancy apartment. I used to turn the music pages for my aunt sometimes during funerals. Anyway, my mother eventually got it together, but I still spent most of my time with my aunt and uncle. When I hit sixteen, I worked in their office in the summers and during the holidays. I saved enough for my first car."

"How do we get from that to negotiation?"

"I'm not certain exactly when I realized the grieving families often behaved worse to one another than a pack of mongrel dogs fighting over a bone. And if money was involved, the worse the fighting became. Here they had lost Momma or Daddy or a spouse or, God forbid, a child, and they dragged out every slight, every remembered pain, every family secret. They fought over everything—which florist was going to do the flowers, what music to play, which preacher to use, what Momma would wear for eternity. Whether she should be buried with her wedding and engagement rings, and if not, who got them. I found myself, at age sixteen, trying to mediate, when what I wanted to do was slap them all silly and tell them they were behaving like rowdy children who should be clinging together, not trying to kill each other."

"At sixteen?"

"Yep. I didn't look sixteen, of course, but since I was the receptionist, I was the first person they exploded at. I found I could sometimes defuse the situation and reconcile them. I hate to say this, but when you pull it off, and people actually start acting right, it's a heck of an ego trip."

"So when you joined the police force…"

"I begged for the job and the training." She suddenly ran out of steam, and for the first time since she'd been shot, and found out that Marlene had been lying dead on her living room rug for hours, Liz felt her eyes begin to fill. "I used to be good at it. I really did."

"I'm sure you were," he said quietly.

"I can't do it any longer. I don't trust myself, and I don't want the responsibility. If I do it wrong, somebody dies."

"Who died?" Again, his voice was soft.

"An abused wife, and the husband who killed her while their daughter watched. I should have read his voice better, picked up the signs. Afterward I freaked. They pretty much made a place for me in Cold Cases. What if I can't handle that, either?" She shook her head. "Don't pay any attention. I'm just tired."

She heard noises in the background, and Colleen's

voice. The teen sounded more like an angry parent than a child. "Daddy, are you talking to that woman?"

Suddenly her voice came loud and clear. "Listen, you. You leave my daddy alone."

There was more noise as Jud reclaimed his phone. "Get back to your room, young lady. You will never do anything like that again, do you hear me? Liz is my friend."

In the background the girl cried, "You don't care about me."

"I care that you don't wind up a miserable brat."

"She hates me."

"I doubt that, but you're making it very difficult for her to like you. Out. And shut the door behind you."

The slam almost broke Liz's eardrum.

"I don't hate her," she said. "I feel bad for her, but she obviously wants nothing to do with me."

"At the moment, her behavior is appalling, and you don't have the memories of when she was cute and cuddly and adorable to carry you through the bad times. Thank God I do, but my patience is wearing thin. I'm afraid she'll quit school, turn to drugs or just, you know, disappear."

Like Sylvia. Of course he'd worry about that. Liz longed to assure him none of that would happen, but of course, she couldn't. She'd arrested too many girls from good families who had done those things or worse. "The two of you should go get some counseling before she acts out any further. I won't call again."

"No! No teenager is going to dictate to me. She's my daughter and I love her, but you're my…"

The silence hung between them.

"Good night," she said softly, and hung up.

The phone rang a moment later. She picked it up.

"My lover, dammit. Somehow, some way, some time." He hung up.

CHAPTER TWENTY

LIZ SLEPT BADLY, so badly that Poirot stalked off and slept on the sofa instead of tight against her back. The questions *should we?* or *should we not?* kept racing through her mind. She woke without a decision. Or at least, a decision she liked.

As an investigator, she knew she shouldn't allow their relationship to develop into anything more than professional. Unfortunately, she had been a woman much longer than she had been a cop. She wanted Jud in her bed as well as constantly in her mind, mucking up her feelings. Every time she thought of being his lover, her whole body flushed. It was like being a teenager again, lusting after that quarterback.

Surely, Jud couldn't be conning her. He could not possibly be a killer. He was too open, too caring, too...

Of course he could. She still had no evidence to the contrary after nearly a week. Speculation, yes. Theories, certainly. Proof? Not an iota.

She dragged herself out of bed at seven-thirty and called the hospital, then spent twenty minutes getting connected to the desk on the floor to which LaPorte had been admitted.

Nobody wanted to speak to her about him, or even admit that he was in the hospital. She turned on what charm she could muster, with no effect. The nurse on the desk made Nurse Ratched sound like Mother Teresa.

Eventually, the woman grudgingly admitted that Detective Gibson was on the list to be given information, then said, "I have no way of knowing whether you are Detective Gibson or not."

"I could give you my mother's maiden name, but it wouldn't mean much to you." Liz heard the edge in her voice and attempted to switch back to charm. "How about I give you my badge number? You can call downtown and check it out. I'll wait, although this early on Sunday morning during shift change, you may be on hold for some time."

Silence. Then, grudgingly, she muttered, "That won't be necessary. But I'd better not get in trouble for talking to you."

Liz sighed. "Not from me, you won't."

"Mr. LaPorte is still somewhat groggy, but the initial MRI was negative for intracranial bleeding. Mr. LaPorte has a very hard head. We'll run another scan on him tomorrow morning to be certain, but at this point, the doctor thinks he should be able to go home tomorrow afternoon."

"Can I see him?"

"If you must." The nurse told her the visiting hours. "He should be thinking rationally by this afternoon."

Next Liz called Jud. "LaPorte's sort of awake. I need to talk to him."

"He'll cooperate. He's an ex-cop."

She laughed. "That may be a reason for him not to cooperate. He probably holds a great many secrets that shouldn't be disclosed. Are you still babysitting?"

"I'm dropping off Colleen's friends from the sleepover and then taking her to Irene's to go to church. Then Irene's taking her to a make-up soccer practice this afternoon, so I'm free until I have to get home to cook dinner."

"I'm surprised you haven't taught her to cook."

"She takes after Sylvia. I actually like to cook, although I don't do anything fancy. Colleen's not interested in learning."

"I guess that's typical of teenagers. So can you meet me at the hospital at two-thirty?"

"Sure. Why don't I pick you up?"

What if she bumped into Randy Randy? "Not a good idea. I need my own wheels. See you there." She could justify having Jud talk to LaPorte. Well, barely. She couldn't justify arriving and departing with him.

She spent the morning on chores such as vacuuming and scrubbing the bathroom, doing two loads of laundry, changing the bed linens and Poirot's litter box, and generally attempting to catch up with everything she'd let slide since she'd started this case.

She had a week left to solve Sylvia's disappearance before Gavigan pulled her from the case. So far she didn't seem to be getting anywhere.

THE ROOKIE COP who had been assigned to guard LaPorte was leaning over the nurse's desk schmoozing with a cute little blonde when Liz interrupted him. He jumped guiltily when she flashed her badge.

"Are you actually trying to get our witness killed?" she asked sweetly.

"No, ma'am. I can see everything from right here."

"Of course you can. If you bother to look anywhere but straight in front of you. Give me a list of the people who have been in and out of that room since you came on."

He glared at her. "A couple of interns and LPNs is all."

"You checked ID? Not just badges?"

"Yeah. One guy said he forgot his ID in his locker. I wouldn't let him in. He hasn't come back yet."

Liz froze. "What did he look like?"

"Big guy. LPN. No hair."

She looked at Jud. "Might have been our boy." She checked the cop's name tag. "Officer Olivet, you were right not to let him in. I hope he didn't sneak in while your back was turned."

"He didn't. Carol Anne was watching over my shoulder." He nodded at the pretty blonde.

Liz stood with her hand on LaPorte's door. From the end of the hall she could hear the rattle of a food cart. She glanced at it, then looked again. There was something familiar about the orderly pushing it. She leaned toward the cop. "Is that the guy?"

"Looks like him."

"Go get him and bring him back. And watch yourself."

"I'll go," Jud offered.

Liz grabbed his arm. "You will not."

The cop walked down the hall. "Hey!"

Without hesitation, the man shoved the food cart into the cop, knocking him off his feet.

It turned over and spilled apple juice, soft drinks, coffee and tea across the tiled corridor, while the orderly sprinted the other direction.

Liz yelled, "Police, stop!" and ran after him, leaping over the mess on the floor. She heard Jud behind her, then a shout and a crash. He obviously hadn't sidestepped in time.

She glanced back over her shoulder to see both the rookie cop and Jud sprawled on the floor. "Call security!" she shouted.

She reached the second bank of elevators just as the doors closed on the broad back of the would-be assailant. This elevator had no floors listed above its lintel, so she couldn't tell whether he was going up or down.

If he was smart, he'd go up. The hospital had over twenty floors. Originally built in the twenties, it had been added to again and again, and was a rabbit warren even for people who worked here. No way would she be able to hunt him down on her own.

She ran back to the nurse's station. "Security's searching," the blonde said. "I told them what to look for." Her tag read Carol Anne Buckminster. "I called housekeeping. He must have snitched a cart. They are going to be so mad about the mess."

Jud and the rookie were trying sheepishly to get the cart back in some semblance of order.

"I could have caught him," Jud grumbled.

"And maybe gotten yourself shot," Liz said as she pitched a sealed half pint of cranberry juice back on the cart. "Officer Olivet, I'm leaving you with this mess. Get me if the security guys find anyone. Come on, Jud, let's see what is making Mr. LaPorte a target."

The P.I. was sitting up in bed, holding an empty bedpan in front of him like a shield. After introductions and explanations, he put it down beside him.

"Anybody I didn't know who came through that door was going to get clocked," LaPorte said. He wore a crown of bandages and both his eyes were black. "When I walked in on him yesterday, Jud, I thought it was you, from the back. Darn near as big as you."

"Could you identify him?" Liz asked. She flipped open her badge case.

He glanced at it and grinned. "They're making detectives prettier these days."

She ignored him.

LaPorte chuckled, then groaned and put his hand to his head. "Hurts when I do that. Doggone it, I barely saw the guy's face. He had on one of those hoodie things. I barely got my gun out before he bashed me. After that, I don't remember anything until I woke up here."

"What do you think he wanted?" Jud asked.

The investigator shrugged. "Damnation, that hurts, too. Usually when somebody gets nasty it's a custody case, but I'm not working on any at the moment."

"We think it might be about Sylvia's disappearance," Jud said.

"Yeah. Timing's right, you just calling me and all. If they were looking for copies of my reports on her, they missed out. I don't keep stuff like that in my office."

Liz grasped Jud's hand. "Where are they?"

"I got a secure storage room in one of those rental places. Too much junk to keep at home, and I never throw anything away."

"Could we have your permission to go into it and find the notes on Sylvia's disappearance? I assume you didn't include all your rough notes in your reports to Jud."

"You think I'd give the cops carte blanche to look through my records? Try getting a court order. We'll both be dead of old age before we find a judge crazy enough to give you one for a fishing expedition. How long you been a detective, honey?"

Liz tamped down her annoyance. He was from the old school. If she got upset with every cop who called her honey or worse, she'd be in a constant state of rage and talking to the employment commission every morning. "Long enough. How about I tell you what we've got. Then we'll talk. Jud has the right to see anything to do with his case."

"I remember my notes. I have a mind like a steel trap. Or I did before I got bopped. So tell me."

When she was finished, he gave a satisfied sigh. "I figured she'd done a bunk, but how? The bicycle makes sense."

"So how would you do it?" Jud asked.

"Buy a cheap car for cash, stash it somewhere close but out of the way, ride the bicycle to it, drive to Nashville or Little Rock or Jackson, abandon the car and the bicycle where they'd likely be stolen and stripped, get on a plane to anywhere under a different name with ID I'd already faked."

"You'd obviously worked all that out," Liz said.

"Except for the bike. Good a hypothesis as any," LaPorte stated. "I traced some twenty clunkers bought for cash around that time and not registered afterward with the state of Tennessee."

"Any of them bought by a woman matching Sylvia's description?"

"Not that anyone remembered. But then, she wouldn't have been that stupid. I did find one car bought by a little old lady down on Airways that wasn't registered. Not reported stolen, and if it was abandoned, it was never reported found, either. Thing is, if she went east, she'd have flown out of

Nashville, probably to Atlanta, but if she drove to Little Rock, she'd probably have taken Southwest."

"That could mean anywhere from Denver to Los Angeles," Jud declared with a groan. "We'll never find her."

"Don't be so certain," Liz said. "Where did you say she went on company trips?"

Jud listed the cities he remembered. "But she had to have money. Nobody ever found any missing."

"Sweetheart, can you pour me some water?" LaPorte asked. "I'm spitting cotton here."

After he had drunk two glasses of water, he leaned back with a satisfied grunt. "Blackmail," he said. "Only answer that makes sense. She didn't embezzle from the bank or strip your accounts. She didn't get money from her parents. Best I could see, she didn't have any friends. Blackmail it had to be."

"I agree. But who?" Liz asked.

"Best guess, one of the men she slept with."

"An obvious one is Trip," Jud whispered. "He treasures his reputation as a good family man, and he'd be anxious not to hurt his wife or kids. That would appeal to Sylvia. She despised Totsy."

"You knew about it, Jud, although Sylvia may not have admitted to Trip that she'd told you. He'd already confessed to his wife," Liz said. "And a sexual peccadillo alone wouldn't seem to be enough."

"If Trip did give her money and Totsy found out…"

"You think she's capable of murder?" LaPorte asked.

"Oh, yeah," Liz said. Jud nodded. "But she'd have no way of knowing where Sylvia was on the night she disappeared."

"How about someone with a professional reputation to lose?" LaPorte said. "A preacher, say, or a doctor…"

"Or a banker," Liz mused. "A banker who was trying to get Sylvia moved to another bank because she was, and I quote, 'nosy' about things that were none of her concern."

"Like good-ole-boy loans," the P.I. said. "Yeah, I thought of that. I had some info on Iams's brokerage account activity from around the time Sylvia died."

Liz raised her eyebrows. "I was going to ask you if you had info on Sylvia's money market and brokerage accounts."

"No activity. They've grown some, but not much. You're not supposed to be able to get that kind of information, and I'm not about to tell you how and where I got it."

"You have a tame hacker."

"I don't know about tame." LaPorte chuckled. "Damn, can't even laugh without my head trying to come off my shoulders. Anyway, about the time Sylvia went missing, so did part of Iams's college fund for his kids. No way of knowing where it went."

"How much?" Jud asked. His face was grim. "I

never knew he and Sylvia were… I guess I shouldn't be surprised after what happened with Trip."

"Sixty thousand large," LaPorte said.

"Why wasn't any of this in your reports?" Jud demanded.

The man held up his hands. "Not info I was supposed to have, and I couldn't tie Sylvia to any of it. You wanted to know whether you could go ahead and have her declared dead. I found no evidence she was alive. People disappear every day. Some are kidnapped, some are murdered, some just take off, often after killing their nearest and dearest. Since most states are now doing a better job of correlating death certificates with birth certificates, it's not that easy to go find some marker in a cemetery for a dead kid and use its birth certificate to get a social security number. Seven years ago, it was simpler."

"And once you have a birth certificate and social security card, you can get a driver's license and even a passport," Liz said.

"Yep. I can cite you half a dozen cases where the cops are certain the missing person is dead, but without a body…" He glanced at Jud. "I'm not saying that's what happened in this case."

"But until we know, I'll always be under suspicion," Jud said.

"Sorry, man."

"If we can make the assumption—and it's a big one—that your attack had something to do with the reopening of Sylvia's case, who do you think hired the thug?" Liz asked.

"The two people you mentioned. Either your business partner, Jud, or more likely Iams. If he did bankroll her disappearance because she was black-mailing him, she had something more important than a love affair on him. Southern bankers have been approving iffy loans for hefty kickbacks since the first bank opened. If Iams was doing that and Sylvia found out, he may think I have more info than I do."

LaPorte lay back. His face looked gray beneath the raccoon bruises around his eyes. "Sorry, Jud. You know, if folks would just do the one crime and leave it alone, we wouldn't catch nearly as many as we do. The Bible says, 'The wicked flee where no man pursueth.' It's the trying to cover up afterward that makes my job a damn sight easier. Go away, now. I'm gonna get some sleep."

His eyes closed, and he began to snore gently. He seemed to have shrunk and aged while they were speaking with him.

They tiptoed out. Olivet sat on a straight-back chair in the hall, and jumped up when he saw them. Down the corridor a cleaning crew was mopping.

"No sign of the guy," he said.

"Not surprising. Has Detective Railsback been by?"

"Carol Ann said he called to say he's on his way."

"Tell him what happened. I'll see him tomorrow at the office. Once LaPorte speaks to him, I doubt the P.I. will be in any further danger, but do what Railsback says."

"Yes, ma'am."

She and Jud started toward the elevators, then she stopped and turned back. "I won't mention that you were off talking to Carol Anne. You did deny the guy access, after all."

He nodded. "Thank you, Detective."

Once the elevator door had closed, Jud shook his head. "The only place Sylvia made more than one trip to was Phoenix. Maybe she's there, or in Albuquerque, as a different person."

"If she is, then you really are a married man."

"In name only. I either have to file for divorce or file to have her declared dead. My lawyer says declaring her dead is better. If that doesn't go through, then I will file for divorce, but I know how much that will upset Colleen. The status quo, no matter how horrible, is still better than either alternative for her."

He ran his hand over his hair and closed his eyes. "I wish I could wake up one morning and find the whole thing over. I want my daughter, my work—and now I want you."

"About that…"

"You can't get involved with a suspect. Yada, yada, yada." He took her shoulders in his big hands. "Face it, Liz. We *are* involved."

"My boss would kill me if he knew. Your daughter would kill you."

"That's a risk I'd be willing to take. What I can't

handle is your not trusting me." Hr brought his face closer to hers. "You either believe I killed my wife or you don't. Which is it?"

CHAPTER TWENTY-ONE

BEFORE SHE COULD ANSWER, the elevator opened on the ground floor. Randy Randy stood waiting, with his hands in the pockets of his jeans. He rolled his eyes at Liz and held the door open. Jud dropped his hands, and moved away.

Liz's face flamed as she brushed by the detective. "LaPorte's awake," she said. "Ask Olivet about the food tray incident." She kept walking.

"Slaughter, give me a minute," Randy called.

Jud stopped. "What?" Railsback sounded impatient. Not surprising.

Instead of waiting for him, Liz sprinted to her car. At least the detective would understand they'd come in separate vehicles.

"Cup of coffee?" Railsback asked.

Jud watched Liz practically fly out of the parking lot without a backward glance. "Fine," he said. He didn't like this man. Too slick, too smarmy and possibly too smart.

They picked up coffee in the cafeteria and sat at one of the tables. Railsback poured a container of creamer into his cup and said, "Word to the not-sowise." He sipped his coffee and made a face. "Yuck. Cop coffee is supposed to be lousy, but the coffee at the precinct is excellent. I buy the beans."

"Good for you."

"Okay, so we don't make nice. Listen up. Gibson is tough, but she's still female, and at the moment she's big-time vulnerable. You, my friend, are messing with her head and her feelings. As her colleague, I do not like that. I also do not like men who kill their wives."

"And you think I did that."

"Dick Sherman and Charlie Lee sure thought you did, and they were good cops."

"Who were wrong."

"Maybe. That's not the point."

"What is the point? And Liz doesn't act so vulnerable to me. She's the most together woman I've ever met."

"Normally, I'd agree, but she's still recovering from getting her butt shot off…."

"I beg your pardon?"

"She didn't tell you? She was on sick leave and limited duty and on crutches for weeks. She thinks she blew a negotiation that got two people killed. She took three in the back of the vest, which broke a couple of ribs, and a fourth hit her in the ass. But she saved an eight-year-old kid. I keep asking her to show me her scar, but so far I've struck out."

Jud wrapped his hands around his cup to stop himself from putting them around Railsback's neck.

The cop would like nothing better than for Jud to create a scene. He'd be pepper-sprayed, Tasered, arrested and possibly shot before he could stand up.

Why hadn't Liz told him? He had to see her right away, but he couldn't walk out on Railsback. "You think if I back off, you'll slide into home?"

"Nah, not really. She married and divorced one cop. She's leery of all of us. Also, she's the kind that plays for keeps. I don't." He leaned forward and dropped his voice to a dangerous whisper. "My partner and I, we've got her back. If you break her heart, hurt her career, make her doubt herself even more than she does now you'll have to answer to us. And, most important of all, if you turn out to be a killer, you won't have to wait for the needle. I'll shoot your ass, and everybody in the department will back me up. Do I make myself clear?"

CHAPTER TWENTY-TWO

TWENTY MINUTES LATER Jud pulled into Liz's driveway, slammed on his brakes in time to avoid rear-ending her car, and a second later leaned heavily on her doorbell. He knew she was there, dammit. He hammered on her door.

He heard her fumbling with the lock and a moment later the door opened wide.

"Why are you here?" she asked.

"Why didn't you tell me you got shot?"

"None of your business."

"The hell it's not. It's my business if you get a hangnail."

"What did Randy want? Other than to blurt out stuff he shouldn't have?"

"Can I come in?"

"Oh, what the heck." She stood aside and shut the door behind him.

"Why didn't you tell me?"

"Should I walk around with a sign on my chest that says, Hey, Everybody, I Got My Ass Grazed by a Rifle Bullet? That's all it was. I'll have a scar on my rump, period."

"Plus a couple of broken ribs and crutches for six weeks?"

"I am going to kill Randy." She glared at Jud. "What do you *mean* it's your business if I get a hangnail?"

"I care about you."

"I can take care of myself. You are not my daddy."

"Obviously you can't."

"Actually, if I could take care of myself, I wouldn't be mixed up with *you.*"

He felt as though she'd punched him in the gut. His anger drained out of him. "Liz, I—"

"Oh, shut up." She came into his arms, molding her body against his, lifting her lips to kiss him, her mouth sweet and open, her tongue searching and meeting his with a hint of honey. His body felt as though he'd stumbled into a blast furnace. He was suddenly hard enough to drill concrete.

He slipped his hands under her rear to lift her. She jerked and pulled away from him with a whimper of pain. "Don't."

"I'm sorry…." How could he let her go now?

"Don't *stop!* Just let me walk."

Instead he picked her up under her knees and shoulders and carried her to her bedroom. He set her down on her feet and pulled her close against him again to taste her mouth.

They began to undress each other slowly, but as they touched one another's skin, the drive to be together grew intense, until sweaters and jeans flew off, shoes caromed into the corners of the room. When they were both finally naked, he leaned down and ran his tongue around the taught button of one of her nipples while his palm caressed the other.

She arched her back and raised her swollen breasts with a soft sound that was part sigh and part moan.

She stroked the muscles along his spine with her fingertips. He shivered when they slid over his flanks.

His soul ached to bury himself in her, to take refuge from all the years of pain and loss.

But not yet. After so long without a woman he knew his ability to hold off was diminished, and he wanted to pleasure her fully, to make her ache for him, feel her wet and open, offering herself without reservation.

She moaned again. He drank in the scent of her and ran his tongue down her body until he knelt before her and tasted her.

She gasped, dug her nails into his shoulders, ran her fingers over his hair.

He wanted to be inside her, encircled by her warmth, looking down into her eyes. He stood and began to pick her up again to lay her on the bed, but she held him off.

"No. Not that way." She pushed him gently onto his back and knelt over him, bending down so that her hair caressed his chest, then his stomach…. He didn't know how long he could hold on if she continued.

"Wait…" he managed to choke out, and started to get up.

"I don't think so," she whispered. "I'm on the pill." A moment later she fitted herself around him and took him into herself. The pace they set was agonizingly slow at first. He gazed up into her face. Her eyes were closed, her lips swollen and parted. Her back arched and she whimpered as he stroked between her thighs. He caressed her breasts, the nipples hard beneath his palms. She was like a pomegranate, taut and tough on the outside, but within, only sweetness.

Then his mind ceased to function rationally as the urge to possess and be possessed overcame him. When at last they had driven together to the peak and beyond, he felt her spasms and heard her scream of pleasure a moment before his body lost its own battle with ecstasy.

She folded over so that he could put his arms around her and hold her, sobbing and breathless, against his chest. Finally she sighed and slid down beside him, to lie on her side with her head under his chin and her left arm across his middle.

"Mmm," she whispered. "We've done it now."

He sucked in a breath so that he could answer, "For better or worse."

"Probably worse. At this moment, who cares?"

"Not me," he murmured, and kissed her hair. He ran his hand down her ribs and over her hip. "This side?"

"Wha…" she said sleepily.

"I want to see your scar."

"Later," she whispered. Within minutes her soft breathing told him she was asleep. He snagged the comforter from the foot of the bed with his toes and pulled it up over both of them without disturbing her.

She might not care at the moment that they had made love, but she might care a lot when she woke up.

Randy said she played for keeps. Jud hadn't played at all for much too long. Now he had let his heart rule his head simply because he wanted Liz Gibson as he'd never wanted another woman. He had desired Sylvia once, but his feelings for her even at the beginning were nothing like this.

He wanted to know everything about Liz. Her joys, fears, good and bad. He wanted to care for her, to take her with him into every aspect of his life, and let her get to know him, as well.

Randy Railsback said he and his partner had her back.

Jud wanted to have her back and know she had his. Forever and ever…

She woke him with a kiss. He wrapped his arms around her to pull her against him. He was ready, willing and able.

"Jud! Come on, wake up."

"Huh?" He opened one eye and smiled up at her.

"You have to go home and cook dinner!"

Instantly, he was awake. "What time is it?"

"Nearly five-thirty. You said you had to be home by six. You're not going to make it."

He released her and rolled out of her bed, yipping when his feet hit the cold wood floor. "Where's my phone? I have to call Irene." He grabbed his jeans, dug into the pocket, found his cell and dialed. "Irene? I'm going to be a few minutes late. Yeah. Tell Colleen I'm picking up a pizza on my way." He listened. "I know. Extra pepperoni, mushrooms and no anchovies. Bless you." He turned off the phone and began to collect his clothes. Liz lay on her side, her head propped in her hand, watching him and smiling.

"Where's my shoe? I can't find my right shoe." He tossed his clothes onto the foot of the bed. His jeans jingled. Keys and change.

"Right there in the corner," Liz said. "Turn on the light."

"No need." He stooped to grab the shoe, stood still for a moment, then sat on the bed and took her in his arms. She dropped her head onto his shoulder. "I'm sorry. I'm no good at this," he murmured. "I want to stay, spend the night…."

"But you have a daughter." She nibbled his ear and whispered, "I think you better take a quick shower, unless you want Irene to realize what you've been up to. Colleen, too, for all I know."

"You're right. How big is your shower?"

"Big enough if we squeeze."

"If we squeeze, I won't make it home before dawn."

"I'm willing to take the chance."

He reached down to pick her up again.

"Stop that. You must not carry me around like a sack of potatoes just because you can."

He gave her his hand and together they walked into her bathroom, their arms around one another's waist.

The shower was marginally large enough for Liz and someone his size. "Having her back" took on a whole new meaning.

"Don't look at my backside," Liz warned. "It is not a pretty sight."

"It'll always be a beautiful sight to me. Damn, the scar is a foot long!"

She turned to face him and began to soap his chest. "I'll probably always have a scar, although they tell me it won't always be bubblegum pink. As a matter of fact, I will probably always have a *groove*."

"Let me kiss it and make it better."

Liz burst out laughing. "You kiss good, caveman, but not that good. I'm nearly healed. Another week or so and I'll be able to sleep on my back again."

"I was thinking of something other than sleep."

Wet mouths and wet bodies met.

"You have to get home," she whispered.

"I'll order the pizza by phone," he whispered back.

The water had begun to run cold when at last they toweled each other off. At the front door, he held Liz with one arm while he speed-dialed the pizza place with his other hand, and stopped kissing her long enough to put in his order to be picked up in twenty minutes. "I wish I didn't have to go," he said.

"But you do."

"I'll call you tonight."

"Don't. I'll be asleep." She grinned. "*Really* asleep."

"Breakfast tomorrow morning?"

"I have to go to work."

"Early? After I take Colleen to school?"

"All right. Same time, same place." She kissed him once again and shoved him out the door. He watched her in his rearview mirror until he turned the corner and lost sight of her. Somehow he had to get her and Colleen on the same wavelength, because he had no intention of letting Liz walk out of his life now that he'd found her.

CHAPTER TWENTY-THREE

WHEN HER PHONE RANG at six-thirty the next morning, Liz tried to ignore it, but finally gave up and answered.

"Get your rear in gear," Jack Samuels said. "We'll be by to pick you up in twenty minutes." He sounded grim.

"What's happened?"

"Tell you then."

She managed to be ready by the time Jack's Hummer drove into her driveway. Randy sat beside Jack in the front, so she crawled into the back.

"What is it?" she asked. Her stomach was roiling. She could tell by their faces that whatever it was, it was bad.

"DB," Jack said. "A couple of poachers found it two days ago, but only decided to report it last night. We just got a heads-up from Homicide. Your bud Cary Williams is doing the autopsy first thing this morning. She thought you'd want to be there."

"We don't do new DBs," Liz said. "Unless… Where was it found?"

"Shallow grave in Putnam Woods. Been there awhile. It's a skeleton."

Liz's heart lurched. "How long? Man or woman?"

"From the remains of the clothes and the hair, it's female."

"Caucasian," Randy said. "Could have been there for years."

Oh, God.

"No ID."

"Manner of death?" Liz asked, afraid to hear the answer.

"Have to wait for the autopsy, but it looks like blunt force trauma."

They pulled into the morgue parking lot. Liz was afraid her legs wouldn't support her when she stood, but she took a deep breath and acted as professional as she could, although she felt her adrenaline pumping so fast she thought her heart would explode.

"You okay?" Samuels asked. Randy glared at her, then ignored her.

She nodded and tried to smile, but knew it was a failure. Jack took her arm. She was grateful for his bulk.

Her friend Cary Williams, a medical examiner, had let Liz watch a few autopsies, and of course she'd inadvertently glimpsed several bodies opened up to be embalmed when she was working at the funeral home as a teenager. She never got used to the smell. And she'd never before seen a skeleton.

Cary nodded to her and pulled down her full-face Plexiglas mask. The skeleton had already been stripped and washed, the water and detritus preserved for further study. The bones were laid out as they had been in life. They were dark brown, not white like Halloween skeletons. Small scraps of sinew still adhered to some of the joints.

Cary picked up the skull and held it out to the detectives. "In medical terminology, I'd say somebody strong gave her a hell of a whack on the right temple."

"From front or back?"

"Probably standing back of her. Probably right-handed, but from the force, I'd say both hands were used. Like a baseball bat, but not quite." She set down the skull. "Haven't figured out what the weapon was yet. Cylindrical, maybe four inches in diameter, with some kind of grooves in circles around it. Maybe a threaded pipe. Her hair was short and not very thick, so the grooves were imprinted on the remains of her scalp and to some extent in the fractures, but there's no evidence as to whether the weapon was metal or wood or something else."

Liz took her first deep breath, and even with a mask on, instantly regretted it. Sylvia's hair had been shoulder-length blond. The hair remaining on the skull was short and auburn.

"Five feet nine. The remains of the clothes are size six or eight, so she was slim."

"How long was she there?" Randy asked. He sounded avid. "Had to be years, right?"

"In this climate, a DB can be skeletonized in four to six months."

"Really?" Liz's spirits lifted. "Can you tell?"

"Not from the bones."

"Could be years?" Randy continued.

Cary shrugged. "Probably no longer than ten from the condition of the clothes. We've got some DNA, but that'll take a few days or a week to process, even with a rush. In the meantime we'll take dental X-rays and casts of her teeth. You're thinking Sylvia Slaughter, right?"

"Have to rule her out," Jack said.

"She's had some work done," Cary stated.

"Work?" Randy asked.

"Plastic surgery. Nose narrowed, possibly bobbed. That kind of nose job leaves marks where the bones were broken and reset. I also found some metal threads, so she probably had one of those wire face-lifts."

"How long ago did they start doing those?" Jack asked.

"A few years. You check. Not my job. Her hair's dyed. I think it may have been lighter, but I won't know until I look at the roots we have. Very professional. Didn't do it herself. An expensive haircut and manicure."

Liz caught her breath again. *Lord, let it not be blond.*

"You got her nails?" Jack asked, astonished.

"Acrylic. Bright red polish."

"What about her clothes? How old were they?" Liz asked.

"Haven't gone over them yet. You can do that

after we finish. She had some stuff in her pockets, but no ID."

"What are those things?" Jack Samuels pointed to a couple of plastic bags at the side of the table.

"Those, my dear detective, are breast implants."

"Sylvia didn't have breast implants!" Liz felt her shoulders lift.

"Your boy toy tell you that?" Randy snarled. "Or maybe not bother to mention it?"

"Breast implants carry registration numbers," Cary said. "I've got a call in to the company to find out whose they were and where the operation was done. Ought to hear by tomorrow. No sense arguing when we don't have the data. Now, shoo while I finish this."

The men started out. Liz lagged behind. "Mind if I go over the clothes and effects?"

"Not alone," Randy snapped.

"I beg your pardon?"

"I'll stay. We'll do it together."

"You don't trust me?"

"Chain of evidence, Liz, just chain of evidence," Jack said. "He's right. Call me when you're done. I'll either pick you up or send a car."

"You really are a bastard," Liz whispered as soon as Jack left the room.

"Yeah." Randy walked over to the table where the muddy rags that had been taken off the body lay in a heap. "And you're an idiot."

"Thanks."

"No prob." He pulled on his gloves and reached

for a stack of paper grocery bags with Chain of Evidence printed on the outside. Then he picked up the tattered linen slacks. Liz took the silk shirt.

"If this happened in November, she would have been freezing," Liz said. "Sylvia was wearing a wool pantsuit when she disappeared."

"Maybe the perp took her jacket when he took her purse and ID."

"Linen slacks mean summertime." She carefully smoothed the tag at the neck of the shirt. "Randy, this blouse is from a boutique in Phoenix, Arizona." She showed it to him.

"Didn't you say she took a bank trip to Phoenix? Might have bought it there."

"I suppose so. What do the slacks say?"

"Same store." He picked up a muddy, flat-heeled shoe.

"That cost a fortune!" Liz took it out of his hand and looked inside. "Jimmy Choo? I don't think anyone in this area even *carries* Jimmy Choo."

Randy reached into the pocket of the slacks and came out with a handful of change and a couple of grotty fifty-dollar bills. "Wasn't robbery, at any rate. No watch, no purse, but a mugger wouldn't overlook a hundred bucks."

"Give me the change." Liz held out her hand. She went over each coin under the magnifying glass on the desk. "Randy, this quarter is only two years old. Sylvia was long gone by that time."

"Damn. I was hoping we'd finally found her."

CHAPTER TWENTY-FOUR

As Liz and Randy were finishing their examination of effects, Jack Samuels pushed the door open with his shoulder. He carried a cardboard tray with three steaming cups on it. He set them down on the steel table where Liz and Randy had been working, handed one to Liz and said, "We have to inform Slaughter."

"We don't have a positive ID yet," she replied. She finished packing everything into bags, closed them and signed and dated them before handing them on to Randy, who did the same thing.

"It's her. Who else could it be? We have to pick his ass up," Randy snapped, as he put the bags into an evidence box and closed the lid. "The minute we find him." He picked up his coffee and started for the car. The other two followed.

Liz glanced at her watch. For a moment she considered not saying anything, but she was either a cop or she wasn't. "I know where he is."

Jud might not still be there. She was nearly an hour late for breakfast. Her phone had been turned off while she worked, but now she clicked it on and saw he'd left three messages, no doubt wondering where she was. "He's probably at Lacy's. He has breakfast there nearly every morning."

Randy climbed into the Hummer. "You coming?"

She had to be there, but God, how she dreaded it. "We can't arrest him," she said.

"Nobody said we were arresting him," Jack said reasonably.

"If it's Sylvia, how do you explain the coin dated two years ago?"

"She's obviously been somewhere else, probably Phoenix, since she disappeared."

Randy turned around. "Yeah, and two years ago for some reason she came back and called him. Maybe wanted to make nice, maybe wanted a divorce. Who's to say he didn't meet her and break her skull? Great place to bury her. It's already been searched a dozen times."

"Why are you so desperate to believe he's a killer?" Liz snapped.

"Children, children," Jack said. "We work on evidence, not on gut feelings, and that includes yours, Randy."

"That's right!"

"As well as yours, Liz."

"What if we can't prove it? We didn't find anything last time," Randy muttered.

"That's because he didn't *do* anything the last time," Liz exclaimed.

"Oh, so he did something this time?"

"Listen, you—"

"Knock it off, both of you," Jack said as he turned into the parking lot at Lacy's. "That his truck?"

"Yes." Suddenly, Liz didn't want to be a part of this. She couldn't face him, not this way. Last night they'd made love. She'd trusted him, believed him. If Sylvia had showed up on his doorstep a couple of years ago, he *might* have killed her.

Would Liz ever be able to believe him again? For that matter, would he ever look at her the same way after she dragged him down to interrogation and went to work on him?

She'd told him at the start that if he was guilty, she'd get him. She had to find out once and for all.

If he didn't kill Sylvia, who had?

When Jud saw her walk into Lacy's, he half stood, grinned and started to wave. When he saw Jack and Randy, he dropped his hand and sank into his seat again. No more smile.

"Mr. Slaughter, may we speak with you?" Jack asked.

"What's this about?"

"Outside might be better."

Every eye in the place, including Bella's, was turned to them. Liz hugged herself and wished she could sink into the ground.

"Can't we talk here? Want some coffee?" He was avoiding Liz's gaze, although the nerve at the corner of his mouth twitched. Fear? Rage?

"Better outside. Give us a little privacy."

"Come on, buddy," Randy said. He was bouncing on his toes, spoiling for a fight. He was just itching to drag Jud out in handcuffs. Liz intended to step in if he made a move, but Jud forestalled her.

"Sure." He dropped a couple of bills on the table, slid from the booth and was first out the door into the parking lot. When he stopped and turned to look at them, his gaze swept over Liz without a change of expression. "What the hell is going on?"

Liz watched his face register surprise, then shock, as Jack told him. He leaned back against the hood of his truck as though his legs wouldn't support him.

"You're positive it's Sylvia? After all this time?"

"Not positive," Jack said.

"But we will be soon," Randy stated.

"She—it—hasn't been there but a couple of years," Liz interjected.

Randy glared at her.

"So it's not Sylvia," Jud said.

"I said we'd know for certain soon." Randy's eyes dared Liz to argue.

"We'd like you to come down to the morgue with us," Jack said. "We need a positive ID."

"From a skeleton?"

"Pure formality. Maybe take a look at her clothes."

That was a crock. They wanted to drag him in to look at what they'd found purely to shake him up. Of course he'd be shaken up. Anyone would be.

"Do I need a lawyer?"

Randy stepped on Liz's foot hard and shook his head at her. "Any reason you might?" he asked.

Liz nodded at Jud and mouthed, *Yes*. Randy glared.

"I'll call my lawyer right now," Jud said. "We'll meet you at the morgue in, say, an hour?"

"We'd prefer to have you ride with us," Jack said. "We'll bring you back after we talk to you."

"Am I under arrest?"

"'Course not. This is just a friendly chat."

"Then I'll wait for my lawyer." He pulled out his cell phone and turned away from them.

Jack gave them a signal and they climbed back into the Hummer.

"Well, thank you very much," Randy snapped at Liz. "Now he's lawyered up."

"He'd be crazy to talk to us without his lawyer, and you know it."

"But you didn't have to let *him* know it."

"Randy, he's been through this before," Jack said. "He knows."

"Drop me at home, Jack," Liz said. "I have to feed my cat, grab some breakfast and head into the office. You two can handle the ID without me."

"Well, well," Randy said. "Abandoning your little project so easily? I warned you."

"I have reports to write."

At her house, Jack climbed out from behind the wheel and followed her to her front door. "Sorry, kid," he said. "I hope this thing with Slaughter hasn't gone too far. If we charge him, it could really screw up the prosecution's case."

"It won't get as far as an arrest, Jack," Liz said.

He patted her arm. "We'll see."

She closed her front door behind her and leaned against it. He was right. Jud's defense would make mincemeat of her if she had to admit she'd slept with him then testified against him.

Liz had told Gavigan after she'd first met Jud that she could believe he'd kill someone in a fit of rage, or to protect someone he loved. Was that what happened when Sylvia turned up two years ago?

She sank to the floor and let the tears flow. Poirot climbed into her lap and butted his head against her chin. She held him and wept into his fur, an indignity he wouldn't ordinarily tolerate.

Obviously, Jud had not killed Sylvia seven years ago. That didn't mean he hadn't killed her when she'd come back. Liz had said he was capable of losing his temper.

How close had the two of them been to her body when they'd found the tire tracks? Had he known all along where she was?

Who else could have known? Would have wanted her finally dead? Jud got the money. Jud was saved from a nasty divorce.

No. He could not by guilty. Liz was trained to read people. He wasn't clever or devious enough to fool her.

She was in love with the man and truly believed he cared for her. Did that blind her totally?

There must be another explanation. Maybe Sylvia had tried to blackmail Rainer Iams again. Or Trip. Or some other lover they hadn't yet identified.

Maybe someone from the new life she'd created had followed her home and killed her. Liz dug into the files in the murder box she'd brought home from the office until she found a studio photo of Sylvia. She scanned it into her laptop, brought up her photo program and began to alter the photo to match what she knew of the skeleton.

She chopped off the hair and turned it auburn. To match the hair, she darkened the eyes from blue to hazel. They hadn't found contact lenses with the skeleton, but soft contacts would have disintegrated. However, if she'd changed her hair color, she might have changed her eye color, as well.

Liz lifted the eyelids, smoothed and lifted the forehead, then shortened and narrowed the nose. Next she tightened the jawline. Sylvia now looked even more beautiful and ten years younger than the original photo. Liz saved the changes and ran off a couple of color prints.

She'd start with Phoenix. Those clothes were not seven years old, so obviously had not been bought on one of Sylvia's trips before she disappeared. Therefore, she'd been in Phoenix since. Someone might recognize the altered photo.

Liz stuffed a box of breakfast bars and a diet cola

into her tote, fed Poirot, rinsed her face and smeared makeup and eye shadow over her red eyelids, then rushed out of the house.

If the woman in the woods was Sylvia, then Liz had to find out who had killed her. Even if Jud was never charged, he'd be under a worse cloud than before. His own child wouldn't completely trust him.

Would Liz?

CHAPTER TWENTY-FIVE

ONE LONE HOMICIDE detective dozed at his desk in the far corner of the room when Liz got to the office. She switched on her computer. Phoenix time was two hours earlier. Probably nobody would be in that detective squad room yet. She sent the altered photo of Sylvia and her query to them before Gavigan came in.

Then she started writing up her notes. The lieutenant liked to read reports before he talked about them.

She was so involved that when her phone rang, she jumped before she answered it, hoping it was Jud.

Not Jud. Trip.

"Jud gave me your office number. He hasn't showed up at the site and I can't get him on his cell phone. I have a message to call him, but he must be out of range. Any idea where he is?"

Should she tell him? If Jud wasn't a killer, then Trip might be. Let Jud tell him. "Not at the moment." It wasn't precisely a lie.

"We've got a big meeting with a lumber supplier this morning. I've got to locate him. If you hear from him, tell him to call me. I hope nothing's happened to him."

"Sure." She hung up. *I hope nothing's happened to him, either.* She probably ought to call Irene and make certain she was planning to pick up Colleen after school, but that wasn't her business, either.

Irene and Herb would be devastated if the skeleton was that of their daughter. To know that she'd been alive all those years, and then had died before she could come home to them would be doubly harsh. Like losing her twice. No matter that they swore they believed she was dead, they must always have harbored hope that she'd show up one day. Even a slim hope for life was better than a certainty of death, wasn't it?

As Liz wrote, she gnawed on a breakfast bar and drank her diet soda. She was ravenous. Some people couldn't eat when they were upset. She always ate everything she could get her hands on. During her divorce, she'd gained thirty pounds and had worked really hard to lose it after the final decree.

If this thing with Jud went bad, she'd weigh four hundred pounds before he was acquitted.

If he ever was. They had no evidence except motive, which didn't prove a thing. Still, plenty of people had been convicted on less.

"Ms. Gibson?"

She looked up. The only word for the man who smiled down at her was *dapper.* He had a neat body, a neat mustache, a neat razor haircut, neither too short nor too long, a proper red power tie, and wore a neat gray suit that had been tailored for him from scratch. You couldn't get that kind of fit across the shoulders off the rack. He held out his hand. "Arnold Jenkins, Actuary Insurance Company. May I sit down?"

She shook his hand. Not too firm, not too soft.

"I heard you've found Mrs. Slaughter's body."

Liz checked the clock over Gavigan's door. Barely nine o'clock, yet Jenkins knew about the skeleton. Civilians couldn't simply waltz into the homicide bull pen. The visitor's pass Jenkins wore clipped to his lapel did not look new. Then she remembered his name. Jenkins was the guy she suspected of being behind the reopening of Sylvia's case. She'd never run into him before, but obviously he was familiar with the building. "We don't know yet whether the body is Mrs. Slaughter's," Liz said. "How'd you find out so quickly?"

He shrugged. "I have friends in the department. Actually, I probably started this reinvestigation with a word to one of the commissioners. I wanted to thank you personally for the work you've done."

"What work? I haven't really found out anything. Thank the poachers who stumbled on the body."

"Oh, I will, believe me."

"I've cost you a million bucks, haven't I?"

He laughed. Liz found the sound chilling. "No one can profit from a crime he's committed, but then, you know that."

"Yes, I do."

"So, if Mr. Slaughter did somehow dispose of his

wife, perhaps accidentally, and buried her body
because he panicked, my company would be off the
hook. The policy can't be transferred to his
daughter."

Liz had wondered about that earlier. She did not
like the answer. "Why are you telling me this?"

"No reason. I was in the neighborhood. I'm sure
Mr. Slaughter never actually intended to kill his wife.
No doubt she drove him to it. If he were to confess
to, say, involuntary manslaughter, he'd probably
serve no more than five years of his sentence. That
would be best for everyone concerned, don't you
agree? It would be in his best interests to avoid
having his family dragged through the court, to have
his daughter listen to all that sordidness. Poor kid.
She's been through enough, wouldn't you agree?"

"So he should confess to killing the mother to
save the daughter's feelings?" Liz fought to keep
her tone even by digging her fingernails into the
palms of her hands.

"No kid wants to know her mother abandoned
her. I'm sure you'll bring that up. I've heard you're
a real crackerjack at interrogation."

"Oh, I am, Mr. Jenkins. Now, if you'll excuse me,
I have reports to write."

"Of course." He stood and offered his hand again.
She ignored it and turned back to her computer.
"Have a good day, Ms. Gibson. We do show our ap-
preciation to people who help us."

Liz gaped at his retreating back. Randy and Jack

were coming in. Jenkins passed them without even a nod.

She called them over. "I think I've just been offered a bribe."

"Did you take it?" Jack asked.

"Put it this way. If that man turns up dead in the next couple of days, arrest me."

CHAPTER TWENTY-SIX

"So you still think Slaughter didn't do it?" Gavigan asked. He leaned back in his chair and pressed his knee against the drawer of his desk to keep from tipping over. He looked completely relaxed, but then this was simply another cold case to him, with no personal involvement.

Liz wished she felt the same way. Everyone had warned her. It wasn't that she hadn't tried to listen. She'd been involved with Jud before she had a chance to resist. Now it was much too late.

"No. I mean yes, he didn't do it," she answered. She sat in the chair across from Gavigan and tried not to fidget. Cool and professional, that was the ticket here, even though she felt as tightly wound as a guitar string.

"Then who did kill her?"

"At this point, we're not certain the victim is Sylvia," she said.

"What are the odds?"

"A million to one for."

"You arresting Slaughter?"

"He's coming in to talk to us of his own free will.

Jack and Randy arranged it at the morgue. Turns out his partner, Trip Weichert, is a lawyer. Real estate law, not criminal, but he called to say he's coming with Jud." After he found him and canceled the meeting with the supplier.

"Weichert won't let him open his mouth."

"Actually, it works out. We also want to talk to Weichert. Sylvia may have been blackmailing him. We think he slept with her and never admitted to his wife that he actually did the deed. He swears it was a near miss."

Gavigan chuckled. "As if." He locked his fingers over his flat belly.

"I might have a line on the life she created after her disappearance."

"Somebody from this supposed new life followed her back here, killed her and knew precisely where to leave her body? Come on, Liz."

Liz felt her face flame. "I still have six days left."

Gavigan stared hard at her. After a long moment he said, "Give me something within twenty-four hours or we turn this directly over to Homicide. Let them sweat Slaughter."

She knew that was the best she was likely to get. As she stood, Jack Samuels knocked on the door, opened it a crack and stuck his head in. "Fax for Liz I think you'll want to see."

She shoved her chair back, got up and followed Jack. She could hear Gavigan's footsteps behind her. "What?"

Jack handed her a printout. "The Phoenix fraud squad wants to talk to you."

"This is an arrest warrant for one Sharon Mitchell, real estate agent, on a charge of kiting escrow funds," Liz said, studying the paper. She looked up at Gavigan. "Issued August the tenth two years ago."

She dialed the return number handwritten on the top of the fax and asked for Detective Jorge Maldinado. When he answered, she told him she was putting him on speakerphone.

"So you found our girl," he said. "I been looking for that *chica* for over two years. It's like she never existed."

"She didn't," Liz said. "You identified the photo I sent?"

"Right down to her perky boobs and hazel eyes."

"Tell me about her."

"She showed up here about seven years ago, maybe a little less," Jorge said. "Passed the real estate license exam with flying colors. Went to work for one of our biggest companies for a year, then went out on her own about five years ago."

"You don't sound as though you're looking at notes," Liz stated.

"Hey, I know her story by heart. At first she did great, but apparently she got overextended. She was robbing Peter to pay Paul. Two years ago she couldn't come up with an escrow payment to close a deal. The whole house of cards fell in on her. By the time we got the arrest warrant, she'd disappeared with the clothes on her back, the money from the other escrow accounts and her personal checking and savings. Not a fortune, but a good chunk of change. So, you got her?"

"In a sense," Liz told him. "She's dead."

"Well, damn," Jorge said.

"Could someone from there have followed her here and killed her?"

"Possible, but I doubt it."

"Unfortunately, so do I."

They made arrangements to swap files. Liz agreed to notify the detective when the ID was firm. She'd barely set the phone down when it rang again.

"Liz? Cary Williams here. We've checked the dental records."

Liz caught her breath. The phone was still on speaker. The others hovered, listening. For Liz, she felt as though she were waiting for the results of a mammogram, only worse.

"Teeth didn't match exactly…."

"It's not Sylvia?" Her spirits rose. *Please let Jud be off the hook.*

"I didn't say that, only that she'd had more dental work in the years since she left here. A couple of new fillings, one cap. The basic work matched. Even without the DNA, I'd say you've found Mrs. Slaughter."

Liz wanted to scream, beat her fists on the desk in frustration—anything. But she didn't dare react with the audience waiting to gauge her reaction. She must show calm acceptance. Good thing nobody could feel her pulse thrum or see the lump in her throat.

"It's all falling into place," Randy said. "I can't wait to talk to Slaughter. Yeah!" He pumped his fist, then looked at Liz. "Oh. Sorry."

"No rush to judgment, people," said Gavigan. "We need forensics, and so far, we don't have any. We need to search his house, his office, any construction he was involved with in August two years ago. Track down the murder weapon. It could be some kind of construction tool we don't recognize."

"What about the attack on LaPorte?" Liz said in desperation. "That wasn't Jud."

"Right. Go make the rounds of his construction sites. Take pictures. See if you can make an identification of the guy you saw at LaPorte's. If you can, show the P.I. an array including the picture, see if he picks out the same man."

"If I can't find the guy working construction, what about Rainer Iams? He might have hired him," Liz suggested. "Can we subpoena his bank records from two years ago? Maybe she blackmailed him again."

"You can try it." Gavigan clapped his hands. "Move it, people. Jack, you handle the interview when Slaughter and Weichert show up. Liz, what are you waiting for? Go."

"I have to talk to Trip and Jud. I don't have a list of their construction sites."

"They're bound to have a secretary or a clerk. Go out to the construction trailer and get a list. Now."

She started to tell Gavigan there'd been no clerk the times she'd been to the trailer before, but decided he wouldn't care. She didn't want to leave, not until she could see Jud, touch his hand, look into his eyes—something, *anything,* to make a connection. Gavigan must realize that, and was doing his best to get her out of the way before Jud showed up.

She ached to do the interrogation herself to see whether she could read any lies in his body language or face. Would she even be able to recognize the signs in someone she loved?

Blast. She loved him. How had she allowed herself to be sucked in so fast, to swing a hundred and eighty degrees from hunter to—well, prey?

She stalled as long as possible, going to the bathroom, touching up her makeup and getting the digital camera set up. Finally, under Gavigan's annoyed stare, she left the office.

Her car was parked in the lot reserved for official police vehicles and officers' personal transportation. She walked around the building to the visitor parking area. Jud's truck was nowhere in sight. Then, at the far end, she spotted Trip's SUV. Jud was climbing out of the passenger side.

She didn't care who saw her; she walked over to him.

He looked as if he was going to wrap his arms around her, then he hesitated and changed his mind. Disappointed, she smiled at him.

He whispered, "It's all right, love."

"It's *not* all right."

"Jud, come on, we're going to be late," Trip said from behind them.

"I did not do it," Jud said.

"I know."

"No, you don't. You *can't*. But trust me. It's going to be all right."

"Let's go, Jud."

"Will you be there?" he asked.

She shook her head. "They're getting me out of the way."

"Just as well. It's not going to be pretty." He took hold of her hand.

When he finally released her, she saw that Trip was staring daggers at her. "With friends like you, who needs enemies?" He pulled Jud's arm. "Not another word, Slaughter. Not one."

CHAPTER TWENTY-SEVEN

TRIP PRACTICALLY HAD to drag him through the door of the station and up to the Cold Case squad room. He'd been afraid he wouldn't see Liz. Or even worse, that if he did, she might cut him dead. Jud had an idea that her public display of support would cost her dearly, but he was grateful for the few moments they'd had together.

The next few hours would be horrible, but he had the memory of Liz's hand in his to give him the strength to get through them.

Trip said they couldn't hold him. They had no evidence, weren't even certain the body was Sylvia's. That wouldn't stop them from treating him like a wife killer. What had that Sherman guy said the first time? "When a woman dies or disappears, it's always the husband."

Always. The law might say "innocent until proven guilty," but in this building, he was guilty until proven innocent. Yet how could he prove his innocence? He'd learned in college that it was impossible to prove a negative. He'd be faced again and again with "when did you stop beating your wife?" questions designed to seem innocent, but in reality trying to make him incriminate himself.

"If they ask for a lie detector test, tell them to stick it up their ass," Trip said. "You did that already."

"Seven years ago."

"I shouldn't have let you do it then. Give them nothing but your name unless I tell you it's okay. Don't volunteer anything. These bastards were out to get you seven years ago, and now they think they've finally done so."

Jud turned to stare down at his partner. "Trip, do you believe I'm innocent?"

"I don't give a damn whether you killed her or not, old friend. If ever a woman deserved killing, it was Sylvia."

"Trip, you didn't…ah, hell, she's still screwing with our heads."

"She is, and I didn't. Remember, whatever you say before they Mirandize you isn't admissible."

THE BEST WAY TO TAKE THE heat off Jud was to find another viable suspect. Liz didn't believe Jud had hired the big man to search LaPorte's office. Checking all the construction sites and eliminating all Jud's workers might go a long way toward convincing Gavigan that someone else was interested in LaPorte's information.

Gavigan's assignment was really an ultimatum. She'd better follow orders if she expected any of the Cold Case squad to keep her in the loop. She headed to Jud's construction trailer.

Liz found a nervous temp holding down the office.

When Liz asked for the list of current construction sites, the girl's eyes widened, and she stammered, "Ma'am, I just got here an hour ago. I don't know whether I should, supposing I could even find them."

"They're a matter of record because building permits were pulled on them. Want me to help you look?"

"It's okay. Give me a minute." She checked in one of the file drawers, came up with a list and made a copy for Liz.

Liz knew she couldn't get a list of employees without a court order, so she didn't try. She drove to the first of the mansions under construction in the cul-de-sac and began snapping pictures of anyone who even vaguely resembled Mr. Big.

Working through that first site took over an hour. Even then, she might have missed a few workers who were not present that morning. Then there were the subcontractors and their employees. It was an enormous task, but she had to keep at it.

She hit the second site during the lunch break and was able to get good shots of nearly everyone. Nobody seemed overly concerned about having his picture taken. A few good-natured teasing comments were all she had to deal with. None of the men came close to being the right size or shape.

On her way to the third site, she decided to swing by Rainer Iams's bank. If he'd been the one who'd hired LaPorte's attacker, it was possible the guy worked either for him or for the bank. Most bankers would not know where to find a thug for hire off the street.

Iams had not arrived, but was due any minute. She decided to wait. In the meantime, she described the man she was looking for to the tellers in as much detail as she could recall. She still hadn't connected with the Identi-kit man. Now she wished she'd found the time.

"Why are you looking for him?" one heavily pregnant young teller asked. "Has he done something?"

"We just want to talk to him about a case," Liz said soothingly. She had caught the startled expression in the girl's eyes when the teller described the man. "He's a really big man. Memorable."

She shook her head. Liz didn't believe her, but had no grounds to question her further. The teller in the next booth finished with her customer and said across the divider, "Might be Nicky. Lord knows he's big enough."

The pregnant teller glared at her. "Shut your mouth, Wanda."

"He's a sweet guy, Cheryl. He wouldn't hurt a fly."

"Who is he?" Liz asked, fighting to keep her voice level.

"He drives for Mr. Iams," Wanda said. "The doctors won't let Iams drive since he had his heart attack."

Great. And I'm about to give him another one.

Cheryl put up the sign that said Next Teller, and slipped out of her booth. Liz glanced at her as she came out from behind the counter and headed for the front door.

Wanda said, "Oh, there's Mr. Iams now."

Cheryl was going to warn him. Liz ran after her. "Not a good idea," she said.

"Listen, you…"

"Go back to your booth, please," Liz told her, and was relieved when she complied.

The security guard watched curiously. Liz stepped through the front door with one hand on her H & K, ready to pull it out should she need it. Rainer Iams's car was the biggest Cadillac sedan made that wasn't actually a limousine. She stood in the shadows under the overhang while the driver walked back to the rear door and opened it, offering Iams a hand out.

"Gotcha," Liz whispered. She'd recognized Nicky instantly as the man from the hospital. She edged down the building, stepped off the curb and moved around the caddy. "Mr. Iams, could I have a word?"

Nicky glanced over his shoulder at her. His eyes opened wide, and he sprinted for the driver's door. She slammed it as he reached for it. "Stop right there."

He was at least a big as Jud, muscle over fat. He could break her in two if he attacked her. Instead, he turned to run. She tripped him, almost exactly as she'd tripped Jud, but with malice. His feet flew out from under him. His chin hit the top of the car and he went down hard.

She holstered her weapon, put a knee in his back, grabbed her cuffs and had him in them before he could clear his head. "Stay down," she said.

"Young woman, what is the meaning of this…this brutality?" Iams shouted.

"Just stay in your car, Mr. Iams. Calm down." She called for backup and stood over Nicky with her gun pointed at his head. Iams sank onto the backseat of the Cadillac.

She looked down when she realized Nicky was sobbing.

"I never meant to hurt nobody. I was just hunting…"

"Shut up, you moron!" Iams shouted.

"He said there wouldn't be nobody there on Saturday morning."

"Who said?" Liz asked gently.

"You're fired!" Iams cried.

"Mr. Iams. He told me what to look for. I didn't find nothin', and then that man had a gun. I got scared. Mr. Iams, he made me go down to the hospital. I was just gonna talk to him. You gotta believe me. I don't wanna go to jail."

Iams had turned puce. Now he looked gray. His shoulders slumped as two squad cars pulled up behind his car. "Take both of them down to the Cold Cases office," Liz said to the officers. "Separate cars. Mr. Iams, if you'll cooperate, I won't handcuff you. However, before we go…" She recited the Miranda warning to each man separately. Nicky was driven off, still sobbing.

"Do you need a doctor?" Liz asked the banker.

"I didn't kill her," he managed to gasp.

"But you gave her sixty thousand dollars to run away, didn't you?"

"How did you…" His shoulders slumped again. "LaPorte." He glared up at Liz. "I want my lawyer."

"Of course. After we finish with you, I suspect the feds will be interested in talking to you about your loan policies."

The cop helped Iams into the squad car. Liz locked his sedan and pocketed the keys. There was likely nothing in it, but they definitely had probable cause to search it, and she wouldn't trust Miss Cheryl for an instant.

CHAPTER TWENTY-EIGHT

"WHY CAN'T I INTERROGATE Iams and Nicky Whatsit?" Liz asked Gavigan. "You said yourself I'm good."

"Three reasons. First, Slaughter and his lawyer are still in Interrogation 1, and I don't want you around when they come out. Second, you *want* Iams to be guilty."

"You want *Jud* to be guilty."

"You're too close to this thing to be objective. Barring forensic evidence, we couldn't charge *Santa Claus,* and I don't believe in browbeating suspects."

Liz gritted her teeth. "Third?"

"Somebody has to tell her parents and her daughter she's dead."

"Me?" Liz felt her hands start to tremble, and clenched them in her lap. In cold cases the notification of death should have been done long ago by the original detectives. The families should have adjusted.

The only reason she hadn't been the one to tell Marlene's parents their daughter was dead was that she herself had been lying facedown in an ambulance at the time. She'd managed to go to the funeral on crutches. Marlene's mother had never said it was Liz's fault her granddaughter had lost both parents, but she'd seen the hurt in the woman's eyes.

"Why can't Jud tell them?" She knew the answer, but she wanted to hear it from Gavigan.

"He's going to be here awhile. I need you to watch the reactions when you tell them and the kid."

"The kid?" Liz's voice rose. "I can't tell Colleen. She'd kill me."

"Two years ago she was twelve, and from what you've told me about her, she was a big girl then. Maybe we need to look a little closer at her." At his office door he turned and said, "Go. Now."

She started toward the room behind Interrogation 1. The one with the two-way mirror. Jud wouldn't be able to see her, but she could check how he looked.

Gavigan said, "No. Jack and Randy are doing fine. You stay out of it. Go."

THE UNPLEASANT TASK of telling Sylvia's family might be inevitable, but at least she could get some food into her stomach before she did it. She stopped at a drive-through for a large coffee with extra sugar, and a burger, then sat in the parking lot cradling the cup between her hands, hoping the warmth would stop her trembling. She unwrapped the sandwich, but tossed it in her trash bag after a single bite.

Until Gavigan forced the issue, she'd avoided thinking about Colleen.

Jud wasn't a killer, but he *was* a doting father, one

who felt guilty about his daughter. Colleen believed her mother had left because of her, and Liz had witnessed Colleen's rage. If Sylvia came back home after five years as if she'd never left, Colleen's mood might have escalated from welcome to fury. She could have picked up some heavy object—there were plenty in that house—hit her mother and been horrified to discover she'd killed her.

What would she do then? Call her father to come rescue her, of course.

Would he?

Absolutely. He would refuse to allow Sylvia to ruin Colleen's life. He might well hide his wife's body, clean up the house and say nothing. Those concrete floors could be scrubbed with bleach and hosed down, then refinished if need be. He had both the skill and the tools.

Even after all this time, the CSIs might be able to find blood spatter on the walls of his house with Luma-lite, but probably not on the floor. He'd certainly be able to carry Sylvia's body into the woods. Woods he knew well.

Liz prayed that Forensics wouldn't find evidence of the crime either in his house or in his car, because she knew he'd go to trial to keep Colleen out of jail. With forensic evidence, he'd be convicted. Colleen wouldn't confess to save him.

Was Colleen enough of an actress to keep up the fiction that her mother was coming back? Maybe she actually believed it. She could have wiped out the entire incident.

Liz's coffee was now tepid. Neither the caffeine nor the sugar had stilled the trembling in her hands or the acid pouring into her stomach. Thank God Colleen would not be home yet.

Liz pulled into the driveway at the Richardson house without calling ahead. She could see the lights on in Irene's workshop, so she walked around and knocked on the door.

"Hello, Detective Gibson, how nice to see you," the woman said. She held a skein of rainbow-dyed yarn in one hand. "Come over by the fire. It's so cold and gray outside today."

If anything could calm Liz's trembling, that room could. She took off her coat and gloves and dropped her tote by the door, then sank gratefully into the shabby club chair by the fireplace. The gas logs both looked and felt real. The only thing missing was the smell of burning wood. The different-colored candles on the mantelpiece burned cheerfully.

"Can I get you something? Tea? Soda?"

"No, thank you."

Irene sat in her rocker. "More questions?" She peered into Liz's eyes and her entire demeanor changed. "What's wrong?"

"I'm sorry to have to tell you this, Irene. This weekend some poachers discovered some remains in Putnam Woods. We're almost positive it's Sylvia. I'm so sorry."

Liz had heard of people being dumbstruck, but she'd never seen it before. The color drained from Irene's face, her mouth sagged, her chest heaved and she began to fold at the waist. Liz caught her shoulders. Otherwise she would have slid out of the rocker to the floor.

"Oh, oh, oh," Irene managed to whisper. "Not now, not after all this time." She leaned her cheek against Liz's shoulder. Liz held her unresisting body and patted her back.

"Shall I go get Herb? Are you all right?"

The woman stiffened. "Herb! Oh, Lord, I'll have to tell Herb."

"I'll tell him."

Irene turned stricken eyes to her. "And Colleen."

"I'll tell her, too. Are you supposed to be picking her up at school?"

Irene rubbed her forehead. "I think… No, it's Emily Morris's turn for car pool. She'll take her home. But…oh, Lord, Jud's bringing her over here to spend the night. He has an early meeting tomorrow morning." Irene covered her mouth with both hands. "I can't tell her. I don't know how. Does Jud know?"

Liz nodded.

"Where is he? Why didn't he come to tell us?"

"He's down at the station talking to my partners."

"They can't believe…not after all this time."

"They have to rule him out, Irene. It's standard procedure." *Calm the voice, relax the shoulders. Convince her.*

"They searched Putnam Woods again and again. Why didn't they find her?"

"She wasn't there when they searched."

"Somebody *moved* her? I don't understand."

"I'm afraid I can't go into it now. I have to talk to your husband."

"I'll tell him. I'm afraid of what he'll do."

"Let me help you." Liz lifted Irene up and kept an arm around her waist. That such a strong woman should suddenly feel so fragile frightened her. Irene walked as if she were a hundred years old.

Red-faced and grumbling, Herb met them at the back door. Did the man run 24/7 on rage? What fun he must be to live with.

"What's the matter with Irene? What'd you do to her?"

His wife straightened. "For once, Herb, shut up." She sank into one of the kitchen chairs. He gaped at her.

For the second time, Liz delivered the news. Almost everyone collapsed when told someone they loved had been killed. Herb was no exception. He sat down hard on another kitchen chair. He didn't look at Irene. "That bastard," he whispered. "I knew he killed my little girl, I knew it." He dragged himself to his feet and howled, "I'll kill him!" A moment later, his eyes rolled back in his head and he fainted.

Liz dropped beside him, put her ear to his chest and her fingers to his throat. Irene hadn't moved.

"Call 911. We need an ambulance. He may be having a heart attack."

Irene sat and stared. Liz called on her cell phone, then began CPR. Herb made choking sounds. Five minutes later, when Irene answered the front door for the EMTs, she had still not said a word nor attempted to help Liz.

The EMTs worked over him. "Heart's strong and regular, ma'am," one told Irene. "Has he had a shock?"

"You might say that," Liz said.

"Looks like he hyperventilated and knocked himself out."

"Not the first time," Irene stated. "He has medicine. I'll call his doctor."

"We'll still transport him. Ma'am?" The paramedic turned to Irene. "You want to ride along or follow us? Might be better to take your own car."

"What? Of course. I'll get my purse...." She picked up a black shoulder bag from the kitchen counter and started after the men. Then she stopped. "Oh, Lord! Colleen. I have to be at Jud's house when they drop her off."

"It's all right," Liz said. "I'll pick her up at school, take her home and stay with her until Jud gets home."

"But the car pool will wonder where she is."

"The school will tell Mrs. Morris that Colleen's gone and why. Go ahead and don't worry, Irene."

"But..."

"The emergency room may admit Herb. Even if

they don't, you're not going to be home until later. I'll tell Colleen she's not spending the night with you."

Irene grabbed Liz's arm. "Please, don't do that. I'm sure they'll send us home with tranquilizers for Herb. That's what always happens when he does this."

"You're not going to want to look after Colleen if you're looking after Herb."

"Herb will be asleep five minutes after we get home. The stuff always knocks him out. I'll call Jud, but I do want Colleen to come here." Irene began to cry softly. "My poor grandbaby. She needs me."

"You call Jud. You two can decide what to do about Colleen tonight. Jud will be home before long."

Liz heard herself say the words but deep down, she wasn't sure Jud would be coming home anytime soon.

CHAPTER TWENTY-NINE

LIZ SHOWED HER BADGE at the school office and told them she was there to pick up Colleen.

"We don't normally allow anyone not on our list to take one of our students," the secretary said.

"I'm a police detective, ma'am. There's been a family emergency. If you like, I can try to get in touch with her father, but he may be unavailable for some time. I plan on staying with her until either he or her grandmother can take over."

After a quick call to the station, Liz received a permission slip to pick up Colleen.

"Classes should be breaking in ten minutes, but I can go to her homeroom and get her for you," the vice principal said. "It's a real crush when all the girls leave."

Liz agreed and stood by the front door.

Two minutes later, the vice principal led Colleen, protesting all the way, down the hall. "I'm not going anywhere with her," Colleen said. "Why's she here, anyway?"

"We'll talk in the car," Liz said. "I'm driving you home."

"I'm *supposed* to ride with my car pool, then Gran's picking me up at home."

"She'll call you about that. Your grandfather had a slight accident. He's at the emergency room. She sent me."

Colleen's eyes opened and she caught her breath. "What kind of an accident? He's not supposed to be driving, because of his blood pressure."

Nice of Irene to mention that before I told him his daughter was dead.

"I'm sure he'll be fine, but who knows how long the emergency room visit will take? I'm driving you home. Come on." She thanked the vice principal and walked down the stairs, not knowing whether Colleen would follow or stand at the door like a mule. Liz heard footsteps behind her and kept walking.

In the car, she said, "Put on your seat belt."

Colleen rolled her eyes. "I always wear my seat belt, Officer, sir. Haven't you heard? It's the law."

As they left the parking lot, the girl asked, "Why aren't you taking me to the hospital?"

"Because your gran asked me to take you home." Good enough answer. "Besides, I have to talk to you about something."

"I knew it. You seduced my father. You bitch."

"Whoa. I did not seduce your father." Liz deliberately used the old-fashioned term. "And please don't call me a bitch."

"Yeah, right. I told you before, he's married, so keep your nasty little cop hands off him."

"Would you like to stop for a soda or something?" Liz had to delay the discussion until she got Colleen safely home, where she wouldn't take a header out of the car when she was told.

"Drive me home and leave."

Liz had no intention of leaving until either Jud or Irene showed up. She started to speak, then realized Colleen had plugged in her iPod and was moving to music Liz couldn't hear.

Jud's truck wasn't in the garage or the driveway. There were no lights showing in the house. Colleen bolted from the car, ran up the steps, unlocked the door and would have slammed it behind her if Liz hadn't been expecting something of the sort. She shoved her shoulder against the door and followed Colleen into the front hall.

The teen bolted for the staircase. "Get out of my house!"

"Stop!"

"No way."

"Colleen, I have some news about your mother," Liz called. The words stopped her in her tracks.

She turned to stare down at Liz. "Wha…"

Liz went to the stairs with her hands in front of her. "We've found Sylvia's body. I'm really sorry to have to give you such bad news."

Colleen sank to the step. "I don't believe you. She's not dead."

Liz felt her heart go out to the teenager. "It's true," she said gently.

"Where? When?" No tears. The girl showed only casual interest, as though they were speaking about a stranger. At the moment she was in shock. Sooner or later, her emotions would break through, but that could take a few seconds or a few weeks. Liz had seen both.

Colleen had clung to the hope that her mother had not abandoned her and would someday return for her. Now she had to let go of that hope. She'd protect her emotions from the pain as long as possible. Liz remembered people who continued to wash dishes or iron clothes after she notified them of the death of a loved one. Anything to preserve normality for a little while longer.

Liz told her simply about the discovery of Sylvia's body.

"Two years?" Colleen asked, puzzled. "Where was she before?"

"Phoenix, Arizona."

"Why?"

"I don't know."

"I said she was dead, but I never believed it, not really. I never felt her dead, you know?" Colleen sounded surprised. "I thought I would. She really did run away from me."

"You don't know that."

"Why else would she leave?"

"Could be a bunch of reasons. Something bad at her job."

"How did she die?"

"I'm sorry, I can't discuss that."

Without warning, Colleen began to laugh. The laughter escalated until she was holding her sides and shrieking.

Liz didn't believe in slapping hysterical people, but she didn't know what else to do. "Colleen! Stop!" she shouted, and moved up the stairs.

Colleen gulped and choked the laughter into snickers. "I prayed for her and talked to her and wished for her and loved her, and all the time she was *dead*."

CHAPTER THIRTY

LIZ TRIED TO TALK TO the girl, and offered to fix her some hot cocoa. Colleen sat on the stairs and glared at her. Finally, she said, "I'm going to my room, Officer, sir. I have to do my homework."

"Your school will let you out of homework."

"Right. They *so* do not care about homework."

"I know you're going to get on your computer and e-mail all your friends about this."

"So?"

"I guess they have to know sometime."

"You'll let me?"

"I can't stop you, but I would suggest keeping the details to a minimum."

"What details? You didn't give me any." She started up the stairs, then stopped and turned. "Where's my daddy?" she asked in a small voice.

Actually, he's being interrogated as a suspect. Liz did not say the words aloud. "He's giving us as much information as he can, so we can catch whoever did this to your mother."

"Somebody really did kill her? You're not just saying that?"

Liz remembered she hadn't told Colleen how her mother had died. "Looks that way."

"Did my daddy do it?"

Liz caught her breath. "No, Colleen, your father did not do it."

"You say." She fled up the stairs. A moment later the door to her bedroom slammed. Probably locked, but Liz couldn't muster the energy to try the handle.

She was still sitting on the steps to the second floor, without lights on, when she heard a car on the gravel drive. It stopped, then a car door slammed and footsteps crossed the porch.

She hadn't locked the front door after she'd shoved her way in. It opened and Jud stood framed against the automatic porch light. His shoulders drooped with exhaustion.

She stood, afraid to take a step toward him.

Then he opened his arms.

She ran to him. They clung to one another in silence for several seconds.

"They didn't arrest me," he whispered, and ran his hand across his forehead. "They wanted to. I am so tired. They're coming first thing tomorrow morning to search the house and the business."

"Colleen's upstairs. I told her." Liz stooped to pick up her tote.

He held her hand. "I don't want you to go, but…"

"You need to be with your daughter."

He nodded.

"Jud," Liz said, and told him about Irene and Herb.

"Irene still wants her to come over tonight?"

"If Herb's not in the hospital. She said she'd call you."

He nodded, turned and walked up the stairs as though he'd run a marathon. "Colleen, baby, I'm home." He said over his shoulder to Liz, "I'll see you tomorrow."

"Maybe."

He didn't react.

She drove out onto the gravel road and turned toward the highway.

If they uncovered forensic evidence in their search of the house, they would arrest Jud. If not, he might avoid arrest but he'd remain the prime suspect. The case would go cold again.

No matter how much they liked him, people would continue to gossip that he had killed his wife and gotten away with it. That suspicion would eat at him, at his family, his child, even his business relationships.

Sooner or later, the media would break the story of Sylvia's death, and any possibility of privacy would disappear.

Liz wouldn't be able to see him except on official business if she intended to stay a police officer. Right now, she didn't give a damn about her blasted career, but he would. He wouldn't put her in jeopardy no matter what she said.

Their lives would diverge, and what they had created would wither. She'd move on to other cases.

But not other loves.

SHE STARED INTO THE flames in her fireplace, but didn't turn on the lights. Poirot sensed her misery and plastered himself to her chest. From time to time, he reached up and patted her chin to comfort her. Under ordinary circumstances, she'd be working her way through her refrigerator, but the box of brownies in the cabinet did not say, "Bake me." If there was no comfort even in comfort food, then she'd fallen as far as she could fall.

Poirot lifted his head and stared at the front door, but didn't move from her lap until Liz heard the tap. Then he bailed out and skittered into the kitchen.

She hadn't bothered to turn on the porch light, but her car sat in the driveway so whoever it was knew she must be home. Maybe if she didn't answer, the person would go away.

"Liz?"

She catapulted over the couch, slipped on the wood floor, slid into the door and yanked it open. "You shouldn't be here." She grabbed Jud's arm, pulled him into the room and slammed the door behind him.

"I'm way past shouldn't. I'm deep into must."

Their lips met, and a moment later their tongues sought one another and reveled in the taste. She clung to him as though she could slip her whole body into his to join in one spirit that could never be sundered. She whispered against his mouth, "Did they follow you?"

"If they tried, I lost them."

Did it matter that Randy Randy might drive by, see

Jud's truck sitting in her driveway and tell Gavigan? No. All that mattered was that Jud was here now, holding her, kissing her, touching her.... She pulled her sweater over her head and felt Jud's fingers unhook her bra. A moment later he began to circle her nipples with his palms. She arched her spine and moaned as heat surged up from her center. She could feel her breasts swell, knew her body was already wet and ready for him, felt him hard and demanding.

They managed to toss their clothes away, and together they sank onto the rug in front of the fireplace. Those educated fingers slid between her legs, tormenting her with pleasure.

Not enough. She held him, guided him. "Now," she begged. "Please, now."

She climaxed less than a minute after he entered her, and then again with a force that stunned her. He lifted her legs to his shoulders. This time she shouted when the spasms hit. A moment later he shouted, too. She slid her legs down to clamp around his hips, holding him inside, willing him to stay joined to her as he collapsed in her arms.

Finally, he lay beside her and ran his thumb down her cheek. "You're crying. Did I hurt you?"

She snuggled against him and draped her arm across his chest. "I'm not hurt. I'm empty."

"Empty?"

"Of the worry and the pain and the anger. All that's left is you in my arms."

"I think they're going to arrest me tomorrow."

"Not unless they find forensic evidence." She lifted herself on one elbow. "There isn't any to find, is there?"

"None that I'm aware of."

Not exactly a resounding no.

"You should be there when they arrive."

He lay back and threw his right arm across his eyes. "I know. I shouldn't have come at all. If Railsback finds out, you'll be in trouble."

"I can handle Randy." Actually, she probably couldn't, but telling Jud that would increase his worries.

He sat up. "I wanted to sleep in your arms, to forget all this for a few hours, but I should go home." He kissed the top of her head, reached for his pants, stood up and dressed hurriedly.

Still naked, and really shivering now, Liz followed him to the door.

He put his arms around her, then stepped back. "Hey, I just realized I was on top. Does that mean…"

"My rear end is pretty much healed. At least I didn't yell."

He grinned. "The heck you didn't. You yelled pretty good."

"But not from lying on my butt." She buried her face in his chest. "This mess has to be over soon."

"For better or worse, remember?" He opened the door and slipped out into the night.

"Then there's *worst*," she whispered.

THE FOLLOWING MORNING she awoke when her alarm went off. She'd slept solidly, without moving or dreaming. Obviously, making love with Jud was a wonderful soporific.

As she was getting ready for work, Irene called. "I wanted to thank you, for yesterday. I couldn't bear to tell Colleen about her mother."

"Thank you for calling. How's Herb?"

"Anxiety attack, as usual. His doctor met us, gave him some medicine and sent us home. He's spending today in bed. Have you talked to Jud?"

"Not recently." It was definitely none of Irene's business how recent was recent.

"Please, give him a little time. He's under so much stress, and being a parent to a teenager is difficult, without the additional stress of a murder investigation and being in love."

"Oh, well, as to that…"

"I mean it. I talk to him every day. He's crazy about you."

"Colleen isn't, and don't say she'll come around, because I doubt that she will."

"She'll need counseling when this is over. So will Jud. Then we'll see. Don't give up on him. He needs you more than he thinks."

She hung up.

Better make that if *it's over, not when.*

THE COLD, RAINY DAY fitted her mood. By the time Liz sat down at her desk she felt clammy, despite using her umbrella. Gavigan had refused to send her along with the forensics team to search Jud's house, so every time the telephone rang in the lieutenant's office, she froze. She had plenty of paperwork to keep her busy, but the minutes dragged, and she found herself filling in the same form over and over.

At eleven, Cary Williams called her direct number. "It's official. DNA came back. It's definitely Sylvia. Sorry."

"No reason to be sorry."

"Of course there is. You are crazy about this guy and I suspect he feels the same about you. I wish I could find something that proved some itinerant tramp killed her, but I can't even identify the murder weapon."

"Could it be some carpenter tool? A funky rasp, say? Some kind of plumber's pipe?"

"Nope. I've never seen anything quite like it. Maybe they'll find it in his house. They're searching today, aren't they?"

"Bite your tongue."

"I will find out what it is sooner or later. I promise you that. Keep the faith. Now, I've got four DBs facing me. I have to go."

Gavigan called Liz into his office at one. "The search of Slaughter's house? Nada. Zilch."

"Nothing?" She wanted to scream with joy.

"No hidden blood on walls or floor. No murder weapon either in the house, the office or any of the construction sites. No arrest for the moment." He pointed his index finger at her. "You stay away from him. Don't talk to him, don't see him, don't e-mail him, don't text him. I mean it."

"For how long?"

"Forever, dammit! Now go get another murder box. This one goes back to closed."

"Not until Friday. My two weeks, remember?"

"Oh, for… Get out of here."

She leaned across the desk and kissed Gavigan on the cheek. He recoiled as though she'd shot him.

She was dying to tell Jud the results of the search, but Gavigan would kill her, and rightly so. She practically danced out of his office, and when the phone on her desk rang, she said hello cheerfully.

"Uh—Liz?"

She sat down hard. "I can't talk to you from here. I'll call you back on your cell phone." She hung up, picked up her tote, ran down the hall to the bathroom, locked herself in a stall and called Jud on her own cell.

"They didn't find anything, thank God," he said.

"Then you're safe."

"Safer, maybe, but not so far as Colleen's concerned."

"What do you mean?"

"She thinks I did it. She accused me last night. She says she isn't coming home."

"Where does she plan to go?"

"She says she'll stay with Irene until I can get her into a boarding school."

"And you agreed?"

"Of course not. Irene'll talk her out of it."

"Jud, you are her father. Isn't it about time you started acting like a parent?" She clicked off the phone. Instantly, she regretted her outburst. Jud didn't need her on his case. He was a loving father, he just had to get beyond the guilt he didn't deserve.

Kids invariably figured out how to push their parent's buttons, and pushed them every chance they got. Colleen wasn't all that different from every other teenager. What Jud didn't seem to realize was that she pushed because she was scared she'd lose him, too.

Liz had tried it with her own mother when she was a teenager, but her mom had gained wisdom over the years and didn't buy her act. "Don't bother, it won't work," her mother had said after one of Liz's more spectacular tantrums. She didn't even remember over what—missing a rock concert, probably.

"What won't work?" Liz had asked.

"You can't make me angry enough either to kick you out or leave myself, so don't bother trying. It wears you out and it infuriates me."

Liz had lost her father as Colleen lost her mother, and though the circumstances were different, the result was the same—deadly and unacknowledged fear of losing the other parent, and a feeling of responsibility for the loss.

One day, years after her mother had successfully confronted her own demons, she had said to Liz, "Having a reason for bad behavior doesn't excuse it, nor give you carte blanche to inflict your bad feelings on people who love you."

As a cop and negotiator, Liz had seen families in unbelievable pain. The ones that survived grew stronger because they refused to allow the love they felt for one another to descend into recrimination or rage. Colleen needed help to see that she was not the only member of her family suffering, feeling angry and guilty.

Unfortunately, getting her that help could only be Jud's decision, not hers.

Liz stamped back into her office, slammed her purse down and attacked her computer.

"Whoa!" Randy Randy called. "Trouble in paradise? Jerk's still not in jail. Be grateful."

"Oh, bite me. I'm going for a late lunch."

"Want company, pretty lady?"

"Not yours."

CHAPTER THIRTY-ONE

LIZ PICKED UP an extra-large barbecue sandwich at a drive-through, stopped by Dinstuhl's for a half pound of chocolate-covered strawberries, drove into the woods at Overton Park and attempted to comfort herself with food. Even the chocolate—absolutely the best in the world—did nothing for her mood.

She knew how tired Jud must be, because she was exhausted. She considered simply driving home. She'd be within an hour of quitting time when she got back to work, anyway.

Nothing waited at home except Poirot. She pictured what it would be like to return there and find Jud waiting for her. She shouldn't have smarted off to him about Colleen, but she'd been right, even though it was none of her business.

Would Irene let Colleen move in? Surely only as a stopgap measure. Still, her grandmother's workshop would give comfort to the frightened, grieving teenager. Liz had a momentary realization that if Jud did actually send Colleen off to boarding school, they'd have more time together.

Great. Just what the kid needed—being abandoned again. *Not worthy of you, Elizabeth Gibson, hormones or not.*

Liz leaned back against her headrest and let her eyes close. Fifteen minutes and she'd go back to work. Maybe she'd drop by Irene's on her way home for a little comfort of her own. She pictured the room in her mind with its smell of cinnamon tea, the fireplace and candles....

"Oh, my God," she said, and sat bolt upright. "How could she *do* it?"

She laid rubber on her way out of the park. She tried to call Randy, but got his answering machine. Same with Jack. Gavigan had gone to a meeting and wouldn't be back. She left a message on Jack's phone, telling him where she was going and why.

She drove to Germantown like a lunatic, without ever seeing a squad car or hearing a radar gun behind her. She didn't dare take her hands off the wheel to call Jud. Would Colleen already be at Irene's?

She stopped in the driveway at the Richardsons' and called Jud. Finally, he picked up. "Where's Colleen?" she asked.

"I told you. She's at Irene's."

"Listen to me. Get in touch with Randy or Jack—I left messages, but they haven't called me back. Tell them I'm at Irene's, and I may need backup."

"Why?"

Liz couldn't tell him until she was certain, and definitely not over the phone. "No time."

"Wait for me. I'll be right there."

"I'll be in the workshop. Stay out of the way."

She clicked off, climbed out of the car and forced herself to walk back to the A-frame calmly. She didn't expect there'd be any trouble, but she loosened her automatic in its holster and let her jacket fall back over it.

"Irene?" she called. "Can I come in?"

Colleen jerked the door open. "What is it with you? Get out of our lives."

"Why, Liz, come in and join us for a cup of tea," Irene said. She ran more water into the electric tea-kettle and turned it on. When she saw Liz's expression, she cocked her head. "Anything wrong?"

Liz took a deep breath. "Just tired." She walked over to the fire, dropped her tote on the hearth and held her hands out. She didn't need to fake being cold and miserable. "As for the tea, not right now, thank you. Maybe later."

"If you're here to drag me home, forget it," Colleen said.

"Your father did not kill your mother," Liz stated, without turning around.

"You go live with him. That's what he wants, anyway. He loves dumping me on Gran. He wants to pack me off to the Jane Eyre School for Girls."

"Colleen," Irene said, the warning heavy in her voice.

"I'm sick of being polite."

"Since when were you ever polite?" Liz said, and this time she did turn to make eye contact.

"Huh?"

"Just because you're miserable, you don't have the right to make everybody around you miserable. Now, I need to speak to your grandmother. Please go up to the house."

"No way! You can't make me." She faced Liz with her arms folded across her chest. "I'm staying here where I can protect her."

Liz laughed. "She doesn't need protection from me."

"Colleen," Irene said quietly, "do as she says." She walked over and took her arm.

"But…"

"We shouldn't be long. Go check on your grandfather. Wait for us in the kitchen. Please." She opened the door, ushered Colleen none too gently into the garden, pulled the door partially closed behind them and wrapped her arms around the girl. Liz could hear her on the front stoop, murmuring reassurances.

In an instant, Liz turned back to the mantelpiece and ran her eye down the twenty or so wooden candlesticks. She was reaching for the largest when she heard Irene come in and shut the door. Liz didn't touch the object, but her hand hovered close to it.

"Was this this one?" she asked. She kept her back to Irene, but every nerve was alert to movement. She didn't think she was in any danger, but this could be one more scenario she might be wrong about.

Irene caught her breath, but her words sounded calm, even casual. "I told you, they're all antique bobbins. That one was used in one of the large mills before the Civil War. It's quite valuable. I found it in an antique store in Harper's Ferry."

"Quite heavy, too. Distinct pattern." Liz turned to face her. "I just remembered where I'd seen that particular pattern before. Embedded in Sylvia's skull."

Irene shook her head and backed up.

"It's impossible to get blood out of wood completely," Liz said. "Even after two years, forensics should be able to identify Sylvia's DNA."

The woman began to moan.

"I should have paid more attention to the statistics about mothers killing their children, but I always assumed they meant babies and toddlers, not grown daughters."

"You can't be serious! Why would I kill Sylvia? I loved her."

One look at Irene's wary eyes, and Liz was certain she was right. "I'm sure you did, but you love Colleen more, don't you? And Jud?"

"Please tell me they haven't arrested him." Irene's hand went to her throat and grasped the strand of pearls around her neck.

Liz expected her to send them flying, but she was still too controlled. "They probably won't arrest him."

Irene pushed past her and sank into her rocking chair, leaned back and closed her eyes. "You see? He's safe."

Liz loomed over her and forced her to look up. "He's not safe. Neither is Colleen. They're already looking at her as a possible alternative suspect. Unless we convict the real killer, both Jud and Colleen will live their whole lives under a cloud of suspicion." She shrugged. "Maybe Colleen did do it. I can hear the prosecutor now telling the jury about her temper. She has as much access to this room as you do. She could have taken that bobbin, used it to brain Sylvia and replaced it before you noticed it was gone."

Irene put her hands over her ears. "No! She's not like Sylvia, who didn't care about anything or anyone. Colleen cares too much about everything. Why would she hurt her mother? She couldn't possibly move Sylvia's body to the woods. She can't even drive."

"Her father can. Accessory after the fact carries a sentence of anywhere from five years to life."

"But she'd never…" Irene wailed. Her face had gone white. She'd aged a dozen years in five minutes. Her fists were clenched on her thighs.

We are getting close, Liz thought. *She wants to tell me, but she's afraid. I don't blame her.*

"That's what I'm asking you," Liz said. She sat in the wing chair and reached for Irene's hand. "You did it to save them, didn't you? Unless you tell me what really happened, they'll still be lost. You'll have killed your own daughter for nothing."

Liz felt Irene's fingers relax and withdraw from hers, to droop over the side of her rocking chair by her yarn bag.

Now. She's letting go. She's ready to tell me.

"She was my responsibility," Irene said. "I've always known there was something basic missing in her, but I didn't know how to fix it." She stared out the front window and into faraway times. "I did love her, but that wasn't enough. She could fake feelings and actions for a short time. She'd watch normal people carefully and do what they did, but she couldn't sustain the act."

"She came back to town and called you," Liz said. "Why not Herb?"

Irene grimaced. "He'd never have forgiven her for putting him through what she did. He likes to punish. Besides, she knew I have money of my own, saved from all those years of teaching. She said if I paid her off she'd disappear again. Otherwise, she'd walk back into our lives with a tale of abduction or amnesia." Irene waved her hand. "It wouldn't have mattered. Sylvia said if she agreed to stay gone, she wanted half of the insurance money Jud would get by having her declared dead. Wherever she'd been for five years, she hadn't been able to sustain that role, either. She needed to create another new identity."

"Why not give her the money?"

"Please! The next time she had to run, she'd be back for more, but I wouldn't be able to give it to her. Jud would never consider putting in for the insurance money if he knew for certain she was alive. She'd show up at Colleen's graduation or her wedding day, or Jud's wedding day."

"Why not call the police?"

"So far as I knew, she wasn't guilty of anything. Besides, I couldn't drag Colleen through that." Irene put her face in her hands, then dropped them over the arms of her rocking chair again. "I picked Sylvia up at the bus station and drove out to the woods—her idea, not mine. Obviously, she didn't want to be seen. That was the sort of thing she thought was funny. The roadway was dry, so I could drive far back. I told her I had the money in my yarn bag in the trunk. When she leaned over I hit her. Just once. I had a terrible time dragging her off the road, but she didn't bleed. I drove to a car wash, had the car detailed and drove home. She was my baby. I couldn't let her hurt anyone else."

"Why not turn yourself in?"

"I'm doing that now, aren't I? Jud and Colleen are in danger because of me. It ends here." From the yarn bag, a pistol materialized in her hand.

Liz jumped and started to get out of the chair.

"Please don't. I know you have a gun, but you're in no danger. Just sit still."

Irene started to lift the muzzle.

She didn't intend to shoot Liz. She planned to kill herself.

"No! You must not kill yourself."

"Why ever not? It'll be simpler for everyone."

"Colleen still needs you. Jud needs you. Even Herb needs you."

"I can't put them through a nasty trial and all the publicity. People wouldn't understand."

"There doesn't have to be a trial."

"Of course there does."

"Listen to me, Irene." Liz leaned forward. The woman raised a hand, indicating that she wouldn't be allowed to get close enough to grab the gun.

This was one negotiation Liz must not blow, for all their sakes. "Let me help you."

"How?"

"Detective Gibson!" The voice sounded as though it was coming through a bullhorn.

Both women jumped.

"What on earth?" Irene said.

"Detective Railsback saw you through the window. He says the woman with you has a gun. Are you all right?"

"Randy must have alerted the TACT squad," Liz said, then called, "We're fine."

Irene looked at her in wonder. "But that's perfect. I'll just walk out and point my gun at them."

"Suicide by cop."

"Pardon."

"It has a name. Suicide by cop. They won't shoot you unless they have to."

"Well, then, I'll fix it so they have to." She stood up.

"Like mother, like daughter."

"I beg your pardon?"

"Aren't you doing what you accuse Sylvia of doing? Bolting? Leaving the problems for the people who love you to deal with?"

"It's not the same thing. If I die, they'll be free to

get on with their lives." She stood up and moved toward the entrance.

Liz managed to slip around her and stand with her back to the door. "If you won't think of yourself, think of *me*."

"You?"

"If we don't both walk out of here alive and together, my career goes up in flames, Colleen will never, ever forgive me and Jud and I can never be together."

"Detective Gibson! Are you certain you're okay in there?"

Liz raised her voice. "We'll be out in a couple of minutes."

Irene laughed. "Sure of yourself, aren't you?"

"You said you're strong. Prove it. You are going to give me the gun. You are going out that door with your hands in the air with me behind you. You'll be arrested and handcuffed, taken down to the jail. I'll be with you the whole way. We'll walk you through the system. You will not open your mouth to say one word—except your name and to ask for a lawyer. You understand so far?"

"Sounds grim."

"Not as grim as being shot to bits in front of your granddaughter." Liz could tell Irene hadn't thought of that.

"Oh, my."

"I'm pretty certain that with my testimony, your lawyer can bargain you down to involuntary manslaughter. You didn't go there intending to kill her, did you? Say no. You took the spindle for protection."

"Only because I couldn't find Herb's gun." Irene looked at the weapon in her hands. "I took it when I heard they'd found that skeleton. I was afraid I'd need it."

Liz closed her eyes. "Don't mention the gun."

"I'm not sorry, you know. It had to be done. Even if she left and never came back here, she'd have ruined other lives. But…"

"Irene, she did threaten you. She threatened to destroy your family. Don't explain, just say she threatened you. You'll plead guilty. There won't be a trial. You stand up in front of a judge dressed like a little old lady—"

"I am *not* a little old lady."

"Dammit, Irene, I know that, but the judge won't."

"I'll go to jail, won't I?"

"Almost certainly. But you have an unblemished record and were under a massive amount of stress. With luck you'll serve no more than eighteen months of a five-year sentence. You'll be out in time to see Colleen graduate from high school."

"She won't want to see *me.*"

"Cross that fence when you come to it. Trust me, alive is better than dead."

Irene looked at Liz for what seemed like an eternity, then she said, "You'll be with me?"

"As long as I can. Definitely until your lawyer is

there. Colleen may not understand, but Jud will. He won't abandon you."

"Herb will."

"Probably."

"Good."

"I beg your pardon?"

"Let him divorce me."

"So, is it a deal?"

"I don't know. You hear so many bad things about prisons. My life will change forever. I'll be a felon. What will my bridge club say?" Irene said. "I refuse to cry, but I am so frightened."

"They won't shoot you as long as I'm with you."

"I'm terrified of afterward. What Colleen and Jud will think of me. I'll be branded a killer."

She stopped talking for a moment. Then looked at Liz and said, "I guess that's what I am." She squared her shoulders and handed the pistol over butt first. "Very well. I'm ready."

Liz heaved a sigh of relief. She'd succeeded in this hostage situation. Nobody had died.

As Liz and Irene crossed the threshold, the TACT team in their battle gear swarmed in with their assault weapons raised.

"Be careful!" Liz yelled at the officer who was about to thrust Irene facedown on her flagstones. Shielding her with her own body, Liz grabbed the man's handcuffs, turned Irene to face the building, and snapped them onto her wrists. "Do you want her to break a hip?"

The cop took a step back, but didn't lower his weapon. "Come on," he said, but whether to Liz or Irene or both, she couldn't tell.

"Gran!"

Irene's head came up as she searched for Colleen in the crowd that had gathered behind the perimeter tape already stretched at the end of the driveway.

"You leave my grandmother alone!"

Two officers tried to hold Colleen as she struggled and kicked and writhed and screamed. They obviously wanted to contain her without pepper spray. Even so, if the reporters had already set up their satellites, the struggle would show up on the evening news, and it wouldn't be pretty. Please God they were too far away to see past the crowd and the police vehicles.

"Please, Liz," Irene said as softly as she dared, "get her away. Take her into the house. Don't worry about me. Please, don't let her see this."

"I'll try." Liz nodded to the cop holding Irene, and ran up the path toward the chaos. She ducked under the yellow tape and blocked Colleen's view. "Your grandmother wants you to wait in the house."

"Wait? Wait for what?" She lunged at Liz. "For you to shoot her dead?"

"Nobody's going to shoot anyone," Liz said.

"You're crazy." The teen turned and shouted over her shoulder at the crowd, "She put handcuffs on my gran!"

Just then, the back door opened and Herb staggered out in pajamas, barefoot, with an old terry-cloth robe wrapped around him. "What is the meaning of this? Get off my property."

"Herb, get back into bed," Liz told him as she continued to struggle with Colleen.

"Grandpop! Help me."

"Colleen? You're arresting my granddaughter?"

By this time Irene and her escort had reached the top of the hill. "Herb, go back to bed before you have a real heart attack," she said. "Take another pill. Colleen, they are not arresting me. I gave up voluntarily, didn't I, Liz? Now, you go into the kitchen with Liz and see to your grandfather."

Colleen lunged and nearly got away before one of the TACT squad guys grabbed the back of her shirt collar.

"I'm not going anywhere with that *cop*. Why are they doing this?"

"Liz will tell you, dear. Go inside."

"Where are *you* going?"

"I'm going to take a ride with this nice young man. Liz will explain."

Colleen glared at her and demanded, "Why?"

Irene smiled at her. "Because I'm asking you to."

Colleen calmed, but she still managed to jerk away from Liz.

"Your father will be here soon," Irene said.

"I don't want to see him ever, ever again." Colleen had morphed from fury to tears. "I want you, Gran," she wailed.

"I'm not available right this minute," the woman said, and managed a shaky little smile.

"Come on, ma'am," the big cop said. "Let me stand between you and all those reporters out there with the cameras, okay? Don't look at them, and walk fast. We'll get you into the car and out of here quick."

"Thank you, young man. Colleen, for the last time, go with Liz. I can't worry about you, too."

Colleen tried to reach out to touch her grandmother as she passed, but Irene kept just out of her reach, huddled close to the cop. Liz saw that tears were rolling down her cheeks. She climbed into the back of the squad car, and was driven away like royalty with the news cameramen chasing after her.

As if her grandmother's presence had been buoying her up, Colleen promptly collapsed. Liz caught her, put her arm around her shoulders and led her up the back stairs and into the kitchen. It was empty. Surprisingly, Herb had apparently gone back to bed as requested. He must still be so heavily sedated he couldn't understand what was happening.

Liz gently pushed Colleen into a chair, pulled a soda from the refrigerator, popped the top and handed it to her.

Colleen turned up her nose. "I drink diet."

"Fine." Liz brought her a can of diet soda, looked at the regular soda, picked it up and downed it in one long gulp. Amazing how thirsty terror could make you. She sat down opposite Colleen, who glared at her.

"What did you do to my grandmother? You

couldn't stand me living with her, so you called the cops?" Colleen's eyes widened. "You're going to take me to juvie and stick me in a foster home so you and Daddy can screw around anytime you want."

"Kid, you have some kind of imagination. That never entered my mind."

"Oh, really. Then—"

"You're not going to believe me, and you're going to hate this when you do. I'll try to explain it, but you're not going to understand."

"What? What? *What?*" Colleen beat her fists on the old wooden table.

Liz took a deep breath and blew it out. "No way to sugarcoat this. Your grandmother just admitted to killing your mother."

"You're crazy!"

"It's true, Colleen."

"You made her confess to save my father. I hate you both."

"'Fraid not. Didn't you wonder why she wanted you to go up to the house?"

Colleen stared at her. "But my *daddy* killed my mother."

"You don't really believe that. Your grandmother admitted it."

"Oh, right. According to you, my gran, the sweetest, most loving person in the world, killed her own daughter. Why would she…"

"She thought she was doing the right thing."

"As if."

"I didn't say she *did* the right thing, only that she *thought* she was."

"She had a stroke or something, right? Oh, God, she's got Alzheimer's."

"I don't know. I'm sure they'll run tests." It might be good if Colleen could believe that. Liz had carefully omitted mentioning the gun. No need for the girl to hear that.

Colleen dropped her head onto the table and began to cry.

"Girl?" Herb's voice. He stood in the doorway to the hall. "Where's Irene? What was all that about?"

"Go back to bed, Mr. Richardson." Liz could see he was unsteady on his feet.

He sounded querulous. "Tell Irene I want her."

"I will, Mr. Richardson."

"Huh." He turned around and disappeared down the hall.

"He's acting really weird," his granddaughter said.

Colleen nodded. "Probably what they gave him in the emergency room last night."

"I can't look after him," Colleen wailed. "Where am I going to stay if I can't stay here?"

"Go home."

"Liz?" Jud burst in the back door, reached his daughter in two strides, swept her into his arms. She clung to him. Over her shoulder he looked at Liz. "Are you all right? What happened? Half the police department is outside. They arrested Irene? That can't be right."

"Daddy?" Colleen looked up at him. "I'm sorry I was mad at you, Daddy." She scowled at Liz. "But it's all *her* fault. She arrested Gran." She burst into noisy sobs. "Everything was fine until *she* came around. She's ruined everything. Why can't she leave us alone?"

Liz turned away.

"No." Jud freed one hand to grab hers. "Stay."

Colleen made a sound that was half sob, half growl.

He wrapped his arm around Liz's waist and held her against his side as he fought to hold on to Colleen. "Everything wasn't fine for any of us, sweetheart. Liz pulled down the curtains and let the sun in."

"But…"

"I've been drowning under suspicion since your mother disappeared. Even *you* believed I might have done it. Isn't it better to know, no matter how hard that is? Liz is the first person who ever really listened to me and then went out and did something about it. We owe her."

"I don't owe her a thing." Colleen pulled away and glared at Liz. "She's ruined our lives."

"Stop that," Jud said. "Your feelings are your own, but you *will* be polite. Liz hasn't ruined our lives, she's saved them." He glanced at Liz and she saw the warmth in his eyes.

Her body glowed with the love she felt for this good man.

"We're all going to need help to work through everything that's happened," Jud continued. "I intend to see that we get it."

Liz gasped. "Help! Oh, Lord, I promised Irene I'd walk her through the system. She must think I've abandoned her. I've got to go. Can you get Trip to meet us?"

"Sure." Jud took his cell phone out of his pocket.

Colleen turned around and started down the hall.

He called, "Come back and sit down, Colleen. No more running away. I love you, baby, and your gran loves you. Together we can face anything. I'm not going to let you cut me out."

She hesitated. "I'll lock my door."

"Since when has a door been a problem for a guy my size?" He smiled. "Of course, if I wake Herb up, he'll probably have me arrested for destroying property."

Colleen yanked the chair out, flopped into it and folded her arms.

"Thank you."

Liz stood on her toes and kissed Jud's cheek, then crossed the room and stopped with her hand on the doorknob. "Colleen, I promise I'll look after your grandmother. May I tell her that you love her and that you're going to be all right?"

"We'll never be all right. Not without Gran."

"But that's not what she needs to hear right now. She needs you to be strong."

Colleen's eyes widened as though the concept was completely foreign to her. Then, slowly, she nodded and reached for her father's hand. He put his arm around her shoulders and hugged her. "Whatever she needs," he said.

Maybe this tragedy would at least bring them together. Liz prayed that would be so.

EPILOGUE

January, One year later

"HI," LIZ SAID. Jud lounged against the pedestal at the foot of the main precinct steps. She came down the stairs, stepped into his arms and kissed him fiercely. He responded with a hug that nearly cracked her bones. She should be used to the power in his arms by now, but still occasionally felt she'd fallen in love with a grizzly bear.

She slipped her arm under his and relished the feel of his sheepskin coat.

"I told Colleen we're getting married," he said.

Liz stiffened. "Uh-oh."

"On our way home from visiting Irene at the prison."

"You took Colleen to the prison with you?"

"Yep. She asked to go. She's come a long way in a year, thanks to Dr. Watkins. I don't think Colleen will ever truly understand. She swears Irene must have had a seizure and maybe I'll just let her believe that."

"Whatever gets her through."

They walked to the parking lot across from the precinct. Jud's SUV sat at the far end under a street-light.

"Jud, there's somebody in the backseat of your car. Oh, Lord, you brought Colleen?"

"Yep. We're dropping her at Andrea's house for the night on our way out to see the new house."

"I can't do this."

"Sure you can. Tough gal like you." He squeezed her arm, clicked the door locks and opened the passenger door for Liz.

"Hey, Colleen," Liz said as she climbed in.

"Hi."

"I told her I'd told you," Jud said to his daughter as he slid into the driver's seat.

"You'll never be my mother," Colleen said, but without rancor.

"No, and I won't try to be. I'll be your father's wife…and your friend, if you'll let me."

Jud pulled out of the parking lot.

"Will you move into our house?"

"No."

"Too many bad vibes," Jud said. "We'll wait until the new house I'm building is ready."

"I don't see why we have to move, anyway," Colleen said with a hint of her old whining.

"You're a contractor's daughter, sport. That's almost as bad as being an army brat, except that you stay in the same general area. Same school, same friends."

"How soon will it be finished?"

"Probably four months or so, depending on the weather. You like the new plans, don't you? You'll have more room."

"When are you going to sell our house?"

"It goes on the market as soon as the other house is ready to move into. We've been through this before, Colleen." Jud sounded exasperated.

Liz figured the girl wanted Jud to go on record with a witness present.

"Maybe it won't sell. You keep saying the market sucks, and it's not the world's most ordinary house."

"Then we'll move anyway, and keep it on the market until it does sell."

"Can I keep Mom's furniture and her portrait?" Colleen hesitated. "And all her jewelry?"

"Sure," Jud said.

"One thing," Liz interjected. "I have a cat. A big, fat black cat named Poirot."

"A cat?" For the first time, Liz heard animation in Colleen's voice. "We never had a cat or a dog. You going to bring him with you?"

"Have to. Nobody else will have him."

"Does he scratch and bite?"

"He's too lazy. He does love to have his tummy rubbed."

"So you won't get married until summer, when the house is done? You think Gran might be able to come to the wedding?"

"Possibly," Jud said. "Would you like that?"

"I guess it won't be the worst thing in the world. And I'll be off to college in another couple of years, if I do summer school and graduate early," Colleen said. "I suppose you'd be lonely." She sat back. "You could probably do a lot worse."

Liz gulped as Jud grabbed her hand. That was as close to a resounding vote of confidence as she was likely to get from his daughter.

After a long and amazingly comfortable silence, Colleen said, "Are you too old to have babies?"

Liz started. "No. Why?" She hadn't expected the question, but should have. She was pretty sure Colleen would hate the idea of having a sibling—more competition for Jud's attention.

But Colleen surprised her again. "Being an only child is nice, but it has disadvantages. Having somebody to boss around might be okay. You better consider it before you get too old." She sat up, crossed her arms on the back of her father's seat and said, "When can I meet the cat?"

"You cold?" Jud asked. Liz wrapped his arm around her and pulled him against her.

"Warmer now. One of your ancestors must have been a grizzly. How come we're stopping by the new house this afternoon?"

"Because we finished the framing this morning. You can finally get a feel for the size of the rooms." They walked hand in hand—actually glove in glove—over the frozen land that would eventually turn into a lawn and garden. At the top of a small rise stood the skeleton of their new house. Jud's green house. The first, and the largest, of the four he planned to build.

The construction crew had left for the day. The January breeze was cold enough to freeze the ground solid, but held a hint of spring. Wild jonquils had already broken through the earth and reached two-inch leaves up to the late-afternoon sunshine. If the weather held, the first blooms would burst open in less than a month. Two weeks later, the trees that dotted the land would begin to put out fragile pale leaves that gave them a sea-foam tint.

He took her elbow to guide her around the construction materials that sat in piles on the concrete floor.

"You really don't mind giving up your dream home?" Liz asked.

"You hated that house. So did I, at the end. Too many bad memories. I should really ask you that question. You have to sell your cottage, your personal space. What do I give up? I get to try new ideas. Best of all, I get you."

"And a twenty-pound cat."

"You get a teenage stepdaughter. Want to trade?"

"We'll manage."

"Secretly, I think she respects you. She may even like you, but she'll never admit that. And I think she's grateful to you for helping Irene face her ordeal. By the way, did I mention that Irene thinks she may be out by June?"

"Irene will be out of jail well before Rainer Iams," Liz said. "No parole in the federal prison system."

"Seven years is a long time for a man Rainer's age, even at a so-called country-club prison."

"The way the feds are going through his loan deals, some of his best farmer friends may become his roommates," Liz said. "I'm glad big Nick only got a year at the prison farm. LaPorte could probably have had his assault charge upped to attempted murder."

"Anybody who meets Nick could see he's really a child, for all his size," Jud said. "Take it from me, guys as big as he and I are have to be careful not to cause serious damage just by walking into a room."

Jud smiled at Liz as they moved around the rough construction staircase being used to reach the second floor.

"Ta-da," he said. "The master bedroom."

"It's huge."

"So am I."

"Don't think this makes you the master," Liz said, reaching up to kiss him.

"To quote Colleen, as if. Now, do you think Poirot will object if I'm the one who shares your bed tonight?"

"He'll just have to get over it."

* * * * *

Silhouette Desire kicks off 2009 with
MAN OF THE MONTH, *a yearlong program*
featuring incredible heroes by stellar authors.

When Navy SEAL Hunter Cabot returns home
for some much-needed R & R, he discovers
he's a married man. There's just one problem:
he's never met his "bride."

Enjoy this sneak peek at Maureen Child's
AN OFFICER AND A MILLIONAIRE.
Available January 2009 from Silhouette Desire.

One

Hunter Cabot, Navy SEAL, had a healing bullet wound in his side, thirty days' leave and, apparently, a wife he'd never met.

On the drive into his hometown of Springville, California, he stopped for gas at Charlie Evans's service station. That's where the trouble started.

"Hunter! Man, it's good to see you! Margie didn't tell us you were coming home."

"Margie?" Hunter leaned back against the front fender of his black pickup truck and winced as his side gave a small twinge of pain. Silently then, he watched as the man he'd known since high school filled his tank.

Charlie grinned, shook his head and pumped gas.

"Guess your wife was lookin' for a little 'alone' time with you, huh?"

"My—" Hunter couldn't even say the word. *Wife?* He didn't have a wife. "Look, Charlie..."

"Don't blame her, of course," his friend said with a wink as he finished up and put the gas cap back on. "You being gone all the time with the SEALs must be hard on the ol' love life."

He'd never had any complaints, Hunter thought, frowning at the man still talking a mile a minute. "What're you—"

"Bet Margie's anxious to see you. She told us all about that R and R trip you two took to Bali." Charlie's dark brown eyebrows lifted and wiggled.

"Charlie..."

"Hey, it's okay, you don't have to say a thing, man."

What the hell could he say? Hunter shook his head, paid for his gas and as he left, told himself Charlie was just losing it. Maybe the guy had been smelling gas fumes too long.

But as it turned out, it wasn't just Charlie. Stopped at a red light on Main Street, Hunter glanced out his window to smile at Mrs. Harker, his second-grade teacher who was now at least a hundred years old. In the middle of the crosswalk, the old lady stopped and shouted, "Hunter Cabot, you've got yourself a wonderful wife. I hope you appreciate her."

Scowling now, he only nodded at the old woman—

the only teacher who'd ever scared the crap out of him. What the hell was going on here? Was everyone but him nuts?

His temper beginning to boil, he put up with a few more comments about his "wife" on the drive through town before finally pulling into the wide, circular drive leading to the Cabot mansion. Hunter didn't have a clue what was going on, but he planned to get to the bottom of it. Fast.

He grabbed his duffel bag, stalked into the house and paid no attention to the housekeeper, who ran at him, fluttering both hands. "Mr. Hunter!"

"Sorry, Sophie," he called out over his shoulder as he took the stairs two at a time. "Need a shower, then we'll talk."

He marched down the long, carpeted hallway to the rooms that were always kept ready for him. In his suite, Hunter tossed the duffel down and stopped dead. The shower in his bathroom was running. His *wife?*

Anger and curiosity boiled in his gut, creating a churning mass that had him moving forward without even thinking about it. He opened the bathroom door to a wall of steam and the sound of a woman singing—off-key. Margie, no doubt.

Well, if she was his wife...Hunter walked across the room, yanked the shower door open and stared in at a curvy, naked, temptingly wet woman.

She whirled to face him, slapping her arms across her naked body while she gave a short, terrified scream.

Hunter smiled. "Hi, honey. I'm home."

* * * * *

Be sure to look for
AN OFFICER AND A MILLIONAIRE
by USA TODAY *bestselling author*
Maureen Child.
Available January 2009 from Silhouette Desire.

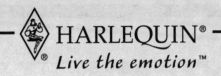

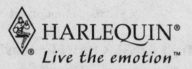

HARLEQUIN®
INTRIGUE®

BREATHTAKING ROMANTIC SUSPENSE

Shared dangers and passions lead to electrifying
romance and heart-stopping suspense!

Every month, you'll meet six new heroes
who are guaranteed to make your spine tingle
and your pulse pound. With them you'll enter
into the exciting world of Harlequin Intrigue—
where your life is on the line
and so is your heart!

THAT'S INTRIGUE—
ROMANTIC SUSPENSE
AT ITS BEST!

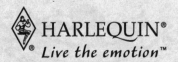

HARLEQUIN®
Live the emotion™

Harlequin® Historical
Historical Romantic Adventure!

*Imagine a time of chivalrous
knights and unconventional ladies,
roguish rakes and impetuous
heiresses, rugged cowboys
and spirited frontierswomen—
these rich and vivid tales will
capture your imagination!*

*Harlequin Historical . . .
they're too good to miss!*